KISSING SARAH

Alex brushed his lips across hers and sent a shiver of delight through her body. Sarah knew she should stop this before it went any further, but as she moved to escape Alex brought his other arm up to stop her.

"Stay," he pleaded. "You cannot ignore what is between us."

Sarah moistened her dry lips, her eyes shying away from the intensity of his gaze. Alex wanted her. There was no denying the attraction between them, but the risk was too high. Sarah could not afford to lose her freedom to any man, especially not the man who was going to wed her cousin.

"We should not be here like this," she whispered.

"It is too late." Alex moved his head closer and Sarah closed her eyes as his warm brandy-scented breath tickled her nose.

He captured her mouth slowly, gently nudging her lips and then easing his tongue in. An exquisite lethargy stole throughout her body. She surrendered to his kiss, allowing herself to be drawn into the web of pleasure he wove . . .

<u>BOOK YOUR PLACE ON OUR WEBSITE</u> <u>AND MAKE THE</u> <u>READING CONNECTION!</u>

We've created a customized website just for our very special readers, where you can get the inside scoop on everything that's going on with Zebra, Pinnacle and Kensington books.

When you come online, you'll have the exciting opportunity to:

- View covers of upcoming books

- Read sample chapters

- Learn about our future publishing schedule (listed by publication month *and author*)

- Find out when your favorite authors will be visiting a city near you

- Search for and order backlist books from our online catalog

- Check out author bios and background information

- Send e-mail to your favorite authors

- Meet the Kensington staff online

- Join us in weekly chats with authors, readers and other guests

- Get writing guidelines

- AND MUCH MORE!

Visit our website at
http://www.kensingtonbooks.com

The Seduction of Sarah

Cynthia Clement

ZEBRA BOOKS
KENSINGTON PUBLISHING CORP.
www.kensingtonbooks.com

To my mom and dad—
Thank you for your support and encouragement.
I love you.

ZEBRA BOOKS are published by

Kensington Publishing Corp.
850 Third Avenue
New York, NY 10022

All Kensington titles, imprints and distributed lines are available at special quantity discounts for bulk purchases for sales promotion, premiums, fund-raising, educational or institutional use.

Special book excerpts or customized printings can also be created to fit specific needs. For details, write or phone the office of the Kensington Special Sales Manager: Attn. Special Sales Department. Kensington Publishing Corp., 850 Third Avenue, New York, NY 10022. Phone: 1-800-221-2647.

Zebra and the Z logo Reg. U.S. Pat. & TM Off.

ISBN 0-8217-7814-5

First Printing: July 2005
10 9 8 7 6 5 4 3 2 1

Printed in the United States of America

Chapter 1

July 1823

Sarah sank down in the cool water, savoring its motion against her bare skin. She closed her eyes and sighed. The birds were chirping and the frogs were croaking their protests to Sarah's daily invasion into their undisturbed privacy. Their sounds calmed and soothed her.

"I had forgotten how refreshing a morning swim could be." A deep, husky, male voice sliced through the early morning silence. "Shall I join you?"

Sarah's head whipped around, cool water splashing her face. She looked into the steely gray eyes of a giant. He stood on the shoreline, leaning against a horse as dark as midnight. Beast and man were perfectly matched. Sarah shivered, her heart beating frantically.

"There is no need to stop on my account." The man moved away from his horse, his strong leg muscles straining the fabric of his tight riding pants. "I have never seen a more beautiful body."

"Please," Sarah begged breathlessly, ducking farther down in the water. "Turn around and allow me to get out."

The man grinned wickedly. "I cannot oblige you."

"Do not be ridiculous." Sarah moved her arms faster to keep afloat. Her initial shock was fast changing to anger. "Your behavior is ungentlemanly."

The interloper shrugged his powerful shoulders indifferently. "Agreed, but living by the rules has always bored me."

"You cannot expect me to leave the water while you stand there." Sarah's chest was beginning to tighten in panic.

He tilted his head toward her and she inhaled sharply when she saw the jagged scar that ran down the right side of his face. Sarah's stomach knotted in renewed fear. She was alone and naked with a stranger who stood between her and safety.

"You have no reason to be modest. I have been watching for several minutes. I do not think I have ever witnessed anything more sensuous. You are one of the most beautiful women I have ever seen."

Sarah's stomach knotted as anxiety crawled up her spine. "You are not easing my fears," she snapped.

He walked closer to the edge of the lake, loose stones crunching beneath his Hessian boots. He stopped at her pile of clothes and bent to pick up her drying sheet. "I will make it easy for you. All you have to do is come and get your clothes."

Sarah shook her head. "I cannot trust you."

"I see your dilemma." The man took the sheet between his hands and spread it out as if to welcome her. "What other choice do you have?"

"I will stay here until you leave," Sarah stated with a lifted chin. "You must have other things to do besides tormenting a helpless woman."

"You are not without power. I would not be dallying with you otherwise." He moved closer to the shoreline, the sheet still held out between his hands. "I have thrown caution away, willing to face rejection just so that I may know your name."

"Will you leave me alone then?"

"Perhaps."

Sarah debated for several seconds before reasoning it would not hurt. In the six weeks that she and her cousin Caroline had been staying at Caldern, they had not met anyone. Sarah would probably never see this man again. "It is Sarah."

"A lovely name for a beautiful woman. I am Alex."

"Now leave," Sarah demanded in a raised voice.

Alex frowned and then shook his head. "No."

"You promised!" Sarah swatted the water with her clenched fist. "That is unfair."

"I did not promise. I said perhaps." Alex moved to a large rock at the water's edge and sat down.

"You are despicable," Sarah hissed. "What do you intend?"

"Nothing," he assured her. "I will not harm you. I give you my word of honor."

Sarah debated her next move while watching his face. It was devoid of expression. She was already late in returning back to the house and Caroline would be furious. Still, she could not trust this stranger.

"All men want something." Sarah shivered as a burst of anger flared in Alex's eyes and then was immediately hidden by half-closed lids.

"You obviously forget yourself," he said coldly. "Who gave you leave to swim here?"

"I did not realize permission was needed," she returned, averting her eyes from the frigid glare of his. She had been swimming in this lake since she had first discovered it a month ago. "I know it is not proper to be swimming . . ."

"You did it anyway," Alex interrupted calmly.

"Yes," she agreed, turning back to him. His impassive face gave her no clue to his intentions. "I hope you will not mention it to anyone?"

"One moment you are questioning my word, and the next you are asking me for it?" Alex queried with a scornful laugh. "I can see you have a pretty strange view of men."

"My views have been shaped by men." Sarah lifted her chin defiantly.

"That may be so," Alex granted smoothly, "but you still have a problem. Are you going to leave the water?"

Sarah's teeth were chattering and she suspected there was nothing that would persuade this man to leave her alone. He was immovable. He had already admitted to spying on her, so she had no secrets to hide.

Abruptly, she swam to the shore, rose and walked to the water's edge. She watched Alex's eyes widen and then warm in appreciation. She straightened her shoulders and scowled at him, but he only smiled.

"Truly exquisite." He stood and handed her the sheet. "I am glad you did not try to cover yourself with your hands. You have nothing to be ashamed of."

Sarah wrapped the sheet about her and then shook her dark hair from her face before moving away. Her cheeks felt warm, but she refused to act embarrassed in front of this man. He would take that as a weakness; one he could exploit.

"I would not have been swimming if I had realized I had an audience." She went to her clothes, but his voice stopped her.

"You have only yourself to blame," he reasoned, walking toward her. "A proper lady would never consider swimming in the nude."

"A proper gentleman would have left when he realized my situation," Sarah retorted. A deep laugh was her only answer. Sarah clenched her teeth together tightly and bent to pick up her clothes, but he was there before her.

"Let me help you." He held out her chemise and drawers. "You cannot stand here all day shivering."

Sarah grabbed the garments and turned away from him. She put the undergarments on with one hand, the other holding the sheet in place. When she was covered, she used the sheet to dry her hair.

"How did you find this place?" Alex demanded in a brusque voice. "Everything is so overgrown on the estate. The lake is not easily seen."

Sarah looked back over her shoulder at the dark stranger. He was a giant of a man, standing over six feet tall with massive shoulders. There was a sense of power and control about him. His face was impassive, but his eyes burned intently as they assessed her. The puckered skin of his scar stood out against the deep tan and dark whiskers of his face.

"I come this way often. It may look hidden, but the pathways are still usable. This is in good condition compared to other parts of the estate."

Alex nodded his understanding, his jaw tightening slightly. She picked up her dress and moved to go around him, but before she could escape, he reached out and clasped her arm. The drying sheet and dress fell to the ground.

Sarah inhaled deeply, her eyes narrowing with

suspicion. Alex's hand touched her cheek softly. Shivers of awareness danced along Sarah's body.

"Will you tell me where you live?" he asked quietly. "I would like to see you again."

Sarah shook her head and pulled against his arm. "There is no need for us to meet."

"I disagree."

Sarah watched breathlessly as Alex's muscles tightened beneath his riding jacket, holding her there effortlessly. He moved closer, his breath tickling the skin of her face. His body loomed over her, blocking out the sun. Sarah felt her heart race.

"Let me go." Sarah's voice caught in her throat, sounding more like an invitation than a demand. A smile of satisfaction spread across Alex's face. He lowered his head and brushed his mouth over hers lightly.

His lips quivered against hers, warm and inviting. Sarah gasped at the stab of pleasure that flooded her body. She swayed closer to Alex, her own lips grazing his before the kiss ended. For a brief second she wondered if it had been real, but her lips still tingled as she ran her tongue over them.

When Sarah looked up, molten silver eyes met hers. The pounding of her heart echoed in her ears, everything forgotten except the man who held her. She tried to look away, but Alex's eyes kept her captive. It was as if she could see into his soul and God help her, she wanted to feel the thrill of his lips again.

His hands eased across her back, drawing her closer to him. A rush of heat exploded in her womb as the long, hard length of Alex pressed against her. A groan escaped her lips as shivers of sensation cascaded and spread throughout every nerve in her body. She ached with a need she had never known before.

Alex lowered his head, letting his tongue slide across her lips before plunging into her mouth. His tongue raked sensuously against hers, stroking and teasing, building a fire deep within her. It burned slow and hot. Sarah trembled, her knees weak as a shock of arousal stirred within her. Her mind warned that the flames would scorch her, but she no longer controlled her reactions. She leaned into Alex, surrendering to her body's wishes and his demands.

Sarah reveled in Alex's hungry exploration, savoring the sensation of her tongue dueling with his. Rational thought was impossible. The only thing that existed was the passion that burned between them. Sarah was lost in the moment, frightened yet enthralled by the awakening response within her. Her body throbbed with need and desire.

Alex's hands roamed across her back moving lower until he cupped her buttocks with both hands. With a swift, deft motion he brought her closer to him. A jolt of intense pleasure twisted inside her.

As if from a great distance, Sarah heard the snapping of a twig and the horse's protesting snort. The spell was broken. She struggled to free herself from the gossamer that held her entranced. Alex eased the pressure of his lips, his hands smoothing her away from him. How long the kiss had lasted, she did not know. Breathlessly she stared up at Alex, her body numb, in shock at her response to this stranger.

"Forgive me," he whispered hoarsely. "I could not resist."

Sarah shook her head in denial. "You should not have done that. You gave your word." She was twenty-seven years old and had never experienced a kiss like that.

"True," he agreed, his hand brushing the hair away from her eyes. "But now you understand why we must meet again. We are explosive together."

"Are you suggesting an affair?" she asked incredulously.

He smiled at her seductively. "It is clearly the next step in our relationship."

Sarah pulled away and slapped his face with a speed that surprised them both. The sound of it reverberated through the air. She covered her mouth in horror as the right side of his face turned red.

"Obviously you did not like my suggestion," he observed dryly. "A simple 'no' would have done."

"I am sorry," Sarah apologized haltingly. "I reacted without thinking."

"You are not a young girl." Alex bent down and picked up her dress. "You are also not inexperienced. Why should my suggestion shock you?"

"It would shock any woman of breeding."

"I had not considered that," Alex admitted with a sneer. "I do not expect to find women of breeding bathing in the nude."

"How dare you!" Sarah felt the anger burn within her and she held her hands tightly by her side. "You have the manners of a boar."

"Now is not the time to discuss it." Alex held out her dress. "You will catch cold standing like that."

Sarah looked down at her wet chemise and felt the heat rise in her cheeks. The thin material clung to her breasts, exposing more than it hid. She grabbed the dress and held it to her chest. This man made her forget herself and that was dangerous.

"I wish to dress in privacy." Sarah noticed a gleam appear in Alex's eyes and her breathing stilled.

She did not understand the effect he had on her, but she must escape.

"Of course." Alex turned to look back at the lake.

Sarah went behind some bushes. Instead of dressing, she crept away from the shoreline, hiding in a small grove of oak trees on the north side of the lake until she heard Alex gallop away.

Sarah looked down and realized she was still holding her dress. With shaking hands, she pulled the dull gray silk material over her head and secured its tape fastenings. She quickly coiled her long brown hair around her head and placed her cap over it.

Sarah almost ran back to the house, barely noticing the magnificence of Caldern. The rising sun's orange glow reflected off the red sandstone of the castle, causing it to burn with a blazing brilliance. The castle came alive under the sun's fiery strokes, but its beauty was lost on her this morning.

When she arrived at the kitchen she was greeted by a flurry of activity. It looked as if all the servants had converged in one place. She waited in the doorway until Cook had finished ladling food onto a serving dish. Johnson, the butler, then barked orders to the footmen, who gathered the dishes from the table. They all hurried out to the dining room and everyone gave a sigh of relief.

"It is busy this morning." Sarah walked over to the Cook who was resting against the table.

"That it is," the plump woman agreed. "What with the Marquess arriving."

"The Marquess is here?" Sarah asked in disbelief. Somehow she had not thought the man real. They had been waiting for him to appear for over a month now.

Cook gathered together her pots. "He arrived

late last night. Never a warning to anyone, but Lady Caldern will be pleased. She has been trying to convince him to return home for the last six months. It certainly will be good to see Master Alex again. Been gone since he was sixteen. He's grown into a fine man."

"I am sure he has," Sarah mumbled, her mind reeling with the news.

"Lady Caroline began ringing a few minutes ago. She'll be anxious to meet the Marquess." Cook handed the pots to one of the kitchen helpers and then turned back to the stove.

Sarah nodded weakly before walking out of the kitchen. When she was safely in the hall, she leaned her head against the dark oak-paneled wall and tried to steady her breathing. The knot in the pit of her stomach grew leaden. The stranger at the lake had said his name was Alex.

Sarah's mind flooded with images of the man who had caught her swimming. She had thought he looked familiar. Now she knew why. When she and her cousin Caroline had first arrived at the remote Cumberland estate of Caldern, they had been shown a picture of the Marquess when he was a boy. The man at the lake was that boy. He was the man her cousin intended to marry.

Chapter 2

Sarah tapped lightly at Caroline's door and then entered. It was a large, bright room with a southern exposure. The floral walls and bed coverings complimented Caroline's willowy, blond beauty perfectly.

"Where have you been?" Caroline demanded querulously. She was sitting in front of a dark mahogany vanity table, brushing her hair. She did not turn around when Sarah entered the room, but glared at her in the mirror. "You have been gone for hours."

"I was outside less than an hour." Sarah walked into the room and sat on the bed.

"It seemed like forever," Caroline cried petulantly, her limpid blue eyes accusing. "I need you here. That is why Father sent you with me."

"No need to talk such nonsense," a voice admonished from the dressing room. Nellie, their maid, came into the room, her arms full of dresses. "Mrs. Wellsley is with you for chaperonage and support. She is your cousin, not your servant."

Sarah smiled at Nellie and stood up. "Good

morning, Nellie. Let me help you with those." Sarah took the dresses and put them on the bed.

"The least she can do is be here when I need her." Caroline slammed her hairbrush down on the vanity top. "The Marquess finally decides to come home and where are you?"

"I was collecting herbs." Sarah began spreading the gowns out on the bed. "Surely these dresses are too elaborate for morning wear?"

"I need to look my best," Caroline exclaimed. "Unlike you, I prefer to attract men. I would never bury myself away from the world if my husband died, no matter how much I loved the man."

Sarah's stomach tightened painfully and her hand froze above the bed. Caroline's last words reverberated in her head. How could her cousin believe Sarah had actually loved her husband? No woman could have loved a man like Stephen Wellsley. A gentle hand on her shoulder nudged her out of her reverie and she looked up to see Nellie's understanding face.

"You go and sit down. I can look after Lady Caroline, Nellie whispered. She led Sarah to a daybed and motioned for her to sit.

"I wish you would pay more attention to your family and less to those herbs," Caroline whined, turning around to look at Sarah directly. "You are always off attending some sick village person or working in the stillroom. You are never here when I need you."

"It is what I do," Sarah explained gently. "People rely on my herbs and healing knowledge."

"Well, I rely on you too." Caroline's full red lips pouted prettily and she tossed her long blond hair behind one shoulder. "You know I am nervous about this meeting. I do not need to worry about you."

"I have never given you any reason to fret,

Caroline." Sarah straightened her shoulders and looked directly at her cousin. "If you are anxious about meeting the Marquess, then why did you agree to your father's ridiculous plan?"

"It is no such thing," Caroline defended. "The Marquess will make the perfect husband. He is rich, titled, and still young enough for me to appreciate him. The rumor in London is that he is quite handsome. That is all I require in a husband."

"You have not met him yet," Sarah reminded. "Perhaps you will not like him." The ruggedly masculine face of the man at the lake flashed through Sarah's mind. There was little chance her cousin would not admire him. He was definitely attractive.

"That is why we are visiting Caldern." Caroline stood up and walked to the bed. She pondered the dresses for a few seconds before choosing a pale pink, silk confection. "We are here to meet each other and see if we will suit. Nothing could be more civilized."

"I suppose," Sarah agreed quietly. "You are talking about the rest of your life, though. This is the man you will have to live with."

Caroline turned around and looked at Sarah in disbelief. "You are such a romantic, Sarah. This is a marriage. We will eventually go our separate ways once the children have been born."

"Uncle John and Aunt Alice do not have a marriage like that," Sarah reminded her cousin.

"They are so provincial." Caroline sighed heavily and then stepped into the gown that Nellie was holding open for her. "I want to live in London with the people who really matter."

"Does that mean your parents are unimportant because they spend most of their time in Somerset?" Sarah asked in outrage.

"Now you are twisting my words." Caroline straightened the bodice of the dress on her shoulders and looked behind as Nellie began to do the tapes up. "Father is an earl, so of course he counts. I just want to have a life that is not centered in the country."

"The Marquess's estate is in the north. It is only hours away from the Scottish border and several days' drive away from London. You will likely never see a social life," Sarah explained patiently.

Caroline looked back at her with narrowed eyes. "I do not believe you can be so silly, Sarah. The Marquess can live wherever he wishes, but I intend to stay in London."

"As your husband, he will have total control over where and how you live, Caroline. Do not rush into a marriage with someone you know nothing about," Sarah pleaded.

"We are hardly rushing." Caroline walked back to the vanity and sat down. Nellie gathered her hair and arranged it on top of her head. "We have been waiting in this horrible drafty castle for over a month now."

"The house is no such thing," Sarah denied. "If you would not insist on staying indoors, you would see how lovely the estate really is. Besides, if you wish to become the Marchioness, you should be meeting the people who live and work here."

"That is hardly necessary. I am not marrying a common vicar like you did." Caroline twisted a ringlet across her bare shoulder and then stood up. "Right now my only concern is securing the Marquess's interest. He still has to propose."

Caroline walked to the bedroom door, but before she opened it, she turned back to Sarah. "You look a complete mess. Please change that gown before you come down for breakfast. I would hate the Marquess to get the wrong impression of my family."

Without another word Caroline left the room. Sarah sat staring at the closed door in silence for a few seconds before she shook her head and smiled. Caroline, as the only daughter, had always been spoiled, but Sarah had never realized how insensitive Caroline had become since being presented in London two years ago.

"Take no mind of her," Nellie said briskly. "She has been cooped up in this place for too long. You know how she needs the company of young people."

Sarah sighed heavily and stood up. "I understand, Nellie. You do not have to be concerned with me. I just hope Caroline does not do anything foolish."

"If you will forgive me, Mrs. Wellsley," Nellie said with a small cough. "Lady Caroline will always take care of herself first."

"True, but I cannot like this plan of my uncle's."

"Lord Hart is very cautious," Nellie advised briskly. "He has few options left with Lady Caroline. She has driven away all the eligible suitors, so he believes an arranged match would suit her best."

Sarah nodded her head. "Lady Caldern and he have been friends for many years. I know Uncle has made certain that Lord Caldern is an honorable man and will not hurt Caroline in any way. I suppose I will just have to trust his opinion."

"It is not easy for you," Nellie murmured.

"I am past that part of my life." Sarah walked over to Nellie and gave her a hug. "I have my herbs and healing now."

"That you do." Nellie moved away to the bed and began to gather up the discarded gowns. "You'd best go and change. Lady Caroline was right about that dress. It looks as if you dragged it through the mud."

Sarah looked down and felt her cheeks burn with embarrassment. There was dirt smeared all over the front of her dress and a small tear at the hem. She had been in such a hurry to escape the lake that she had not realized the condition of her clothes.

"I will go and change immediately." Sarah left the room quickly and went to her own bedroom in the north wing.

She was in an older section of the house and even though Caroline would have abhorred it, she loved her room. It was large, with the stone exposed on the outer wall. The bed was at least a hundred years old and the dark burgundy tapestry window and bed coverings were probably the same age. Sarah relaxed the moment she set foot in the room.

She shed her dirty gown and selected a clean one from the wardrobe. She dressed and then took her cap off to redo her hair. It took her a few minutes to rearrange her braid and then to cover it with another gray silk and lace cap. When she was satisfied, she left her room and went downstairs to the dining room.

Caldern had been built over several centuries and now consisted of several wings and additions. The formal dining room was in the newest addition in the south wing. It was a large room that could easily accommodate fifty people. The oak paneling added an air of elegance that was enhanced by the numerous works of art that hung on the walls. Each successive generation of Calderns had left their touch on the room.

Sarah entered the room quietly and walked to

the first of three ancient sideboards that stood against the wall. It was closest to the doorway where the servants carried in the food. Breakfast was informal at Caldern, with people wandering in whenever they rose in the mornings. Sarah helped herself to a poached egg and a slice of ham before sitting at the table.

Caroline was not in the room, but that did not surprise Sarah. Her cousin was seldom awake at such an early hour and she never ate much in the morning. Her quick departure meant the Marquess had not been in the dining room. The rest of the household was present, though.

"Good morning Mrs. Wellsley," Lady Caldern greeted stiffly. "You are later than usual."

Lady Caldern sat at the end of the table. She was in her late fifties and still retained a portion of the beauty that must have been truly spectacular in her younger years. She had pale brown hair, heavily streaked with gray, but it was covered with a dark mauve turban this morning. She wore a matching mauve morning dress.

"Lady Caroline needed my help," Sarah explained, accepting a cup of hot chocolate from Johnson. "I understand Lord Caldern arrived last night."

"It is high time my exalted half brother returned," Lord Bryan Norward snapped from across the table. He was a young man of about twenty-eight who always wore a slightly bored expression. He had light brown hair and green eyes. His looks and charm were rumored to have captivated most of the women of the area.

"I agree," Lady Caldern said with a nod of her head. "It has been a year since he inherited the title. His indifference to his responsibilities is unacceptable."

"But Mother, he was in India when Douglas

died," Lady Julianna Norward objected in a timid voice. "You cannot fault him for that."

"True," Lady Caldern admitted. "He has been in London for the last six months, though. I sent numerous missives demanding his attendance at Caldern and he saw fit to ignore them all. I cannot forgive that."

Privately, Sarah agreed with Lady Caldern. The general state of disrepair and neglect that pervaded Caldern was atrocious.

"He left Caldern very angry with Father," the quiet, hesitant voice of Lady Julianna reminded them.

Sarah looked at Lady Julianna Norward with surprise. She was a shy, fragile, beautiful young woman of twenty. Sarah had never heard her answer her mother back before. She usually accepted her mother's criticism and faded into the background.

"What would you know of such matters?" Lady Caldern snapped loudly. "You were nothing more than a babe still in the nursery."

"Mary used to tell me about Alex."

"I will not have that woman's name mentioned in my house." Lady Caldern glared at Lady Julianna until the young woman hung her head in defeat. "I am ashamed that a daughter of mine would associate with a creature such as her."

Sarah glanced questioningly at Lady Julianna, but the young girl's face was expressionless. The only Mary Sarah knew lived in a small cottage on the estate. She was well liked by the villagers and had a grown son who had made his fortune in the Americas. Sarah could not imagine why this woman would cause such a reaction in the Marchioness.

"Now that Father and Douglas are dead, you should have her removed from Caldern land," Lord Bryan stated.

"If it were within my power, I would." Lady Caldern's knife clattered on her plate as she put it down. "I have heard enough this morning. Mrs. Wellsley, if you are finished I would like to show you the tapestry I need repaired."

"Certainly," Sarah replied. She put down her napkin and rose from the table to follow Lady Caldern from the room.

"I am so happy Lady Caroline mentioned your skill with the needle." Lady Caldern stopped outside the dining room door and turned to Sarah. "The work you have done with repairing the linens and bedcovers has been appreciated."

"Thank you, Lady Caldern," Sarah murmured. The household mending was another area that had been neglected for years and Sarah had been spending a good portion of her day in the fourth floor sewing room.

"I enjoy handwork. The quiet gives me time to think about the best treatments for my patients."

"Yes, of course," Lady Caldern harrumphed. "You have been making yourself quite useful. I am glad your uncle insisted on sending you along with Lady Caroline."

Sarah smiled slightly and remembered the coldness of Lady Caldern's initial greeting. They had reached the stairs and she started to climb them. She turned to speak to Lady Caldern, but stopped when someone cleared his throat.

"Fanny." A firm male voice echoed in the large hallway.

Sarah saw Lady Caldern stiffen, her eyes narrowing and her mouth grimacing into a thin line of disapproval. Footsteps came toward them.

"I am busy, Alex."

"As am I."

Sarah's stomach tightened into a knot and her

breath stopped in her throat. Panic threatened to overcome her and she gripped the balustrade to prevent herself from falling. The tall, dark figure of the man she had met at the lake swam before her eyes and she quickly lowered her head to avoid his glance. She felt his eyes turn her way and her hand tightened on the railing as she waited for him to recognize her.

Chapter 3

Alex leaned against the solid oak newel post. His eyes scanned Sarah and then turned back to Lady Caldern. "Why have you not answered my summons?"

"I am attending to a household matter." Lady Caldern walked down the stairs and stood in front of him. "I will be with you shortly."

"I asked you to come to the library when you had finished your breakfast. I am not in the habit of waiting."

"When I have finished my duties, I will meet with you," Lady Caldern replied in a voice hardened with reprove.

"You have no duties at Caldern unless I say so," Lord Caldern explained in a deceptively soft voice before bowing to his stepmother. "We will discuss this now." Without another word he walked into the library.

Lady Caldern stared at the open door for a few seconds before she looked at Sarah. "I must apologize for my stepson's rudeness. It seems that his years away have not been to his benefit."

"I understand." Sarah loosened her grip on the railing. "I will find the tapestry on my own. There is no need for you to trouble yourself."

Lady Caldern nodded and then walked to the library. She entered the room and shut the door quietly behind her. Sarah sagged into the stair railing and took a deep breath of relief. The Marquess had not recognized her. Perhaps if she remained in the background and did not call attention to herself, she would be able to successfully avoid the man.

Sarah spent the rest of the morning repairing the tapestry. In the afternoon she visited with her patients in the village. She had successfully avoided the Marquess all day, but when she went to her room to dress for dinner she knew there was no escape. She prayed he would not tell anyone about her swimming.

Sarah sat down at her vanity and looked into the mirror. She frowned and rubbed her hands across her face. For the first time in years, she did not feel pleasure in her appearance. Her brown hair was tightly wound around her head and all that remained was to cover it with the gray satin cap sitting on her vanity. She looked like the nondescript servant her family wanted her to be. No one would notice her, but that brought little solace this evening.

"You look unhappy." Nellie's strident voice broke into Sarah's musings.

"Just nervous," Sarah explained. She stood up and went to the bed where Nellie was waiting with her evening dress. The dress was a plain gray gown without lace or frills.

"I know it was hard for you to come with Lady Caroline, but your uncle was right." Nellie adjusted the skirt of the gown and then began to fasten it at the back. "Caroline needs guidance and you would never disappoint your family."

"I owe them too much." Sarah straightened the collar of the dress and then picked up her cap. "Uncle John gave me a home after Stephen died and now I only want to live my life in peace."

"It might feel safer that way, but I am not fooled." Nellie took the cap from Sarah's hands and placed it on her head. "I have known you a long time. Do not let one man destroy your dreams of children."

Sarah moved away from Nellie. "I am older. I have everything I need to keep me content."

Nellie shook her head and put one hand on her hip. "You are hiding from the world."

Sarah unconsciously pulled at her cap, moving it until it was almost in her eyes. "I must go. I cannot be late for dinner."

Sarah turned away and left the room swiftly. She did not want to dwell on Nellie's words. They had been too close to the truth. Sarah had almost reconciled herself to a life without children until she and Caroline had arrived at Caldern. Everything had come flooding back during her first days here. All the memories and dreams she had once believed in.

Perhaps it was the newness of the area or the people she was meeting, but for some reason she could not bury her sense of loss. Visiting Caldern had reopened a wound that had not fully healed. Many nights she had gone to bed crying, something she had not done in years.

Sarah took a deep breath and forced herself to think about tonight's dinner. She would again be meeting the Marquess. There was a slight possibility of him recognizing her from this morning, but Sarah brushed that thought aside. He would have eyes only for Caroline.

She approached the drawing room doors quietly and slipped into the room unnoticed. She was moving toward the window seat where she usually sat, when Lady Caldern's voice halted her.

"Mrs. Wellsley, please come here," she demanded in an imperious tone.

Sarah turned to Lady Caldern. She stood with Lady Caroline and two men near the fireplace. When Sarah reached them, Lady Caldern took her arm.

"You must meet my stepson and his friend Mr. Stanton."

Lady Caldern moved her to a man wearing a bright sea blue waistcoat and black evening suit. His attire was shockingly bold and Sarah thought he was a dandy until she glanced at his face. His soft, brown eyes were bright with curiosity, his eyebrow quirked questioningly.

"Mr. Stanton, this is Mrs. Wellsley," Lady Caldern announced.

"Mr. Stanton," Sarah murmured as she curtsied.

"Delighted to make your acquaintance, Mrs. Wellsley." Mr. Stanton made a neat bow and then turned back to his conversation with her cousin.

"This is my stepson, Lord Caldern." Lady Caldern's strident voice forced Sarah to turn and look at the tall dark man who stood beside Mr. Stanton. Her heart beat rapidly. He seemed indifferent and bored, his dark eyes barely glancing in her direction.

Anger replaced Sarah's fear. For some inexplicable reason his indifference was an insult. She forced herself to look at him directly, daring him to recognize her. His eyes darted over her appearance quickly and his head inclined politely at Sarah's slight curtsey.

"Mrs. Wellsley is Lady Caroline's cousin," Lady Caldern explained. "She has been gracious enough to visit with the villagers and help them with her herbal treatments. I am afraid we have trespassed on her kindness, too Her skill with a needle has been most useful in repairing the household linens."

"A marvel among women," Lord Caldern agreed. "The estate has been sadly neglected of late. Any effort to help is appreciated."

"I trust that things will improve now that you have arrived," Sarah murmured quietly as he began to turn away.

Lord Caldern paused in his movement and glanced back at Sarah. "Have we met before, Mrs. Wellsley?"

"I am certain we have not," Sarah answered quickly. Her breath caught in her throat at the searing glance Lord Caldern gave her. She lowered her head in an attempt to escape it.

"Perhaps in London?"

"Sarah has never been to London," Caroline interjected. "She refuses to go anywhere. Father had to insist she accompany me to Caldern."

Sarah cringed at Caroline's words, her cheeks blushing with mortification.

"We are grateful to your father." Lord Caldern spoke indifferently, but when Sarah glanced back at his face, his eyes were sparkling with amusement. He recognized her!

"No need to be," Caroline said with a scornful laugh. "She is always helping others, even if it means neglecting her family."

Sarah looked at Caroline with a frown. Her cousin was being more cruel than usual and she did not understand why. Caroline glared back at her and then tossed her head defiantly. Sarah could see no obvious reason for her anger. Caroline looked stunning in a light blue gown that matched her eyes perfectly. Mr. Stanton seemed mesmerized by her. His eyes had not left her face since he greeted Sarah.

"You have described a paragon of virtue, Lady Caroline," Lord Caldern observed dryly. "It seems unlikely that such an angel would neglect her own family."

Sarah flinched at Lord Caldern's sarcasm. She looked at him boldly before speaking. "I believe you exaggerate, my lord."

Lord Caldern inclined his head slightly. "You may be correct, Mrs. Wellsley. I am certain that you have a few faults. Perhaps something done in privacy that you would not like others to know about."

"You are mistaken, my lord." Caroline disagreed with a shake of her head. "My cousin has always been above reproach, even when she was a young girl."

"Perhaps, Lady Caroline," Lord Caldern admitted. "We all have secrets, though."

"Nonsense." Lady Caldern interrupted with a snort. "You are making Mrs. Wellsley extremely uncomfortable."

Sarah held herself still, her heart beating frantically. Lord Caldern seemed determined to bait her, his very look threatening to uncover her secret. She could not allow him to continue in this manner. Her initial anger had changed to fear. She took a deep breath and reminded herself that she had vowed never to let a man terrorize her again.

"As we have not met before, Lord Caldern, your comments are extremely rude. I resent your attitude." Sarah looked at him directly, daring him to reveal her swimming.

Caldern tilted his head to one side, a small smile played across his mouth, as he seemed to debate her words. "Perhaps you are right, Mrs. Wellsley," he agreed smoothly. "I believe I have mistaken you for someone else."

"Whom could you possibly mistake my cousin for?" Caroline demanded incredulously.

"That is hardly kind," Caldern admonished severely.

"Enough," Sarah insisted in a strangled voice. Her cheeks were red with embarrassment and all she wanted was to escape. "I do not wish to be spoken of in such a manner. Please excuse me."

Sarah turned abruptly away and walked to the window seat. She sat down with a sigh of relief and barely noticed when Lady Julianna sat next to her.

"How are you?" she asked quietly.

Sarah smiled and turned to the timid woman beside her. "An introduction to your brother was more of an ordeal than I expected. I will be fine shortly."

"Alex is my half brother," Lady Julianna corrected. "You were lucky. He treated you better than your cousin."

Sarah frowned. No man had ever been able to resist Caroline and it seemed unlikely that Lord Caldern would be immune. "There must be some mistake."

Lady Julianna shook her head. "I was present when they met in the library. Alex was indifferent to Lady Caroline's flirtations and told her they would deal better if she did not try so hard to please him."

Sarah closed her eyes and grimaced. Caroline's temper had sent many of her suitors running. "What happened?"

"Lady Caroline picked up a vase and flung it at Alex and then asked if that pleased him more. Alex said that at least it was honest." Lady Julianna paused for a few seconds before continuing. "I am afraid Lady Caroline flew into a rage and then stormed out of the room."

"How did Caldern react to that?"

"He shrugged his shoulders and went back to his papers."

"No wonder Caroline is being so cruel this evening. She cannot bear to have her will thwarted."

"Alex was wrong," Lady Julianna insisted. "A gentleman should not treat a lady in such a manner."

"Perhaps not," Sarah agreed with a sigh. "But your brother does not seem to be fooled easily."

Sarah glanced at Caroline, noting the artificial gaiety in her laugh. Her back was turned to the Marquess and her attention was focused solely on Mr. Stanton. Lord Caldern seemed totally impervious to Caroline's attempt to make him jealous. He was speaking with Lord Bryan and raised his glass to his mouth to take a drink when his eyes collided with Sarah's.

Her mouth went dry as the noise of the room faded away. There were only two people in the world, their eyes locked in a moment of recognition. Sarah felt as if the world were spinning. Nothing in her ordered life had prepared her for the rush of emotion that welled up inside of her. Thankfully, Alex looked away. He inclined his head slightly and then turned back to his half brother.

Sarah took a deep breath, clasping her hands together to hide their trembling. She had never experienced such an intense or private moment before. She wanted to run and hide, but Lady Julianna's quiet voice brought her back to the present.

"I visited Bates today and he seemed much improved. He mentioned that you had given him something for his cough."

"I gave him a tea made from elder flowers," Sarah explained. "It should relax the muscles in his lungs and help with the cough."

"He could not sing your praises enough," Lady Julianna added with a smile. "He thinks you are an angel sent from heaven."

"Another person who believes you a paragon of virtue?"

Sarah jumped and her heart lurched in her chest at the sound of Alex's voice. She had been looking at Lady Julianna and had not seen him approach them.

"My apologies, Mrs. Wellsley. I did not mean to startle you." Lord Caldern gave a slight bow and then turned to Lady Julianna. "Who has been singing our fair guest's praises?"

"Old Bates," Lady Julianna explained. "Do you remember him?"

"Of course I do." Caldern grinned broadly. "He used to chase me out of the gardens. I was constantly underfoot when I was a young lad. He must be in his eighties now. How is he doing?"

Lady Julianna bowed her head and looked at her hands before answering. "He lives in a tiny cottage by the village, but his pension is small and I am worried about him surviving the winter."

Lord Caldern's mouth hardened into a thin line and he shook his head. "I saw those cottages this morning. They are in deplorable condition."

Lady Julianna looked up at Caldern and nodded. "Mother did not believe they needed improvement, but Bates cannot handle another winter there. Mrs. Wellsley has been helping him with his lungs, but she will not be here come winter."

"Perhaps we may persuade her to leave us her remedies."

Sarah felt her cheeks redden. Lord Caldern was looking at her inscrutably, his eyes never wavering from hers. "I will do everything in my power to help Bates. There is no need to worry on that account."

"I will make certain his cottage is improved," Lord Caldern stated.

Sarah was about to ask Lord Caldern about the

other cottages when Johnson announced dinner. She stood up and moved to take her place in the dinner procession when Lord Caldern held his arm out to her.

She looked up at him. His eyebrow was raised slightly, highlighting the gleam in his eye. Sarah's heart started to beat quicker.

"Did you think I would let you escape?"

Chapter 4

"You cannot lead me into dinner," she insisted in a whisper.

"There is no reason to follow society's dictates at a family dinner."

"What are you about?" Lady Caldern demanded from the other side of the room. "Alex, you must lead Lady Caroline in. She takes precedence over her cousin."

"This is hardly a formal dinner, Fanny." Caldern placed Sarah's hand on his arm.

The Marquess seated her on his right side and motioned for the servants to begin serving the meal. He cleared his throat before saying conversationally, "Does your interest in herbs extend to other aspects of nature, Mrs. Wellsley?"

Sarah looked up to see a pair of laughing gray eyes. He did not appear to be menacing, but his every word seemed to suggest a delight in torturing her. Sarah shook her head in confusion.

"Mrs. Wellsley has spent a great deal of time restoring the kitchen garden," Lady Julianna interjected. "It had fallen into a terrible state since Mother had to reduce the gardening staff."

"I was told that was my mother's favorite place," Lord Caldern mused quietly. "I am thankful you are working on it."

"Sarah is only doing it for her precious herbs," Caroline advised sarcastically. She was seated on the other side of the Marquess.

"I am still grateful," Lord Caldern stated with a cold glare at Lady Caroline.

Sarah closed her eyes briefly, her stomach clenched tightly in a knot. Everyone seemed determined to make her uncomfortable this evening. The footman brought her the platter of Florentine rabbit and she accepted a small portion of food. Her hand shook slightly as she used her fork to push the food around her plate. She did not believe she would be able to swallow anything this evening.

The Marquess leaned close to her. "I did not think anything would embarrass you," he said in a low whisper.

"What can you mean?" Sarah asked sharply.

"You hardly blinked an eye when I met you this morning," he explained quietly. The chatter and laughter of the others gave a perfect cover for a private conversation. "Surely a woman as bold as yourself would be used to this game?"

"I do not play games," Sarah insisted in a tight voice. "I believe you are mistaken in your opinion of me."

"I understood you this morning. Your actions were very forceful, but women usually say one thing and mean another. Your swimming gave me a very clear indication of your character." Lord Caldern winked.

"You are wrong. I did not realize anyone was about or I would never have risked discovery." Sarah turned back to her food, thankful that Caroline demanded the Marquess's attention.

A few minutes later Lady Julianna leaned toward her. "You should not have angered Mother."

"I had no choice," Sarah advised in a low voice, her eyes glancing sideways to be certain the Marquess's attention was elsewhere.

"She always gets what she wants." Lady Julianna sighed and Sarah felt a twinge of sympathy for the young woman. Her life was not easy.

"You stood up to her this morning."

Lady Julianna nodded. "Mother was upset, though. She banished me for the rest of the day."

Sarah's eyes opened wide in astonishment. She glanced down the table to where Lady Caldern sat. "Hardly a punishment."

Julianna giggled. "I spent the day roaming the house. I even went to the roof," she confided. "Father used to take me up there before he was ill. He said it was the best place to see Caldern."

"It is a spectacular view." Sarah had only visited the roof once. The old battlements and stone walls from the original castle had made her feel as if she were walking back in time.

"Mother is looking at us," Lady Julianna whispered. "We must stop talking."

The rest of the meal passed in relative peace for Sarah. Lord Caldern's attention was focused on her cousin. He seemed to be engrossed in his conversation with Caroline, but every time Sarah looked up, she found his eyes on her. As the desserts were being removed, Lord Caldern leaned to her once again.

"I understand what your beautiful cousin wants, but you puzzle me. Why have you dressed yourself in such a fashion?" Caldern asked in a whisper.

"That is hardly any of your business, sir."

"You are wrong," he insisted. "You are my guest."

Sarah's breath caught in her throat at the intense gaze Alex gave her. "I do not need a man to care for me," she insisted, standing to follow Lady Caldern from the room.

Sarah pleaded a headache and went upstairs to the sewing room to work. Several hours later she squinted, straining to see where to put the next stitch. The flickering candlelight made it difficult to see the pattern of the tapestry. She slanted it toward the light before pushing her needle through. A short stab of pain pierced her finger.

"Ouch!" She pulled her hand away, putting the wounded finger in her mouth to stop the flow of blood.

"You should be more careful with such a dangerous tool, Sarah," a quiet voice advised.

Sarah's heart jumped with surprise. The large figure of the Marquess was blocking the doorway. His face was in the shadows, but she knew it was him.

"Do not look so horrified," the Marquess said quietly. "I will not harm you." He moved slowly away from the door and into the room, his eyes scanning the piles of household items waiting to be repaired.

"Fanny was not lying about the linens." Lord Caldern walked to one of the tables and examined a torn sheet. "Would it not be better to replace these?"

Sarah released the breath she had been holding. "Lady Caldern says it is not possible. I believe it has been several years since anything has been refurbished."

"Then it is time we had new. There is no need for you to waste your efforts on these rags." Caldern moved away from the table and began to walk around the small room. The wall sconces provided enough light that Sarah could discern his features in the darkness.

"I will sort through them." Sarah's eyes followed the Marquess's progress until he stopped at a window and looked out.

"I came to apologize." He spoke with his back to her, reaching up a hand to close the curtain before turning toward her. His face was expressionless, but Sarah noticed his jaw tighten, making his scar stand out in the faint light.

"Apologize?" Sarah repeated in surprise. "I do not believe I have ever heard a man do so."

"Then perhaps you have not known the right men," he suggested coldly.

Sarah raised her hand to her mouth. "I should never have said that, my lord. I spoke without thinking."

"You were being honest." He moved away from the window and stood near the wall with his hands behind his back. "I thought I had asked you to call me Alex."

"It would not be proper." Sarah protested. "Caroline would never understand."

"I prefer Alex," he said with a grin. "At least when we are in private. Am I forgiven now?"

"For what?"

"My rude behavior this morning," he explained. "I had given you my word. I should never have touched you."

"Why did you then?"

"You saw no reason for us to meet again." The Marquess looked at her intently, his eyes unwavering. "I wanted to prove you wrong. It will not happen again."

"Your conduct this evening suggested otherwise." Sarah leaned back in her chair and eyed the Marquess carefully. His face was expressionless. "You did nothing but bait me in front of my cousin. If you feel that you must let Caroline know about my swimming, I understand, but I prefer not to be teased."

"Again, I apologize." Caldern sighed heavily. "I had misjudged the situation."

"What did you believe?" Sarah asked curiously. She folded the tapestry and placed it on the table.

The Marquess started to move around the room again. His pacing reminded Sarah of the caged animals she had read about in books. He exuded a strength and power that the room could not contain. She shivered when she considered how closely she had come to being in this man's control.

"I thought you would welcome my advances," the Marquess explained after a short pause. He turned abruptly to face her. "You must admit your swimming was hardly ladylike behavior."

Sarah looked down at her hands and felt the heat flare in her face. She closed her eyes and grimaced. Swimming was bad enough, but to be found in the nude was beyond the pale.

"It was wrong of me," she whispered. "Can you not forget it?"

"I do not believe I will ever forget the sight of you in that lake. It will stay with me for the rest of my life. I was wrong to use that to make an assumption about your character, though," he replied quietly. "I realized at dinner that you were uncomfortable. I would like us to begin again."

"I suppose we will have to see each other frequently." Sarah looked at the Marquess and felt her mouth go dry. Just the sight of him sent her body spinning out of control. "It would be better if we could at least be civil to each other, my lord."

"More than civil, I hope." The Marquess smiled seductively. "I asked you to call me Alex. Tell me why you risked the chance of being caught swimming?"

"It is exhilarating and gives me a sense of freedom," Sarah admitted hesitantly. "For years I have permitted myself these tiny liberties. Stephen, my husband, was constantly lecturing me about the evil I allowed into my life, but when I saw the lake, I could not resist. It was so inviting and peaceful. Before long, I had made it part of my daily ritual. I did not see any harm in it."

"I can understand that."

"You can?" Sarah asked in astonishment.

"I have spent most of my life on the water. I joined the navy when I was sixteen."

"I did not realize," Sarah confessed apologetically. "You must find it very different being on land after all those years."

"Not really." Alex sauntered to the table. He pulled out one of the vacant chairs and sat down across from her. "I have been out of the navy since Napoleon's final surrender. After that, I spent my time in India."

"India," Sarah repeated in awe. "I have read so many books about it. I have dreamed of visiting there one day. What was it like?"

"Hot and dry," Alex answered with a frown.

"If you found it so disagreeable, why did you stay for so long?" Sarah found herself struggling for breath at the nearness of the Marquess. A sudden heat suffused her cheeks, only to intensify at the Marquess's quirked eyebrow.

"I was the second son." Alex's tone was devoid of emotion, but his lips had thinned into a tight line. "My father and I fought before I left, so I had no expectations."

"After all those years surely your father would have forgiven you?" Sarah could not imagine a father neglecting a child in such a manner.

"I was dead to my father," Alex stated firmly. "It was the way I wanted it."

"You had no wish to see your family?"

"None."

Sarah could only stare in amazement. Her father had died when she was barely ten years old and she still remembered the pain of the loss. She could not understand how someone would deliberately distance themselves from family.

"You look amazed," Caldern noted with a slight laugh. "You cannot tell me that you enjoy your cousin's treatment?"

"No," Sarah agreed, "But I understand her and I would never be happy knowing that I could not see her."

"Perhaps your family is more loving, but other than my brother Nathan, I have not kept in touch with mine."

"I have not heard mention of a Nathan Caldern." Sarah had only heard of an older brother Douglas, who had died a year ago.

"It is Nathan Carter. You have not heard of him because my beloved stepmother, Fanny, would never permit him or my brother Samuel to be mentioned."

Sarah stared at Caldern in confusion. "I do not understand."

"My brothers were born on the wrong side of the blanket," Alex explained. "My father was a notorious philanderer, but he had always treated his sons equally, until he married Fanny."

"You have illegitimate brothers?"

"My father raised them with us until he remarried when I was six. Fanny insisted they be sent away." Alex looked down at the table and was silent for several minutes before he continued. "Samuel went to school. Nathan and his mother, Mary, were moved to a small cottage on the estate."

Sarah suddenly remembered the conversation at breakfast concerning Mary. Perhaps this was the

Mary to whom Lady Caldern was referring. It would certainly explain Lady Caldern's behavior.

"Does Mary still live on the estate?"

"Yes. She was our nanny and my father pensioned her off." Alex sighed and frowned down at the floor. "Samuel was not so lucky. His mother had died when he was born, so he was sent away to school. When he graduated, my father gave him a small parish with the stipulation he never visit Caldern."

"How horrible for him."

The Marquess looked up, his eyes piercing Sarah almost to her soul. "I do believe you mean that."

"Of course I do," Sarah cried indignantly. "Your brothers cannot be blamed for their birth."

"No," Alex agreed. "Many women would, though. Fanny was within her rights to demand my father send them away. Society does not look kindly on a man's bastards."

"Society has always dealt with the weak harshly," Sarah declared vehemently. "That does not make it right."

The Marquess stared at her intently. "You are an unusual woman, Sarah. We have talked enough about me. Tell me why are you still unmarried."

"I am much too old to be marrying," Sarah declared swiftly, confused by the abrupt change of subject. "What could possibly interest you about me?"

"Lots of things interest me," Alex stated, picking up the tapestry she had been mending. "Humor me."

"There is nothing to say," Sarah answered cautiously. "My husband died and I returned to my uncle's home."

"How old were you when your husband died?"

"Eighteen."

"Now that is unusual." Alex raised his head quickly. "Did you love him so much that you could not bring yourself to remarry?"

"Love?" Sarah choked out in surprise.

"Obviously not," Alex surmised quietly, his eyes never leaving her face.

"My life is of no concern to you, my lord," Sarah advised firmly. "I can answer any questions you have about Caroline, though. I am sure you would find that much more interesting."

"Why would I want to know anything about Lady Caroline?" the Marquess asked as he leaned forward in his chair.

"You are considering marriage to her," she answered. "I would have thought that you would like to know everything about her."

"And you would give me an unbiased view?" he asked with deliberate care.

"Of course," Sarah answered, blushing when his right eyebrow lifted in doubt.

"I will remember that. However, I believe I know as much as I need to about Lady Caroline."

"Then you have decided to wed Caroline," Sarah stated with a nod. It would please her cousin, but for some reason her own stomach sank at the thought.

"I must wed," Alex agreed.

Sarah's mouth went dry as Alex continued to watch her. She sensed that he wanted to say something more. He reached across the narrow table and touched her hand. Shivers raced up her arm and Sarah's heart started to beat frantically.

"You have no need to fear me," he insisted, stroking his finger across her hand. "I can see you are unsure. I think we should start out by becoming friends."

"Of course. We are to become family." Sarah's breath caught in her throat as lethargy spread throughout her body. Alex gathered her hand in his and brought it to his mouth. His lips caressed it gently before he turned it over.

"You have beautiful hands." Caldern traced a finger over her palm, sending a tingling weakness up her arm. "So capable and strong. Is there anything you cannot do?"

"I do not understand," Sarah whispered. She licked her lips in nervousness. In an effort to catch her breath she inhaled deeply. The strong masculine scent of the Marquess tickled her nostrils and stirred fluttering sensations in her lower abdomen.

"You garden, sew, heal, and care for your family." The Marquess looked up at her, his eyes burning with an inner light. "You also have the ability to arouse a man's desire. A truly remarkable woman."

Sarah shook her head in denial. "You should not talk to me in such a manner. You are to marry Caroline."

"What does that have to do with us?" Caldern gave her a crooked smile and released her hand. "Marriage is purely a business arrangement, but desire is another thing."

"But Caroline . . ." Sarah began, until she remembered whom she was speaking about. She could not refute what he had said. Caroline had expressed the same sentiment about marriage this morning.

"Very wise," Alex advised dryly. "Your loyalty to your cousin does you credit, but I am not yet engaged. I am still free to do as I please and you please me very much." The Marquess stood up and walked to the door. When he had almost reached it, he stopped. "Perhaps I should ask Lady Caroline about you?" he asked without turning around. "I wonder if she will be quite as honest."

Without another word, he left the room and Sarah let out the breath she had been holding. The Marquess was definitely a man she must stay away from.

Chapter 5

The bright July sun beat down upon Sarah, forcing her to move into the shade of the trees. She pushed her bonnet off her head, swiping her hand across her forehead impatiently. It was unbearably hot and she was walking along the laneway that led from the village to Caldern. She slowed down as she passed the house of Mary Carter.

Two large stallions were pastured in the side yard and Sarah recognized one of them. It was Alex's horse. She quickened her pace, putting as much distance between her and the house until the heat forced her to slow down. It had been a week since Alex's visit to the sewing room and Sarah had made every effort to avoid the man. He was dangerous.

The unmistakable sound of a horse galloping broke into her thoughts and made her move closer to the trees. She was about to duck into an opening in the bushes when the deafening noise of a shotgun blast stopped her.

Sarah turned and saw the horse rear up in the air and toss his rider before bolting past her. She did not stop to think; but gathered her long skirt in one hand and ran back to the man on the road.

Sarah's heart was racing as she drew near him. It was the Marquess. She collapsed on her knees beside Alex and forced herself to steady her hands. She would be of no use to him if she became hysterical. He lay still on the ground, eyes closed and blood oozing from his right arm.

Sarah took a deep breath and placed her hands under Alex's neck. She felt it carefully, taking note that no bones were protruding. She moved down to his shoulders and then his back. Everything seemed to be fine.

Next she focused her attention on his arm. She tried to see where the wound was, but the Marquess's riding jacket interfered. She sat back and started to pull on the arm of the jacket when the sound of running feet stopped her.

"What the hell happened?"

Sarah looked up at the man panting for breath and leaning over her with his hands on his knees. He was dark and large like Alex and his face was furrowed with worry.

"I do not know." Sarah turned back to Alex. "Right now we need to get this jacket off him."

The man knelt down beside her. "It looks bad. How can I help?"

"Lift him while I pull the sleeve off."

Together they struggled to pull off the tight jacket. Blood had soaked the sleeve of the shirt underneath. Sarah sat forward and gently removed the shirt from the wound. It was bleeding profusely, but there was no bullet hole.

"The bullet only grazed his arm. Hand me my basket."

Sarah waited as the man looked around quickly

and then reached for her basket. "I am Nathan Carter." He handed her the container.

Sarah stared at him a second before she took the outstretched basket. "You are the Marquess's brother."

"Yes." He looked at her with raised eyebrows. "And you are?"

"Mrs. Wellsley." Sarah put her basket down.

"I have heard the villagers speak of you."

Sarah looked up at him, but there was only curiosity in his eyes. She turned back to her medicines and pulled out a bandage and a small bottle of whiskey to cleanse the wound.

"Hold his arm still," she commanded. She sat up on her knees and bent over the Marquess again. She poured the liquid over it. Immediately the Marquess jumped in protest.

"God's blood!" he shouted. "What the hell are you trying to do to me?"

"Quiet." Nathan held his brother's arm tighter. "Mrs. Wellsley is only trying to fix you up."

Alex chuckled quietly. "I should have guessed it was you, Sarah. Are you enjoying yourself?"

Sarah felt a flash of heat rise in her cheeks when Nathan looked at her with a raised eyebrow. "Nonsense, my lord." She ducked her head and continued to tend to the Marquess's wound until she was satisfied it was clean. "You were lucky."

"You call this lucky?"

"The bullet missed you."

"The bullet?" the Marquess exclaimed. He struggled to sit up, but Nathan pushed him back down. "I only remember Fury throwing me."

"I was walking to Caldern when I heard the gunshot." Sarah's head was bent and her hands were busy winding a bandage around the Marquess's arm. When she was finished, she secured it with a knot.

"Your horse reared and threw you. That is all I know of the matter."

"I too heard the shot, Alex. I was at the cottage and when I looked down the laneway, you were on the ground." Nathan straightened away from his brother and stood up. He brushed the dirt from his leather breeches. "I came running, but Mrs. Wellsley was ahead of me."

"Where is Fury?"

"Probably at the stable by now." Nathan held his hand out to Alex. "Can you stand up?"

Alex brushed Nathan's hand away and sat up. "I am not an invalid." In a rush to prove his words, he leaned over on his injured arm and winced in pain. "Damn," he hissed.

"You never did know when to accept help," Nathan observed dryly. He placed his hands under his brother's arms and heaved him up. "You weigh more than you used to."

"It has been twenty years."

"That is no excuse," Nathan countered. "I thought the navy would have toughened you up."

"Toughened, yes," the Marquess agreed. "The extra weight is all muscle."

Nathan tilted his head at Alex. "Perhaps a bit of it is."

"You should talk." Alex straightened his shirt and then bent to retrieve his jacket. "You have filled out, too."

Sarah looked at the two brothers and felt a twinge of jealousy. Even after so many years apart there was a playful camaraderie between them. She would have loved to have had a sister, or even a close friend, but there had been no one. Caroline had never treated her kindly and the only one she was close to was her cousin Jack, Caroline's older brother. Still, it was not the same as having a sister.

The Marquess's outraged voice broke into her thoughts. "What the hell have you done to my jacket? This is the first time I have worn it. My valet will have my head if I bring it back to him in this condition."

Nathan pointed to Sarah. "Mrs. Wellsley demanded we remove it."

Alex turned to Sarah, a slight grin on his face. "A bit impatient, was she?"

Sarah blushed hotly. "It was no such thing, my lord. I needed to tend your wound."

Alex bowed his head slightly and winked. "I see that I will have to find another explanation for Hobson. I would not like to ruin your reputation."

"Leave be," Nathan said with a growl. "Mrs. Wellsley is not amused by your witticisms, Alex."

"You are right. We have other things to worry about." Alex shrugged into his jacket with a grimace and then turned back to Sarah. "Let me help you up."

Sarah put her hand in his, suppressing a yelp of surprise at the shock of sensation that ran up her arm. She looked at him, but his face was expressionless. She stood quickly, turning away to hide her confusion.

"Thank you, my lord." Sarah moved a few paces back and bent to retrieve her basket.

"Did you see anything, Sarah?"

Sarah shook her head. "I am afraid not. I was turning to go across the fields when I heard the gunshot. By the time I reached the road you were already on the ground and no one was in sight."

Alex nodded and then turned to his brother. "What about you, Nathan?"

"I was almost at the door of the cottage when I heard the shot. At first I thought it was a poacher until I heard Fury gallop off. Mrs. Wellsley was here when I arrived."

Alex looked behind him toward the cottage and then to the wooded area near the road. "Someone must have been shooting in the woods." He walked toward the wooded area a few paces and then shook his head. "It is sheer lunacy to be shooting across the laneway."

Nathan nodded his agreement. "They were taking a chance."

Alex was about to say something else when he glanced at Sarah. He gave her a quick smile. "There is no need for you to worry, Sarah. I believe you were on your way home?"

Sarah understood the dismissal. "Yes, my lord. You should change your bandage when you get back to Caldern. I would hate for infection to set in."

"I am not one of your patients," Alex denied. "This is a mere scratch."

"Perhaps," Sarah agreed mildly. "I am more concerned about your head, though. You had a serious fall and it would not do if you did not take precautions."

"I have had many falls in my life," Alex smiled crookedly. "Thank you for your concern. I will take care of myself."

Sarah stared at him for a few seconds before deciding that it would be best not to say more. He was a grown man. "As you wish, my lord. I must get back to Caldern." With a quick curtsey to the two gentlemen, Sarah set out for the house.

She walked through the opening in the bushes and pulled her bonnet back on her head. She was already late for tea. The sooner she forgot about Alex the better. Since meeting the Marquess, Caroline was more determined than ever to marry him.

Chapter 6

Alex watched Sarah walk away with mixed feelings. He had not spoken to her in nearly a week. She was at dinner every evening, but avoided him and was never in the drawing room when the men joined the ladies. He supposed that was his fault.

He had heard much about her from his tenants, though. They viewed her as an angel of mercy, tending their needs and listening to their worries. She was a remarkable woman. She had treated his wound and then left when he asked. No questions or incessant chatter. Neither were there tears or hysterics.

When Sarah disappeared into the opening in the bushes, he forced himself to look away. He had other things to worry about. He turned back to Nathan, who was staring down the laneway.

"What are you thinking?" Alex asked with a frown.

His brother looked at him and then glanced at the wooded area behind him. "You were well beyond the woods when the shot hit you. The angle that you were hit from suggests the shooter was near the road."

Alex grimaced. "I had thought the same thing. Anyone aiming in that direction must either be a very poor hunter or deliberately trying to scare me."

"Any reason you need to be warned?"

"Not that I know of." Alex started to walk to the small woodlot. "I would like to find where he was standing."

Nathan fell in step beside him. "You were deliberately trying to bait Mrs. Wellsley."

Alex looked at his brother sheepishly. "Most unfair, I agree. I cannot seem to help myself."

"You two seem to be very familiar."

"We met under unusual circumstances."

"Continue."

Alex shook his head. "I am bound as a gentleman not to divulge anymore. All I can say is that the quiet Mrs. Wellsley is not all that she seems."

"Now you have piqued my interest."

"It is nothing bad, I assure you." Alex stopped and looked at his brother. "I suspect she has been forced to hide her feelings for so many years that few people ever see beneath the surface."

"You told me this morning you were almost convinced that you and Lady Caroline Hart would deal well together." Nathan looked at him intently, his eyes full of questions. "I hope you know what you are about."

"I have not changed my mind. I need a wife and Lady Caroline will grace my home perfectly."

"You also need a companion," Nathan reminded. "You will be married many years. Do not choose someone who will make you miserable."

"Are not all marriages the same?" Alex asked

cynically. "I do not expect to be happy, only to produce legitimate heirs."

Nathan shook his head. "You can do your duty and be happy. Do not settle for less."

"I do not have the luxury of time." Alex patted his brother on the back. "Do not worry."

They stopped as they reached the woodlot and Nathan looked at him doubtfully. "If that is what you wish."

"It is." Alex walked off the laneway and stood at the edge of the woods. "Do you see anything unusual?"

Nathan stopped beside him. "I am probably not the best person to ask. I have only been home a couple of months."

"That is two months longer than me. Surely we should be able to find where he was shooting from?"

"Perhaps Jenkins should take a look."

"Jenkins's abilities as a gamekeeper are in serious doubt. He has allowed the poachers to run wild." Alex moved some of the long grass away with his foot and walked into the woods. It was cool and the trees blocked the light from the sun.

He paused while his eyes adjusted. "Are you coming?"

"Yes." Nathan stopped a few feet behind. "It looks as if the undergrowth has been disturbed over to the right."

Alex glanced in the direction Nathan pointed to and nodded. His brother had sharp eyes. The ground was dry, but there appeared to be an area where the grass had been smoothed out, almost as if someone had placed something there. Alex knelt down to examine it closer.

His fingers moved lightly across the surface, stopping when they reached a slight indent. "I think the barrel of the rifle rested here." He looked up at his brother with a frown. "Why stop here?"

"He was waiting for something or someone," Nathan advised grimly.

Alex stood up and looked out at the road. It was a perfect vantage point. The branches of the trees and undergrowth sheltered one from prying eyes and yet provided a clear view of the laneway. Whoever waited here had wanted to aim at something on the road, or beyond.

"I think it would be best if we did not mention this to anyone."

"You are not serious?" Nathan asked incredulously. "You cannot allow someone to run around the estate shooting at you."

"I do not know that they were shooting at me," Alex stated mildly. "They may have been aiming across the lane."

"Nonsense." Nathan shook his head and put his hands on his hips.

"Whether you believe it or not," Alex stated quietly, "I expect you to honor my wishes. There is no need to mention that I was shot."

"What about Mrs. Wellsley?"

"Leave Sarah to me." Alex moved away from the vantage point and started to walk out of the woods. "I think we should go back to the house now."

"I am hardly dressed for visiting." Nathan followed his brother out to the laneway.

"I am expecting you for dinner tonight. Do not disappoint me."

"I will be there as promised." Nathan looked at his brother with a raised eyebrow. "What do you intend to do about today?"

"Nothing for the moment," Alex advised. "I think I would like to see what happens."

"You always liked to stir up trouble." Nathan turned back to the cottage. "You have enough problems with the changes to the estate and Fanny. Let someone else look into the shooting incident."

"I will consider your advice."

"But you will not use it." Nathan grinned at his brother and shook his head. "I would despair of you if I did not know you better. You are going to enjoy surprising Fanny this evening."

"You wrong me, brother." Alex put a hand to his chest in mock outrage. "I would never knowingly cause my stepmother pain."

"You will offend her sensibilities, though."

"I lived with her sensibilities for almost ten years. That was one of the reasons I left Caldern," Alex admitted. "It is my home now and I will do as I please. Our father did not leave Fanny destitute. There is the dower house if she wishes, or she could rent a house anywhere she pleases."

"You know Fanny will never willingly leave Caldern. It is her whole life."

"I find that hard to believe. She has let it fall into such disrepair." Alex glanced down the lane, running one hand through his hair distractedly. "I am grateful you wrote me, Nathan. I might not have come home otherwise."

"You are needed here, Alex. These people have always relied on the owner of Caldern. Do not let them down."

Alex glanced back at his brother and nodded. "I will not."

"I know it was hard to return, but it is where you belong."

"Thank you, Nathan." Alex heaved a large sigh. "It is time I returned home. I will see you at dinner."

Alex turned away and started down the laneway. He cut through the same opening in the bushes as Sarah had used. It was one he had used a thousand times before when he was young, seeking the haven of Mary Carter's cottage.

Mary was the only mother he had ever known and she provided the comfort he needed after his father's marriage. Fanny's rules were stifling and his father was always too busy to be bothered with his whereabouts. Nathan and he would spend their days together and often even the nights.

Alex touched the back of his head and winced. The fall had wounded more than his pride, but he was not about to let anyone else know that. It was bad enough that Sarah had witnessed the accident. He must make certain she did not speak of it to anyone else.

Alex reached the stables about fifteen minutes later and stared at the flurry of activity that greeted him. There were several horses in the outer yard in various stages of being saddled. His own horse, Fury, was being led away by one of his grooms.

"What the hell is going on?" Alex shouted above the noise.

Almost immediately, everyone stopped and looked at him. "My lord!" his groom, Jacobs, exclaimed. "We were about to go out looking fer you. We didn't know what to think when Fury came riding in without you."

"Fury sent me flying," the Marquess admitted with a grin. "Something spooked him and off he went. Next time I will be more prepared."

"Are you hurt, my lord?"

"Just my pride. Get these animals back to their stalls."

Jacobs nodded and ordered the stable hands to

help. Alex watched until the last horse was led into the stables. He started to walk to the house when he was hailed.

"Alex?"

The Marquess turned in the direction of the voice. A large man in a black coat was walking toward him. He was about the same height as Alex but thinner. Alex frowned, searching his memory for the visitor's identity.

"It has been too many years," the man said as he came closer. "I would never have recognized you."

At that moment Alex knew him. "Samuel," he greeted his half brother enthusiastically. "I have not seen you since I was six years old. It is amazing how different, yet similar you are."

"You have grown too, little brother." Samuel hugged Alex close to him and then released him. "Thank you for the invitation to Caldern. I have longed to see it again."

"I am glad you accepted." Alex threw his arm around his brother's shoulders and led him away from the stables. "We must hurry if we are to make tea. Fanny is still a stickler for the rules."

"I am amazed I have been allowed to visit. What was Lady Caldern's reaction?"

"We shall soon find out," Alex confessed. "I have not yet told her."

Samuel stopped and stared at Alex. "How could you not inform her?"

"I was about to ask the same question," a sour voice asked from behind them. Both men turned to face Lord Bryan Norward.

"Bryan." The Marquess inclined his head briefly, his eyes noting his brother's muddy boots, leather jacket and rifle. "Where have you been?"

Lord Bryan glared at Alex and raised his rifle

slightly. "Hunting. Jenkins said the rabbits were overrunning the north wood."

"Any luck?"

"None," Bryan answered sullenly.

"I do not think you know our brother Samuel Black." Alex nodded in Samuel's direction.

"I have not had the pleasure." Bryan scowled at the Marquess, ignoring Samuel's outstretched hand. "I do not believe Mother will approve."

"It is not up to your mother to approve," Alex explained coldly. "Caldern is my home and I have the right to invite who I wish."

"How can you admit to such a relationship?" Bryan spat indignantly. "He is a bastard."

Alex felt his stomach knot in revulsion at Bryan's condemnation. Anger replaced his disdain. "He is your brother, too," Alex snarled. "Samuel will be staying at Caldern as my guest and I expect him to be treated with respect."

"You are not serious?" Bryan retorted. "Mother will never permit it."

"Lady Caldern has no say in this matter," Alex explained. "Caldern is my home, not hers. I will say who is invited and who is not."

Bryan stared at him with an open mouth for several seconds before pushing past the two men. "You will regret this," he threw back over his shoulder before disappearing around the corner of the house.

"I apologize." Alex sighed and gripped Samuel's shoulder. "I had not expected Bryan to react in such a manner."

"Perhaps I should visit another time."

Alex shook his head. "No. We have been apart too long."

Samuel looked at him intently for several seconds and then nodded. "I will stay. I only hope you do not regret angering Lady Caldern."

Alex secretly agreed, but only smiled at his brother's words. Fanny would not be pleased. He could do nothing about that, though. He was determined to right things at Caldern. Having Samuel and Nathan accepted was one of the things he wanted rectified. He would succeed in this, despite his stepmother's objections.

Chapter 7

Sarah looked out her bedroom window, mesmerized by the beauty of the clear night sky. The stars were shining bright and the slight breeze brought with it the scent of roses. Everywhere Sarah looked there was peace, but the knot in her stomach grew tighter.

She had returned to Caldern and gone to the stillroom to work on her herbs. It had always been her refuge from the world. Today it had not helped, though. All she could think about was the Marquess lying on the laneway, his arm bleeding and his face deathly pale.

To make matters worse, Alex's invitation to his brothers to dine at Caldern was all the servants could talk about. The whole house was in an uproar. Lady Caldern had taken to her room, but Alex had forced her to appear for dinner. Her maid Hilda insisted her mistress would end up having an apoplexy.

Sarah moved away from the window, her white dressing gown billowing behind her as she walked to her desk. She picked up a piece of paper and then put it down. Her hands fluttered over her inkstand and then moved to the book she had been reading. She flipped open the cover and then slammed it shut.

She picked up her flickering candle and started to bed. It was ridiculous to worry about the man. She would be up early in the morning collecting lavender, so she needed her sleep. She walked to the bed and placed the candle on the night side table, but before she could pull back her sheets her door crashed open.

"I cannot believe what happened this evening."

Sarah looked at Caroline's crossed arms and pouting mouth and put aside her thoughts of sleep. "What is the matter?"

"Caldern inviting his brothers to dinner." Caroline walked into the room and sat on the bed. "Worse than that, he has actually invited one of them to stay here."

"There is nothing wrong with that." Sarah went to the door and closed it.

"You have spent too much time with the villagers. The man has insulted me."

"It is his house," Sarah soothed. "I am sure he was not thinking of your opinion when he invited them."

"They are not even real brothers." Caroline pounded her fist on the bed. "I will not tolerate this kind of behavior when we are married."

"You do not want to entertain his family?"

"They are not family," Caroline insisted. "They are bastards."

"They are his brothers and he recognizes them," Sarah reasoned. She sat down on her desk chair. "I think it would be easier if you accepted that."

"I will not be laughed at by society."

"Do you not think he has a right to see them?"

"Not if it affects me." Caroline stood up impatiently. "It is alright for you to be so understanding. You will never have a position in society."

Sarah sighed and looked down at her clasped hands. Perhaps Caroline was right. It was easier for her to understand. "What if they were only his friends? Would that make it any easier to acknowledge them?"

Caroline paused in her pacing and looked at Sarah with narrowed eyes. "It is not the same thing." Caroline grimaced. "You will never understand about sensibilities."

"They are men, Caroline." Sarah stood up and took her cousin's hand in hers. "He wants to see them. If you wish to be his wife, then you will have to accept his wishes in this matter."

"Father did not tell me about this." Caroline pulled her hands away from Sarah. "He should have warned me."

"Perhaps he did not wish to offend your sensibilities," Sarah offered primly.

Caroline glared at her for a few seconds. "Your tongue will get you in trouble one day."

Sarah smiled. "It is getting late and I think we should try to get some sleep."

"That is not the only reason I am here. Caldern insists that you stay in the drawing room after dinner," Caroline announced.

Sarah felt the color rush to her cheeks and her heart began to beat furiously. She turned away from Caroline and walked to the window. She did not want her cousin to guess how affected she was by Caldern's actions.

"Why would he do that?"

"I have no idea. He seems to think I was to blame for your disappearance." Caroline picked up the book on the desk, turning it over in her hands before throwing it down. "I hope you will be more circumspect."

"I have done nothing wrong," Sarah insisted, turning to face her cousin. "Your behavior only makes the situation worse."

Caroline looked at her through narrowed eyes. "What are you talking about?"

"You spend all your time with Mr. Stanton. You make it very obvious that you have no wish to be with Caldern."

"I do no such thing," Caroline cried indignantly.

"You are trying to bring Caldern to heel and your plan is not working."

"Even if that were the case, you do not need to push yourself onto the man. Lady Caldern will not countenance any forwardness by you," Caroline reminded her in a smug tone. "You are here because she sees you as my companion. You must act as one."

"I believe I have always behaved properly," Sarah asserted. "Your father was adamant that I accompany you because he was worried about your conduct."

Caroline tossed her head and walked to the door. She paused with her hand on the handle. "I have done nothing to be ashamed of."

"Neither have I," Sarah defended quietly.

"Stay clear of Caldern. He has strange manners and ideas about how people should be treated." Caroline opened the door. "It must be all the time he spent in India, but I will change him once we are married."

Caroline left the room, closing the door behind her. Sarah could only shake her head at her cousin. She did not believe a man like the Marquess would bend his convictions because his wife insisted.

Caroline would find herself frustrated in her attempts.

Sarah went to her bed. She pulled the sheets back and tossed her robe to the foot of the bed before climbing in. There was no point in worrying about Caroline. Sarah needed her sleep. She pulled the covers over her shoulder and blew out the candle.

Sarah tossed and turned, sleeping on and off until she finally threw back the covers in exasperation. She could not ease her mind about Caldern's wound. She had heard the hall clock chime three and knew there would be no further sleep until she had checked the Marquess. He was her patient, she reasoned. It was her duty.

Sarah lit the candle beside the bed and threw on her robe. She picked up her basket of medicines and left the room. Walking quickly, she arrived at the Marquess's bedchamber. It was one of a large suite of rooms that had been the master's for several generations. Adjoining it were the mistress's rooms. Caroline was already making plans to redecorate them.

Sarah turned the handle slowly and opened the door wide enough to look inside. The room was shrouded in darkness. Her candle provided enough light to discern the bed and its occupant. She entered the room, silently closing the door behind her.

Taking a deep breath, she forced her legs to move. Even though she felt that she needed to make certain Alex's wound was healing, she still hesitated. She was not certain Alex would be happy with her concern.

Sarah crept toward the large four-poster bed, the darkness closing around her with each step. She saw Caldern's massive frame rise and fall evenly. Sarah held her breath, wincing at the creaking floorboards, yet still moving forward. She needed to be certain his head injury was not serious.

When Sarah reached the bed she put the candle on the nightstand. She leaned over the Marquess, straining to hear if his breathing was regular before checking his bandages. When she was certain there was no need to be concerned she reached her hand out to his arm.

Suddenly, she was caught in the tight grip of the Marquess. She grimaced as pain shot up her arm. He dragged her close to him. She could feel his rapid heartbeat and his breath was hot on her face.

"What the hell are you doing?" Caldern's voice was quiet, but his tone menacing.

"You are hurting me." Sarah's heart beat frantically and she tried to pull his fingers away from her arm. They were immovable.

"Answer my question."

Sarah looked into his steely eyes. He had no intention of freeing her. She did not want to admit her concern, but she had no choice. "I wanted to see you."

"So you sneak into my bedchamber?"

"I did no such thing," Sarah denied hotly. Her anxiety was swiftly changing to outrage.

Caldern's eyes narrowed. Sarah felt the color rise in her cheeks and she began to struggle against his grip. Instead of being released, she found herself dragged off her feet and held tightly in Alex's arms. She tried to push herself away, but he only held her closer.

"I thought you were not interested in an affair?" he whispered in her ear. His breath tickled her face. She inhaled his musky scent and a shiver of desire ran through her. She opened her mouth to deny his words, but before she could speak his lips closed over hers in a searing kiss.

Sarah tried to stop him, but he overwhelmed her with his unrestrained passion. He stroked her tongue with his, teasing and enticing her. Pleasure radiated from her lips, spreading throughout her body until Sarah felt her whole being throb with excitement. Her resistance melted and she relaxed.

Alex tightened his arms, moving her closer to his heated body. Sarah savored the feel of his hard muscles against hers, burning with an inner yearning that she had never felt before. Within seconds she had lost her inhibitions, responding to his silent urgings, moving restlessly in his arms.

His hands began to caress her body, pulling at the thin fabric of her nightgown until he had exposed the sensitive skin beneath. Sarah gasped in surprise as a jolt of electricity shot through her. His hand trembled against her skin, lightly stroking her back. With a swiftness that took her breath away, Alex shifted her in his arms so that she rested against the bed. She found herself looking up into his glimmering eyes.

"You look good in my bed. I knew you could not resist coming to me."

His words slowly penetrated the fog in her brain. "You are wrong," she stammered.

"Nonsense," he said with a satisfied smile. "There is no need to explain. We are both old enough to know what we want."

"You think I desire you?" Sarah shook her head in denial.

"Your lips tell me all I need to know."

"You took me by surprise." Sarah struggled to sit up, but his body blocked her escape.

"You cannot deny that you enjoy kissing me." Caldern brushed his lips over hers before lightly nipping them with his teeth.

"I have already told you that I am not interested." Sarah's voice shook. She pounded her fist against Caldern's chest. "Let me up."

Caldern's eyes hardened and Sarah suppressed a shiver. He moved away from her and she sat up. She could not allow herself to succumb to his seduction. He was going to marry her cousin.

"It seems I misjudged the situation once again." Caldern leaned against his pillows. His voice was devoid of emotion, his body stiff with indignation.

"I should never have come tonight."

"Why did you?"

Sarah was about to answer him when a noise from the hallway stopped her. She strained her ears to listen to the slight shuffling sound. Caldern clasped her arm and motioned her to be silent.

The noise came closer and stopped outside his door. Caldern pushed her from his bed and motioned for her to go to the dressing room. Sarah moved swiftly. The last thing she wanted was to be caught in a compromising situation with the Marquess. She opened the door and slid into the room with a quick backward glance at Caldern.

He had repositioned himself in bed, the covers over his body and her candle now blown out. To an outside observer he looked to be sleeping. She peered through a slight opening, watching as the door to the bedchamber opened slowly.

Chapter 8

Alex lay in bed, forcing himself to breathe evenly. This was the second time this evening he had hidden, but he doubted this assailant would be quite as lovely as his first. With closed eyes, he listened until the footsteps stopped. Alex's heart beat furiously in anticipation.

A hand pulled back the covers and Alex grabbed it. The startled cry and the frightened face of his valet, Hobson, greeted him. "Damn."

"My lord!" Hobson cried. "You startled me."

"What the hell are you doing?" Alex glared at his valet, leaning over to light Sarah's candle from the candle Hobson had brought with him.

Hobson had been with him since Alex returned to England a year ago. The man had impeccable references and to date the only complaint Alex had about him was his insistence about jewelry. Alex abhorred wearing more than his signet ring and a stickpin. Hobson was constantly trying to press him to adorn himself with jeweled fobs, rings, and chains.

"I was worried about you." Hobson moved away

from the bed and straightened his shirt. "You have a nasty bump on your head from the fall this afternoon."

"I am more than capable of taking care of myself." Alex sat up, his covers slipping to his waist. He eyed Hobson silently. He was a short dark man, neatly dressed in black pants, white shirt, and gray waistcoat. "I appreciate your concern, but it is unnecessary."

"I can see you are doing fine," Hobson agreed. "I did not mean to disturb your sleep."

"Of course not." Alex waved Hobson away.

Hobson bowed and turned toward the dressing room.

"Where are you going?" Alex asked sharply.

"I think it might be best if I spent the night on the cot in the dressing room," Hobson explained. "You do not seem yourself."

Alex rolled his eyes and sighed deeply. "I am fine."

"If you will forgive me for saying so, you are extremely irritable, my lord. That is not a good sign."

"You startled me out of a deep sleep. How the hell do you expect me to react?"

Hobson tilted his head and eyed Alex seriously. "Are you certain, my lord?"

"Very."

"As you wish." Hobson bobbed his head and left the room. The clicking of the door shutting reverberated throughout the room.

Alex sat back in the bed and rearranged the covers under his arms. He frowned at the closed door. Hobson's story may have been true. It was part of a valet's job to keep an eye on his master. More confusing was Mrs. Wellsley's appearance.

When Alex had first grabbed her arm, he had been certain he had captured the person who had tried to harm him this afternoon. It would have been impossible for Sarah to shoot him. Nathan would have seen her running out of the woods.

When he had seen her wide blue eyes staring back at him and her mouth twisted in indignation he had reacted without thinking. Alex had been unprepared for the flash of passion that had flared between them. He had lost himself completely in the heated excitement of their kiss.

Sarah's rebuff had doused his ardor like a bucket of cold water. Once again he had misjudged her intentions. Damn. Just the thought of her sent a surge of heat to his loins. It had been a long time since he had met a woman who could do that. If he were honest, he admitted ruefully, he had never been this affected before.

"It is safe," he called to Sarah. "You can come out."

Sarah had been holding her breath in the small dark room, waiting for Hobson to leave. She opened the door cautiously, peering around the side to be certain the room was empty. All she saw was Caldern sitting in the bed. The light from her candle was not enough to dispel the shadows that surrounded him.

"He has gone," Caldern assured her, lounging back against the pillows.

"I must not be found with you."

"No," Caldern agreed. "Why did you risk coming?"

"I could not sleep," Sarah explained. She moved out of the dressing room and closed the door.

Caldern smiled. "Yet you refused my solution."

Sarah felt the color rush into her cheeks. She tightened her hand around the neck of her night robe, swallowing nervously. "You misunderstood my intentions."

"I gathered as much," Caldern replied dryly. "Perhaps you could explain?"

"I was worried about you."

"Ah," Caldern said with a nod. "It seems I have that effect on people. Both you and Hobson found it necessary to forego your sleep for my sake."

"It was not like that," Sarah objected. She walked to the bed. "I did sleep."

The Marquess raised his eyebrow quizzically. "Yet I invaded your dreams?"

Sarah blushed hotly at the tone of his voice. "Must you embarrass me at every turn?"

Caldern reached out and clasped her hand. "Forgive me." His tone was contrite.

Sarah looked at his face, noting the seriousness of his expression. There was a warmth seeping up her arm from the touch of his hand. She could not resist his appeal and nodded her agreement.

"Continue," Alex coaxed.

"You are my patient," Sarah explained. She lifted her small basket of medicines from the table and placed it on the bed. "I could not sleep until I knew you were well."

"I am fine."

"Your head injury does not appear to have left any lasting effects," Sarah agreed. "I need to rebind your wound, though."

"It was the merest of scratches."

"True, but I did not have a chance to clean it properly." Sarah looked up from her medicines. "It will only take a few minutes."

Alex stared at her silently for several seconds before sighing deeply. "If you insist." He held out his injured arm.

"Could you sit on the edge of the bed?"

"I could, but I am afraid I would only embarrass you more."

Sarah frowned at Caldern. His eyes were twinkling and his mouth was turned up in a smile. She shook her head in confusion.

"Have you forgotten already?" he inquired teasingly. "I am wearing nothing beneath these sheets."

Sarah brought her hand to her mouth. For the first time she noticed his bare chest. When he sat up, the sheets had fallen away, exposing a wide expanse of firm muscles covered with short dark hairs. "Please stay where you are."

Alex hefted a sheet closer to his chest and stretched his arm out. "I would have expected you to be more prepared for the sight of a man's naked body."

"Men are usually more modest than you." Sarah took his arm and unwound the bandage.

"I find that hard to believe." Caldern's voice was low and husky. "You are a very beautiful woman."

Sarah stopped unwinding the bandage to look up at Alex. His eyes seemed to be smoldering with an inner fire and she felt her breath catch in her throat. He was looking at her with desire. She shook her head in denial. "You are mistaken, my lord."

"Alex," he corrected. "Why do you not believe me?"

"My late husband made it very clear that no man could ever desire me." Sarah bundled up the old linen and then brought the candle closer to examine the wound.

"He was a fool."

"He was a very learned man and well respected by his parishioners." Sarah put the arm down. "It looks as if it is healing well. I would like to put some comfrey on it to be certain."

"Do as you wish." Alex flexed the muscles in his

arm before allowing Sarah to continue with her ministrations. "Even learned men can be fools."

Sarah frowned as she applied a small amount of cream to Alex's wound. "My uncle assured me that Mr. Wellsley was not. That was the main reason he wished me to marry him."

"What about you? Did you wish the marriage?"

Sarah put down the jar of comfrey lotion and pulled out some clean linen from her basket. "I was only seventeen and without a dowry."

"You had no say in the matter."

Sarah glanced up at Caldern, captured by his piercing gray eyes. She saw understanding and compassion. "You are correct. I had no choice."

"Do not let one person affect your opinion of men."

Sarah wound the new linen around Caldern's arm and then tied it off. "Should I judge men by your actions?" She looked at him with raised eyebrows.

"If you must, yes." Caldern moved his arm away and lay back against the pillows. "At least I see you for the woman you are."

"You have not known me long enough."

"You are wrong. I knew everything the moment I first saw you."

"That is impossible." Sarah picked up her basket and turned away, moving toward the door. The man was insane to talk to her in this fashion.

"I saw a beautiful and sensuous woman who enjoyed life and was not afraid to take risks. I have seen nothing since to make me change that view."

"How can you possibly think that of me?" Sarah denied, stopping to look back at Alex. "I have never taken chances."

"Swimming in the lake was dangerous," the

Marquess countered. "Bathing nude was sensuous and you were definitely enjoying yourself."

Sarah began to fidget with the lid of her basket. She brushed a strand of hair from her eyes. "You must promise not to speak of it again."

The Marquess regarded her solemnly. "It is not something you need be ashamed of."

"It was unladylike."

"But very womanly."

Sarah looked at him sharply. "It was still wrong."

Alex shook his head. "I can see I will not convince you tonight."

Sarah smiled at him. "You need your sleep. Your invitation to your brothers has sent the house into an uproar and you will need your energy for tomorrow. Lady Caldern is not pleased."

Caldern covered his face with his hand and groaned. "I had almost forgotten."

Sarah frowned and walked back to the bed. "If it is such an effort, why did you invite Mr. Black to stay?"

"It is my house."

"I understand, but perhaps you could wait until your stepmother has left Caldern."

Alex shook his head. "That will never happen. Fanny would be lost without Caldern. It is her whole life."

"Then why does she not take better care of it?" Sarah's eyes widened as she realized how impertinent her remark was. "Forgive me. I should never have said that."

"There is nothing wrong with the truth," Alex asserted. "Fanny is also very concerned with money. To maintain the estate would have meant spending money."

"Finances were a problem then?"

Caldern looked at her quizzically and tilted his head to one side. Sarah straightened her shoulders and moved back from the bed. She had overstepped the bounds and Caldern had every right to ignore the question.

"I am still investigating that," Caldern answered finally.

"I must return to my room." Sarah fiddled with the lid of her basket, forcing her eyes to remain on the floor. The Marquess's silence and manner were making her uncomfortable. She had stayed too long as it was.

"In a hurry to leave?"

Sarah glanced up quickly. Caldern was lounging back on the pillows and the sheets had once again fallen to his waist. He appeared to be totally relaxed, but when Sarah looked at his eyes a shiver ran through her. They were shuttered, holding no emotion.

"It is best." Sarah turned and walked to the door.

"Have you spoken to Lady Caroline?"

Sarah paused. "I saw her this evening," she answered without turning around.

"Then you know that I wish you to remain downstairs after dinner?"

"Yes, my lord."

"Alex," the Marquess insisted.

"Yes, Alex." Sarah reached her hand out to the door.

"I want you to become better acquainted with my brother Samuel."

Sarah looked over her shoulder at the Marquess. He was smiling slightly, but she had no other hint as to his meaning. "Is there any particular reason?"

Alex shook his head. "None. He is a minister, though. Perhaps the two of you will have something in common?"

"Are you trying to be a matchmaker?" Sarah gaped at Caldern, her mouth open in astonishment.

"Would that be so horrible?"

"Your brother is a minister. He would never want a wife such as me."

"He would be lucky if he could get you." Alex leaned forward in bed. "You are not only a beautiful and desirable woman, you also care about people."

"I have no wish to marry."

Lord Caldern frowned. "Never?"

Sarah shook her head. "I will not marry again. It does not suit me."

"What about love?"

"I have survived this long without it. I have my work to keep me busy."

"Yet you refuse my offer of an affair." Caldern shifted in the bed. "You cannot cut yourself away from men."

"Why not?" Sarah clasped her hands together. "Men do not consider women's needs. Why should I allow them into my life?"

"It is unnatural to live alone, especially for a woman as sensuous and responsive as you." Alex reached over the blankets and grabbed a robe from the bottom of the bed. He put it on hastily and then threw back the covers. "What has made you think this way?"

"Men," Sarah answered sharply. "There is no need for you to leave your bed. I am going now."

"Not until I understand."

"What is there to understand?" Sarah sighed deeply. Alex was determined to get his answer. She walked back into the room. "I have no wish to be controlled by another person. Surely you can see that?"

Alex stood up from the bed and walked toward her. "Is that how your marriage was?"

Sarah nodded and then sat down in a dark brocade chair. "Stephen always knew what was best. My wishes were never heeded."

"That is not the way of all marriages."

"It is the way of most." Sarah hugged her basket closer to her. "I vowed after Stephen's death that I would never put myself in such a position again. I have my freedom as long as I stay unmarried."

"A husband who loved you would give you freedom."

Sarah shook her head. "I would always have to consider his wishes first."

Alex pulled up another chair and sat down in front of her. He took one of her hands in his. "In a loving and caring marriage, there is sharing. Not all men are selfish."

Sarah's eyebrow rose at Alex's words. Surely he did not actually believe that. "Has that been your experience?"

Alex paused for a few seconds before shaking his head. "No, but I am certain that it exists. I have known men who would happily die for their wives."

"Would they give their wives the freedom to follow their dreams?"

Alex shook his head in confusion. "What are you talking about?"

Sarah looked away from the Marquess and sighed heavily. He was no different from all the other men she had met. "If I were married and a patient required my care, do you think a husband would understand that I had to be elsewhere?"

"Of course he would."

"Would he understand if it meant I could not be at an important dinner party he was giving?"

Alex opened his mouth to answer, but closed it again. His eyes narrowed in concentration before he shook his head. "No. He would insist his wife be with him. It is a wife's duty."

"Is it not also her duty to be true to herself?"

"Yes," Alex agreed in exasperation. "Surely there is some room for compromise."

"Why could not the husband accept his wife's absence?"

"You said it was an important event, so naturally he needs his wife there."

"Tending the sick would be just as important to me."

Alex stood up and walked over to the window. He pushed the curtain back and stared out for several minutes. "I understand what you are trying to say. You believe a husband would never allow you freedom. If a wife loved her husband she should be willing to put his needs first."

"But the husband does not need to put his wife first?"

Alex turned away from the window. "If he allows her the freedom to care for the sick, he is putting her needs first."

"So long as they do not interfere with his life."

"It sounds completely selfish and mean-spirited when you say it like that." Caldern rubbed the back of his neck with his hand. "You are deliberately twisting my words and suggesting impossible situations."

Sarah shook her head. "I wish I were. Many a time I had to let a patient suffer because Stephen refused to let me leave the house. Sometimes he did not have a reason other than he did not wish it."

"I see." Alex heaved a sigh. "He was a cruel man then."

"No," Sarah denied quietly. "He was no different than most men. His needs were all that mattered and he had married so that he would have a wife who could cater to those needs."

"Not all men marry for that reason."

"True," Sarah agreed. She clasped her hands tightly around her basket and took a deep breath before continuing. "You are marrying because you want an heir, but will you treat Caroline with any more respect than I was treated?"

The Marquess stood perfectly still. His eyes turned dark gray and a muscle in his chin twitched just below the end of his scar. Sarah hugged the basket closer and held her breath.

"I believe you have forgotten who you are speaking to." Caldern bit his words off in a cold unemotional tone. His lip curled slightly. He clenched his fists by his side.

"No, my lord." Sarah stood up from the chair and backed away. "Lady Caroline is my cousin and I am concerned about her well-being. You are not marrying for love, so will you respect her needs?"

"You have said more than enough, Mrs. Wellsley." Caldern turned back to face the window. "Kindly leave."

"As you wish, my lord." Sarah moved swiftly to the door. She left the room, heaving a sigh of relief when the door was closed behind her. It was not until then that she remembered her candle. She would have to return to her room in the dark.

She had deliberately provoked the Marquess on the question of marriage, yet she did not regret it. His naïve assumptions had been too much to bear. He was a man and did not have to live under the same rules as a woman. He could never understand how powerless she had felt in her marriage.

Chapter 9

Alex looked out the large library window and frowned. It had been over a week since his return home and he still was not used to the unkempt grounds. In his father's day the gardeners had kept everything immaculate. Now the drive was overgrown with weeds, the lawn needed trimming, and the hedgerows and shrubbery had been allowed to grow wild.

"Something amiss?" a familiar voice asked.

Alex turned around and smiled. "David."

"This is the first time in days that you have been alone." David Stanton walked up to the worn leather chair by the desk and sat down with a sigh. "Are you accomplishing anything?"

Alex shook his head. "Can you believe my stepmother let things go to such ruin? It will take years and an army of men to restore the gardens alone."

"The estate and house are deplorable, but you will fix it in no time," David assured. "Lucky we made our fortunes in India."

Alex walked to his desk and sat down. "That is

what is so outrageous. There was no need for any of this to happen."

David frowned and sat forward in his seat. "Surely it was a matter of finances?"

"No," Alex denied with a twisted smile. "Fanny has increased the family coffers enormously during her years of control. Caldern does not need any of my money."

"Everything is falling apart," David exclaimed incredulously. "I can understand the tenant cottages, but to let your own house deteriorate is ridiculous."

"I find it hard to believe also." Alex leaned his arms on the desk. "The roof is falling in on the west wing. Rooms have been closed off and plaster from the ceilings covers the furniture. The house is crumbling all around. The only areas maintained are the formal rooms on the main floor and the family bedchambers. It is as if nothing else mattered to Fanny."

"She probably wanted to hide the dreadful condition of the estate from your father."

"I never thought of that," Alex muttered. "You are right, though. Even sick, Father would not have allowed the place to be ruined. I suppose Fanny had the ultimate revenge."

"Why should she desire that?"

"Everything was entailed away from her precious son, Bryan." Alex leaned back and sighed. "Father left him a small estate in the south, but that is nothing in comparison to Caldern."

"Nonsense," David reasoned. "Lady Caldern knew how things stood when she married your father. At least Bryan was left something. That was more than he gave you."

"True," Alex agreed, "But I never wanted anything from him."

David nodded his head and then rested it against

the back of his chair. "You were able to survive without his help. I am not certain that Bryan would fare so well."

Alex grinned mischievously. "Bryan has spent too much of his life near his mother. I would not underestimate him, though. He is still my father's son."

"I will remember that," David assured. "What will you do now?"

"Get to work on the repairs," Alex stated grimly. "I was foolish to linger a year before returning home, but there is no way to remedy that now."

"You were in India when you received the news of Douglas's death and your succession to the title. We had business to finish and the long trip home."

"I suppose." Alex sighed heavily and pushed his chair back from the desk. David spoke the truth, but Alex still felt guilty for lingering in London. If Nathan had not sent him a missive demanding he return, he would still be there.

"Everything that is wrong with Caldern can be fixed. Something else is troubling you," David declared shrewdly.

Alex stood up and walked to the window. He leaned his hand against the glass and looked out. "I never could fool you."

"We have known each other too long."

Alex continued to stare out the window for several minutes before turning to face his friend. "I have been considering my marriage."

"Having second thoughts?"

Alex shook his head. "Nothing like that. I must marry. Caldern needs an heir."

"You have an heir. Bryan would be only too willing to step into your shoes." David tapped his fingers against the chair arm. "Does the thought of marrying the beautiful Lady Caroline upset you?"

"How could I be upset?" Alex grinned at his friend. "She is perfect. I cannot imagine a more beautiful Marchioness."

"She is exquisite," David declared calmly. "Are you certain you two will suit?"

Alex frowned and looked closely at his friend. David seemed indifferent to the conversation, but he sensed an inner tension. "Why?"

"Because you are constantly fobbing her off on me." David calmly brushed away some lint from his pantaloons. "That is not the action of a man considering marriage."

"I must and will marry." Alex walked back to his desk and leaned against it.

"What of Lady Caroline? Will she be happy in this marriage?"

Alex crossed his arms and eyed his friend seriously. "She desires a husband who is titled and rich."

"What of love?"

"It has no place in a marriage such as ours." Alex clamped his teeth together tightly to rein in his temper. David's words were reminiscent of Sarah's words last night.

"Have you considered how Lady Caroline will react to living in the north of England?"

"I have no intention of leaving Caldern. I was forced to spend nineteen years in exile, but no more."

David nodded his understanding. "I know how much you love this place."

"I will not change my life for her," Alex stated firmly.

"You surprise me, Alex." David stretched his legs in front of him. "Usually you are more considerate."

"I have never thought of marriage before." A

sudden vision of Sarah rising from the water flooded his mind. His body tightened in response.

"This is a woman you will have to see every day of your life. Someone who will have needs and desires of her own."

"She will have a husband who can provide for her."

"Will that be enough?"

Alex sat down in his chair with a heavy sigh. He rubbed his eyes with his hand, hoping to erase Sarah's image. It refused to leave. "You think I am selfish. What about Lady Caroline? Is she not also selfish?"

David shook his head and frowned. "She does not have the same options as you."

"That does not make it right." Alex crumpled a piece of paper on his desk and then pushed it away. Sarah's words had echoed in his head all morning, forcing him to reevaluate his decision to marry.

"No," David stated firmly. "Women look to men to protect them. I am certain her father has insisted on this marriage."

Alex stared at David for a few seconds and then burst out laughing. "You do not honestly believe that?"

"A woman has very little choice about marriage."

"Lady Caroline is a spoiled and pampered young lady. I doubt her father would force her to do anything." Alex pushed his chair back. "Lady Caroline is not a victim."

David sighed. "No, she is not."

"I really see no other choice." Alex had thought about this for most of the night. Sarah's stinging condemnation had forced him to reconsider his motives.

"Do you think you could learn to love Lady Caroline?"

Alex shook his head and looked down at his desk. Despite Lady Caroline's beauty, she did not arouse his interest. Marriage to her would be strictly duty. "I am not certain."

"She is a very beautiful woman and despite her behavior, quite endearing." David eyed Alex seriously. "Spend more time with her to see if you will suit."

"I must marry, David." Alex frowned. The memory of Sarah in his arms, her lips against his, sent a shiver down his spine.

"You do not have to rush." David reasoned.

Alex nodded abstractedly. He doubted that time with Lady Caroline would change his mind. "Enough about this," he declared firmly. "Did you enjoy dinner last night?"

"Extremely entertaining." David grinned and lounged back in his chair. "What are you planning for this evening?"

"I have insisted that Mrs. Wellsley be present in the drawing room. I think she will do famously for Samuel." Alex forced back a stab of regret. Sarah was not for him.

"Samuel will be visiting for a while?"

"Yes. I think Fanny should rather enjoy the company."

"Be careful how much you provoke her." David Stanton sighed heavily and stood up. "Are you accompanying us to the lake this afternoon? Lady Caldern has arranged a picnic."

Alex shook his head. "No, I have promised to visit with Nathan and his mother."

David smiled and turned toward the door. "Give him my best."

"I will. Enjoy yourself."

David looked back with a grin. "A whole afternoon spent with the beautiful Lady Caroline? How could I not enjoy myself?"

David left the room and Alex shook his head. David was in danger of developing a serious attachment for Lady Caroline. He might be enormously wealthy, but without a title, Alex doubted that she would consider marrying him.

Alex turned back to the window and squinted up at the sun. It was getting late and he had promised Mary a visit. She was the only mother he had ever known and he could not refuse her. Nathan would be there also. With a heavy sigh he turned away from the window and closed the ledger book on his desk. He would sort out the problems of Caldern later.

A few minutes later Alex was saddled on Fury and galloping down the laneway toward the Carter cottage. He reined in when he saw another rider approaching, grinning when he recognized Nathan.

"Did you think I forgot?"

"No, but Mother said I should hurry you along." Nathan turned his horse and moved beside Alex. "She was afraid you would let estate business delay you."

"She was right." Alex felt himself relax. Even after nineteen years, Mary still knew his weaknesses. It was wonderful to be among people who cared. Alex was filled with a sense of homecoming and belonging for the first time since he had returned to Caldern.

"So what was the important business that delayed you?"

"Marriage."

Nathan eyed him sideways for a few seconds before looking back at the laneway. "You have made it official?"

"Not yet." Alex shrugged his shoulders and turned his head to Nathan. "David waylaid me in the library and we chatted about its merits."

"I am surprised you are not later." Nathan looked at his brother seriously. "Marriage cannot be discussed quickly. Are you having doubts?"

"Not about marriage," Alex denied. "David thinks I should reconsider my choice, though. What is your impression of Lady Caroline?"

"She is a very beautiful woman." Nathan's tone was cautious.

"That sounds more like a condemnation."

"She does not seem interested in the estate." Nathan looked across at the woods. "She is never seen outdoors and the tenants have been asking questions."

"I do not believe she likes the countryside."

"So you are planning to live in London?"

"No." Alex shook his head and sighed. "I will not leave Caldern again."

"I see." Nathan reined in his horse. They had reached the cottage, but instead of going to the stables he looked at Alex. "That could be a problem."

Alex nodded his head. "That is what David thinks, too."

"You have yet to mention love," Nathan pointed out quietly.

"There is no love."

"Then wait," Nathan advised.

"I am thirty-five years old. It is time." Alex looked at his brother. He sensed Nathan was holding something back. "What do you know of love?"

Nathan glanced off to the stables, his mouth twisted in a wry grin. "I thought we were discussing you?"

Alex sighed deeply. He dismounted from Fury

and waited for Nathan before walking to the stables. He tied Fury to a post and then looked back at his brother. They had gone through a lot in their childhood, but nineteen years separated them. Both had gone on to make their fortunes, he in India and Nathan in America. Perhaps his brother no longer felt he could confide in him.

Nathan took the saddle off his horse and walked the animal to its stall. When he returned, he kicked the dirt with his boots and snapped his riding crop against his leg. "I was in love once," he began hesitantly. "I actually considered marrying her, but I thought I needed more money to support a wife. She deserved the best in life."

"What happened?"

"She married someone else. He could not support her either," Nathan spat out bitterly. "She had to earn extra money doing laundry and cleaning. She was too fragile for that kind of life. Within two years she had died of pneumonia."

Alex's stomach tightened at the agony he heard in his brother's voice. "You were not responsible for what happened."

"I blame myself every day of my life." Nathan looked up at Alex, his eyes burning with intensity. "I would have taken better care of her. Instead I did what I thought was prudent and I lost her. Forever."

"I am sorry," Alex said gently. He could not even imagine the devastation of Nathan's loss.

"Duty is not always the best decision." Nathan gripped his brother's shoulder. "If you find love, hold onto it no matter what."

Alex nodded. There was little chance of finding love. He had given up on love when he was a boy and he did not think anyone would change his mind now.

"Come." Nathan pushed him ahead. "Mother is waiting."

Alex smiled and forced thoughts of marriage from his mind. He still had time to make his decision and right now he wanted to concentrate on pleasant things. Alex was the first to reach the house and he yanked the kitchen door open without ceremony.

"Here we are," he called, waiting for his eyes to adjust to the darkness of the room.

Nathan pushed him through the door. Alex closed his eyes and inhaled the scent of freshly baked bread and herbs drying from the rafters. Memories of his childhood washed over him. He opened his eyes, expecting to see Mary, but his smile froze and he nearly stumbled when he saw who was sitting at the kitchen table. It was Sarah.

Chapter 10

Sarah stood up from her chair, grabbing the edge of the oak kitchen table as she struggled to breathe. When Nathan had invited her to stay for luncheon, she had never imagined that Lord Caldern would be visiting. There was no way to escape now. His massive frame blocked the doorway, his head almost touching the blackened ceiling beams. She felt trapped.

"Alex!" Mary exclaimed, running to the Marquess. "I was afraid you would not make it."

"I said I would." Alex clasped Mary to him in a hug, lifting her feet from the ground and swinging her around. "Surely you have more faith in me?"

"I do." Mary patted him on the back. "But I know Caldern has all of your attention."

"I never refuse an invite to enjoy your cooking." Alex put Mary down on the floor and moved aside to let Nathan enter the room.

"Alex was already on his way, Mother." Nathan put his riding crop on the wooden dresser beside the door. "Mrs. Wellsley, I hope you will not mind sharing luncheon with Alex?"

Sarah bobbed a quick curtsey. "My pleasure." There was nothing else she could do. To leave would be rude.

Alex inclined his head at her words, his eyes glaring at her coolly. Sarah tightened her grip on the table and took a deep breath. He was still angry about last night.

"What brings you here?" the Marquess asked nonchalantly. "I would have expected you to be tending one of the villagers."

Nathan smiled slightly and led his brother away from the doorway. "Mrs. Wellsley does more than tend the sick."

Sarah sensed the rebuff in Nathan's words and was grateful for his support. "Mr. Carter asked me to stop and visit. Mary is greatly respected among the tenants and villagers."

"Thank you, child." Mary hurried to the stove. She opened the lid on a pot and the room was filled with the aroma of the simmering stew.

Alex peeled off his riding gloves. "That smells heavenly."

"It is your favorite." Mary turned from the stove and smiled. "Rabbit stew."

"No one can cook like you, Mary." Alex put his gloves and riding crop on the dresser beside Nathan's and walked over to the stove. He bent down and inhaled deeply. "During my first year aboard ship, I would go to bed at night dreaming of your meals."

"You should never have left."

"I needed to." Alex put his arm around Mary's shoulder and squeezed. "When do we eat?"

"You carry this to the table and then we can all sit down."

Sarah watched as Alex grinned at Mary and then heaved the large iron pot off the stove. All the tension had left his face and he seemed to be years younger. It was amazing how quick the transformation had been.

"Come and sit down." Nathan touched her arm gently.

Sarah was startled and turned away from the Marquess. Nathan was smiling at her, his blue eyes soft with understanding. Sarah felt her cheeks flush with embarrassment. She had not meant to study the Marquess so closely. She bowed her head and allowed herself to be led to a chair at the table.

"Alex has recovered from his wound," Nathan observed. He pulled the chair out for Sarah.

"It does not seem to have affected him at all." Sarah sat down.

Nathan sat down beside her. "He is tough. He has been like that since he was a child."

"Are you two talking about me?" Alex put the pot of stew on the end of the table.

"Just about your health." Nathan tilted his head at his brother. "You have recovered remarkably fast."

"It was a mere scratch." Alex pulled out a chair on the other side of the table and then waited for Mary to join them before sitting down.

Mary sat at the head of the table and began to fill bowls with the steaming stew. When everyone had been served, they bowed their heads and said a quick prayer of thanks before eating.

"This is wonderful." Sarah complimented, savoring her meal. Rabbit and root vegetables were nestled together in a rich, thick broth. It was delicious.

"Mother always had a way with food," Nathan agreed. "She should have been put to work in the kitchen instead of the nursery."

"I do not agree." Alex smiled mischievously at Mary. "I would have been at a huge disadvantage."

"How so?" Nathan paused, his spoon halfway to his mouth.

Alex grabbed a piece of bread from the center of the table. "Father never knew most of the things I did, thanks to Mary."

Nathan raised an eyebrow at his brother. "I seem to remember Father being closeted with you numerous times."

"True, but it would have been far worse if Mary had not protected me." Alex squeezed Mary's hand briefly. "I am truly grateful."

"You're talking nonsense." Mary shifted uncomfortably in her chair, her cheeks pink with delight. "I did what any good mother would."

"That you did," Alex agreed softly. "You were the only mother I ever knew."

Sarah looked down at her bowl, feeling as if she were intruding on a private family moment. The Marquess was being warm and relaxed, something he had never been at Caldern. It was as if he were a totally different person.

Nathan cleared his throat beside her. "I hear that you have been extending your care beyond the estate and helping the villagers, Mrs. Wellsley."

Sarah looked up from her bowl. Nathan was smiling at her, but when she glanced across the table, the Marquess was scowling. "They need my help also."

"You are no longer confining your work to the estate?" Alex asked sharply. He put his spoon down and leaned back from the table. "That is unsafe."

"Where is the danger?" Sarah clenched her hand in her lap. The man knew nothing about her work.

"Here you are protected because you are a guest." Caldern tapped a finger on the table. "The villagers will not see you the same."

"I have been doing this work for years," Sarah

explained patiently. "No one has ever tried to harm me."

"You have been lucky," Caldern spat out. "If you insist on visiting the villagers, then you must have a footman accompany you."

Sarah stared at the Marquess openmouthed. She was at a loss for words. The man had no right to interfere with her life in such a way. She was perfectly safe.

"You will do as I ask, or stop visiting the village." Alex glared at her coldly.

"This is ridiculous."

"Nevertheless, you will do it."

"I do not wish to have someone following me." Sarah sat up straight in her chair. "I am often called out at odd hours."

"Even at odd hours, a footman is available." The Marquess put his open hand on the table. "You are under my protection and I insist you abide by my rules."

"Perhaps it would be best," Nathan interjected quickly. "You have not worked in the north before. Feelings run high in this country."

Sarah turned to Nathan and saw only concern in his eyes. She turned back to the Marquess and nodded her agreement. "I still believe it is unnecessary. No one would harm me."

"At least it will stop you from taking risks." Caldern gave her a twisted smile. Sarah caught her breath and flushed at the hidden meaning of his words. How could he think she would risk bathing in the lake after the humiliation she had already endured?

"It cannot hurt," Mary Carter insisted softly.

Sarah inhaled deeply, trying to steady her voice before answering, but all she could manage was to nod her head.

"A man to carry things can be most useful," Mary added. "All of your baskets of herbs and medicines must be heavy. Just think of how light your load will be."

Sarah smiled at Mary's advice. "I am beginning to see the advantages."

"Good." Caldern began to eat again. "I would hate to confine you to the house."

Sarah opened her mouth to answer Caldern's outrageous claim when Nathan put his hand over hers and squeezed lightly. "Alex, I think you should stop teasing Mrs. Wellsley."

"Who said I was teasing?"

"Mrs. Wellsley's work is very important to the tenants." Nathan moved his hand away from Sarah's. "I know you want to do everything to help them."

Alex looked up at his brother and frowned. "Are you suggesting otherwise?"

"Boys," Mary pleaded. She pushed her chair back and went to the stove. "I have pie for dessert, so no more arguments."

Mary brought a strawberry pie to the table and further conversation ceased until the meal was finished. Sarah was glad for the respite. The Marquess appeared to be relaxed, but Sarah sensed that he was still upset with her. His insinuation that he could prevent her from doing her work had angered her. Only Nathan's intervention had prevented her from saying something she might regret later.

When the table was cleared, they made their way into the parlor. It was a small room with a fireplace at one end. The furniture was comfortable, but threadbare and the plaster on the walls was darkened with age. It was warm and welcoming. Sarah relaxed immediately.

"Who are you visiting this afternoon, Mrs.

Wellsley?" Alex sat down in a cushioned chair and adjusted his legs in front of him.

Sarah sat with Mary on a faded blue settee. "Mr. Bates needs my attention. Afterwards I plan to gather some comfrey."

"A busy day." Alex raised an eyebrow and leaned forward in his chair. "I will accompany you."

Sarah's stomach tensed. "I do not need your protection," she advised tartly. "Bates lives on the estate."

Alex smiled. "You misunderstand. I need to see Bates and now would be a good time. Do you object?"

Sarah clenched her hands together and blushed. The man had made her look a fool, deliberately misleading her. "Of course not."

"Alex, I need to show you something in the stables." Nathan stood up from his seat and motioned for his brother to follow him. Caldern stood and followed his brother from the room, but not before he turned and winked at Sarah.

"Don't let Alex upset you," Mary said looking up from her darning when the brothers left the room. "He has spent too many years commanding men."

Sarah forced herself to look away from the empty doorway and concentrate on Mary's words. "He told me he had been in the navy before he went to India."

"Joined when he was sixteen." Mary turned to Sarah, her friendly face full of concern. "Once he had made up his mind to leave, there was no talking him out of it."

"I thought the navy had been his choice." Sarah knew it was common for second sons to choose the military or navy as a career.

Mary shook her head. "No. He had planned on a diplomatic career."

"Why the navy then?"

"He had a fight with his father and there was no convincing him to stay. The Norward men are a stubborn lot."

Sarah privately agreed with Mary, but thought it was best if she kept silent. "That must have been difficult for you."

Mary nodded her head slowly, keeping her head down while she spoke. "I knew he would leave one day, but I expected him to be older. His father, the Marquess, had always kept Alex on a tight leash. The only freedom the boy had was when he went away to school."

Sarah tried to imagine the cold, arrogant Marquess as a young boy, but had difficulty doing so. "I imagine it was hard for Lord Caldern."

"Yes." Mary looked up and then glanced out the window on the far wall. "I knew both my boys would leave eventually. It happened so quickly. I wasn't prepared for the loneliness."

"Did you not have other family here on the estate?"

"I was an only child and my parents died when I was fourteen." Mary turned to Sarah; a sad smile twisted her lips. "That was when I went to work at the big house. At first I enjoyed looking after Douglas and Samuel, and Lady Caldern was such a nice woman. I wish it could have stayed that way."

"What happened?"

"The old Marquess," Mary sighed heavily, her fingers twisting the darning yarn. "He noticed me one day and that was the end of my peaceful life."

Sarah reached over and clasped Mary's restless hands. "It must not have been easy. You were so young."

Mary nodded her head. "The other servants ignored me. I suppose they were grateful he wasn't looking at them. There was no escaping him."

"There never is," Sarah whispered. "They have all the power."

Mary glanced at her quickly. "You understand."

Sarah nodded her head. "My late husband was a man who was forever reminding me of his authority over me."

"At least he married you."

"True," Sarah agreed. "A small consolation for all the pain he put me through."

"The old Marquess left me alone after I became pregnant and that was a blessing." Mary's voice caught on a sob. "My mistress was devastated. She never recovered."

"She died in childbirth?"

Mary brought her hand to her mouth and nodded her head. "Three days after. She lingered long enough to see Alex take to me and then she made me promise to care for her boys. After I agreed, she smiled and told me she never blamed me for her husband's betrayal. Then she closed her eyes and was gone."

Sarah blinked back her tears. How tragic for Alex. Sarah shivered at the thought of never knowing her mother. At least hers had been with her for most of her childhood. "So you became Lord Caldern's mother."

"I was all he had, but he was such a joy to raise." Mary wiped her tears away and her eyes shone with pride. "He never gave me any trouble, always helping and eager to learn. Those first six years were wonderful, but everything changed when her ladyship came to Caldern."

"You mean his lordship's stepmother?"

"Yes," Mary said with a shake of her head. "She

had different ideas about how the house should be run and who could live there. The old Marquess tried to protect us, but she was a strong woman. Nathan and I were lucky, we were given this cottage."

"It must have been wonderful to have something of your own, though." Sarah almost envied Mary her freedom.

"I missed the big house, but Alex was with us almost every day." Mary was silent for several minutes, looking out the window with a frown. "Master Douglas used to visit, too. He grew up to hate the old Marquess. He went to London and spent most of his time chasing the women, drinking, and gambling. His death was a shock."

Sarah nodded her agreement. If Alex's brother had not died without an heir, she would never have been forced to come here. Caroline would have been in London chasing a different man. Sarah was surprised at how low she felt at the thought of never meeting Alex.

A clock chimed two and Sarah jumped. The afternoon was passing rapidly and she still had work to do. She stood up and straightened the skirt of her muslin gown. "I thank you for the lunch, but I must be on my way."

"Of course, child. I have been rambling." Mary stood up and led Sarah into the kitchen. "I packed some food for you to take to Bates."

"Thank you." Sarah took the food wrapped in cloth and carried it with her to the door.

Mary hugged her and opened the door. "You stop and visit anytime. I am always here."

"I will," Sarah agreed with a smile. She put her straw bonnet on her head and picked up her basket before stepping out the door. The bright sunlight forced her to squint and raise a hand to shield her eyes until they had adjusted.

The fragrance of roses and lavender assailed her and Sarah inhaled deeply. Flowers grew in wild abandon around Mary's small cottage, creating a riot of color. Sarah stooped to cup a small pink rose in her hand. She closed her eyes, letting the perfume tickle her nostrils. When she straightened up, no one was in sight, so she began to walk down the drive. She had just passed the stables when a familiar voice stopped her.

"Were you planning on leaving without me?"

Chapter 11

Sarah jumped at the voice behind her and swung around, her heart beating frantically. "You frightened me," she accused.

Caldern bowed slightly. "My apologies."

Sarah straightened her shoulders and relaxed the hand clenched to her chest. "I thought you had returned home."

"I was waiting in the stable," Alex explained. "I am a man of my word."

Sarah glared at the Marquess. "I would disagree. You said you would leave me be."

Alex raised his eyebrow and smiled. "Do you honestly think I am visiting Bates just to annoy you?"

Sarah shook her head. She had heard the tenants talking about the Marquess all week and he seemed to honestly care about them. "You have been working hard to improve the estate," Sarah admitted. "Bates has been eager to see you. I would be insensitive not to realize that."

"Then we will call a truce for this afternoon." Caldern reached over and took Sarah's basket from her. "Let me help you."

"I can carry it."

"I insist. It is the least I can do as a gentleman."

Indignation threatened to choke Sarah. "That is not how you acted the first time we met," she sputtered.

"You were hardly behaving ladylike," the Marquess reminded her in a smooth voice.

Sarah's cheeks burned with heat. "You are insufferable."

Caldern shook his head. "It is useless to fight me on these matters. What can it hurt if I carry the basket?"

Sarah sighed heavily with resignation. As much as it hurt to admit it, he was right. "This is silly. Carry the basket, but remember I do not need a man to control my life."

"You made that abundantly clear last night."

Alex offered her his arm. She ignored it and started to walk down the laneway. Bates's cottage was probably a mile away and she wanted to get there early. Already she had allowed a good portion of her day to slip away. Now that the Marquess was coming with her, she doubted she would have a chance to collect any comfrey.

"What is in the basket? You always seem to be carrying it with you." The Marquess had matched his pace with Sarah's, his glossy Hessian boots fast becoming dusty.

"Just an assortment of herbal tinctures and creams, linens, and some dried herbal teas," Sarah explained patiently. "I carry it so that I am prepared for most any emergency."

"As you were yesterday."

"Yes." The image of the Marquess's ashen face and bloody arm almost caused her to stumble. "I seldom have anything as serious as that, though. Usually a bad cough or an inflamed wound."

"So I added some interest to your day," Alex teased.

"We can both live without that kind of excitement," Sarah commented dryly. "How is your arm doing?"

Alex shrugged. "It was only a scratch. Tell me why you are so interested in herbs."

"My mother taught me." Sarah's voice softened and her lips turned up in a gentle smile.

"You loved her very much," Alex said quietly. "How old were you when she died?"

"Fourteen." Sarah clasped her hands together tightly. "My parents died within two weeks of each other. First my father and then my mother." Sarah glanced at the Marquess. "Influenza."

Alex nodded. "That must have been difficult for you."

Sarah frowned and shook her head. "It was best for them. I do not think my mother could have lived without my father. They loved each other too much."

"That is rare."

Sarah glanced at the Marquess quickly, but his expression was sincere. "Mother defied her family to marry my father. He was a younger son who had gone into the church. He only had a small living, but they were happy."

"You were happy, too."

Sarah sighed. "Very."

They walked in silence for several minutes. Sarah listened to the faint rustling of the leaves and the chirping of the insects and breathed deeply of the scent of freshly cut hay. It was a perfect summer day.

"I remember running up and down this laneway as a boy." Alex stopped, looked around and pointed to a grove of oaks. "Nathan and I would play soldiers in those trees until it was time for dinner."

Sarah looked at the Marquess and was suddenly struck by the animation in his face. He truly loved Caldern. Her breath caught in her throat as she recognized the same emotion within her. In the few weeks that she had been here she had grown to love it too.

Alex looked at her intently. "I always swore I would never leave, but when I was sixteen I could not get away fast enough. Now that I am back, I know I will not leave again."

"It means too much to you."

"It is not just the house or the land, but also the people."

"They are very loyal to you." A vision of Caroline flashed through Sarah's mind. Her cousin had made it perfectly clear that she had no intention of staying in the country. She knew Caroline's determination too well to believe she would alter her plans.

"I intend to make everything right for them again. It may take a couple of years, but Caldern will once again be prosperous."

"You are very serious about your responsibilities." Sarah pushed her bonnet off her head, letting it swing around her neck. "You remind me of my Uncle John, Lord Hart. He has spent his whole life working on his estate."

"That is the commitment that Caldern needs."

"Did your father neglect the estate?"

"No." The Marquess shook his head. "My father only neglected his family."

Sarah frowned. She had thought the reason Alex had left Caldern was because of an argument with his father over the estate. "What about your brother?"

"Douglas refused to live at Caldern while my father was alive." Alex began to walk again, his pace unrushed. "Douglas wasted his time gambling and drinking in London. He should have married and settled down."

"Is that why you want to marry so quickly?"

"Caldern needs stability and I need an heir."

"What about happiness?"

"The only thing necessary for a marriage is civility and respect."

Sarah shook her head. "My husband was always polite to me, but never kind. He had promised my uncle he would care for me, but in the end he was disgusted by the sight of me."

"I cannot imagine any man not enjoying looking at you."

"Stephen should not have married. He blamed me for his unhappiness." Sarah felt her chest constrict in remembered pain and humiliation.

"Why?"

Sarah closed her eyes tightly, memories of her marriage washing over her. She struggled to breathe, her words tumbling out in a whisper. "He said I distracted him from God. I was an instrument of the devil and my child would be born in sin."

Sarah opened her eyes. The Marquess was watching her, his face expressionless, but his eyes had darkened to almost black. Her stomach tightened in regret. She had revealed more than she had intended. "Forgive me. I should not have told you that."

"There is nothing to forgive." The Marquess took her arm, urging her to continue walking. "You mentioned a child. What happened to him?"

Sarah's body started to shake and she took a deep breath to gain control. "The baby died in the same carriage accident that killed my husband."

"I am sorry." The Marquess spoke softly and squeezed her arm gently.

Sarah brought her clenched hand up to her stomach. Her whole body tightened against the onslaught of anguish and tears that threatened to overcome her. This was the first time she had spoken openly of the secret she had buried deep within her.

"The carriage overturned and I was pinned under a wheel. When I regained consciousness several days later I had lost my baby."

The Marquess was silent for several minutes. Tears slid down Sarah's face, but she was too caught up in her sorrow to notice. When Alex finally spoke there was tenderness and understanding in his voice. "Your baby was not born yet?"

Sarah shook her head and wiped away the tears. "Stephen had been upset when he had learned that I was with child, so I suppose he got his wish in the end."

"Nonsense," Alex said sharply. "It sounds like the man was insane. You were too young to deal with his problems."

Sarah had accepted that fact, too. She remembered how Stephen would lock himself in his study for weeks at a time, only emerging in the evening when he would demand his husbandly rights. He could not fight his desire for her, but in the morning he would turn away from her in disgust, washing his hands repeatedly, trying to cleanse himself of her scent.

"I was left with a generous stipend, but my uncle insisted I live with him." Sarah smiled slightly as she recalled her uncle's outrage at her intention of living on her own. She had only agreed after he had promised he would not force her to marry again.

Sarah felt drained, her thoughts consumed with painful memories. She continued to walk quietly beside the Marquess until they reached a small stone cottage. The pathway was overgrown with weeds, a neglected garden on either side of it. Red poppies were scattered throughout, while the holly-hocks and foxgloves fought for space amongst the weeds.

"Bates has been too ill to go outside this year." Sarah walked to the door. "I do not think he has been able to garden for several years."

The Marquess looked around and shook his head. "I will send one of the gardeners from the house to work here."

Sarah's hand stopped on the door handle. Sur-prise at the Marquess's generosity overwhelmed her. "Bates would love that," she agreed quietly.

"Do not look so shocked. I spent a large part of my youth with servants and tenants. I would be a very selfish person if I did not care for them." Alex stood in the middle of the path, his hands on his hips, his head tilted at her. "Bates spent his whole life tending the gardens at Caldern. It is only fit-ting that his garden be kept up."

Sarah felt her heart tighten with sympathy for the lonely young boy the Marquess had been. She had not seen this side of him before and it amazed her that a man so stern and determined could be so sensitive to others' needs.

"Having his garden in order will probably do more to heal him than my teas."

"Let us hope so." The Marquess gestured for her to knock at the door.

A gravelly voice yelled, "Come in."

The two entered the darkened cottage. The smell of dampness and a cold chill greeted them.

Sarah paused a few seconds to allow her eyes to adjust.

"I am sorry I am late, but I brought a visitor with me," she explained. Sarah took her basket from the Marquess and put it on the cluttered table by the hearth.

Bates turned his head, his face breaking into a toothy smile when he saw the Marquess. "Master Alex!" Bates struggled to get up from his bed until a coughing fit forced him to lie back down.

Alex walked over to him and put a reassuring hand on his shoulder. "You are too sick, Bates. Stay put."

Bates nodded his head, lying back until his coughing subsided. "Aye, it is best."

Alex moved a chair over to the bed and sat down. "I hope Mrs. Wellsley has been taking good care of you."

"The best," Bates agreed. "Her medicines have helped some and her pretty young face has soothed my heart."

Alex chuckled. "I agree. Best to keep that to ourselves, though."

"Aye," Bates chortled. "You always were the man to notice the ladies."

"And you always pointed them out."

"We made a good pair back then." Bates sat up slowly. Alex pushed the pillows up behind Bates's back until he had settled himself comfortably. "I can see the navy didn't do you no harm."

"It taught me a lot," Alex agreed. "My only regret was leaving Caldern."

"No regrets, Master Alex." Bates cleared his throat. "Yer here now and none too soon."

"I know," Alex said quietly. "I will not leave again."

"No need to tell me that. Haven't I known you since you could walk?"

Alex laughed. "That is what I am afraid of. You know too many of my secrets."

"No need to worry on my account. You just see that those gardens are straightened out. What her ladyship done to them would give a lesser man an apoplexy."

"I am working on it. Soon everything will be in order again."

Bates harrumphed loudly and then settled back onto his pillows. "I'm too old to waste time. The sooner those gardens are in order, the better I'll feel."

Sarah listened as she worked at the hearth, preparing a small fire and heating a kettle of water. She smiled at Bates's comments. Even though he had been pensioned off for more than ten years, he still considered the gardens to be his domain.

"I tried to tell Lady Caldern that she couldn't be skimping on the men, but she wouldn't listen to me." Bates shook his head in disgust. "I'm just glad you finally came home, Master Alex."

"So am I." Alex patted Bates's hand. "Everything will be put to rights now. I have hired about thirty extra men for the gardens alone."

"They'll be needing at least that many. The rose garden is a disgrace."

Sarah finished brewing her tea of elder flowers and brought a cup to Bates. "Sip this," she said, placing the cup in the gnarled hands of her patient. "I left you enough tea for the next few days."

"Thank you." Bates blew on the hot liquid before taking a sip. He grimaced in protest. "Wish it didn't taste so horrible."

Sarah smiled in sympathy. Many of her medicines tasted strange, but their benefits made them necessary. "Mary Carter sent food and I brought soup from the main house. That should take away the taste."

The Marquess stood up from his chair and straightened his riding jacket. "You do whatever it takes to get better, Bates. I expect to see you outside soon."

"I'll try." Bates took another sip of the tea.

The Marquess went to the table and picked up Sarah's basket. "I will be back to check on you. Soon the workmen will finish repairing the cottages and that should make things easier for you."

"Much obliged, Master Alex." Bates leaned back against his pillows. "I'll just take a nap now."

Sarah took the tea from Bates's hand and put it on the table beside the bed. She then brought the food over and after covering her patient she backed away. "I will see you in a couple of days."

Bates nodded his agreement and then closed his eyes. Sarah turned away and followed the Marquess from the cottage. When she was outside she took a deep breath of fresh air before closing the door. She joined the Marquess on the laneway.

"He is looking worse than I imagined." Alex looked back at the cottage and then down the laneway. "He was an old man when I left Caldern, but somehow I never expected to see him so defeated."

"He is doing much better than when I first came." Sarah started to walk back to Caldern.

"Thank you for that." The Marquess fell in step with her. "So much has changed."

Sarah nodded her understanding. "You expected Caldern to be the same."

"Crazy, I know, but somehow I never envisioned things being so different."

"You were gone for a long time," Sarah said

softly. "You will have things the way you want them soon enough."

Alex nodded his agreement and the two of them walked back to Mary Carter's cottage in silence. The warm sun relaxed Sarah and she felt at ease with the new understanding she had of the Marquess. He might be a man determined to have his own way, but he seemed to care how his actions affected others.

When they reached the cottage, the Marquess stopped and turned to Sarah. "I have some other visits I need to make before I return to the house. I enjoyed escorting you this afternoon."

Sarah adjusted her bonnet on her head and reached her hand out for her basket. "It was a very enlightening afternoon."

Alex raised an eyebrow. "How so?"

Sarah shrugged her shoulders slightly, trying to avoid the Marquess's probing gaze. "You were genuinely concerned for Bates. I had not expected that."

"What kind of person did you think I was?"

Sarah looked at the impassive face of the Marquess and felt her stomach tighten. She sensed she had somehow angered him. "I did not know what to expect," she explained hesitantly. "Before today I have only seen your behavior with your Lady Caldern and my cousin."

"And you of course," the Marquess finished.

Sarah nodded. "You have been less than patient in the past."

"I hope that means you do not suspect my motives anymore."

"I think it best I watch myself around you, my lord, but I will never doubt your sincere commitment to Caldern."

The Marquess grinned. "You are still a skeptic

where I am concerned. I will have to show you my intentions are only honorable."

"I will take your word for it, my lord."

"Very wise, Sarah." The Marquess reached out and stroked the blue ribbon of her bonnet. "I would hate to give you reason to distrust me," he teased silkily.

Sarah's heartbeat quickened and her stomach fluttered nervously. Her breath had caught in her throat and she could only nod her head and watch as a flare of heat sparked in Alex's eyes. He leaned toward her, his breath skimming across her cheek and Sarah tensed in anticipation of his kiss. Instead, he cleared his throat and moved away.

He turned to go, but paused and looked back. "I think you and my brother Samuel will deal very well together."

Sarah could only stare at the Marquess in amazement as he turned away and walked to the stables. She could not believe the audacity of the man. She had told him how horrible her marriage had been and still he thought to match her with his brother. Anger at his insensitiveness raged within her. She had no desire to be married.

Chapter 12

Sarah shrugged her shoulder, easing the pain in her neck. She flexed her cramped fingers and then picked up her embroidery needle again. She had been sitting in the corner of the drawing room since the ladies had retired from dinner. The candlelight was poor, but she was away from Lady Caldern's condemning eyes. She bent back to her work when the strident voice of her cousin forced her to look up.

"I do not approve of Mr. Black, Sarah." Caroline stood with her arms crossed and her mouth pinched into a grimace. "But setting your cap at him keeps you away from Caldern."

"I never did any such thing." Sarah pushed away her needlework. "I was seated next to Mr. Black at dinner. It would have been impolite to ignore him."

"There are worse things than being rude," Caroline countered. "I suppose we must recognize the man, though. I have already spoken to Lady Caldern about the changes I intend to make once I am married to the Marquess."

Sarah was saved from making a reply by the appearance of the gentlemen. Caroline straightened her dress with her hands and turned a broad smile to them. "It has seemed an age since we left you in the dining room," she pouted.

"Nonsense," Mr. Stanton countered heartily. "We could never stay away from you for long."

Sarah looked up at the men, scanning their faces until her eyes rested on the Marquess. He was frowning slightly, but glanced at her immediately, quirking an eyebrow questioningly. A rush of heat raced through her body. She could only stare at him, her mouth dry and her heart pounding frantically. His gaze never wavered until Mr. Stanton claimed his attention.

Caroline started to move toward the men, but stopped and looked back at Sarah. "Remember you are to serve the tea. Lady Caldern was very explicit about your duties."

Caroline left in a swirl of silk and Sarah sighed deeply. She picked up her handwork, trying to thread her needle, but her hands shook. She still felt the searing penetration of the Marquess's eyes.

"I have never understood how women can see those things."

Sarah jumped at the voice of Samuel Black. He stood in front of her, his hands behind his back. He was attired in the black garb of a clergyman and the gray scattered throughout his dark hair only added to his aura of somberness.

"You surprised me, Mr. Black. I did not hear you approach." Sarah felt her cheeks redden in embarrassment, thankful he could not read her thoughts.

"Too intent on your work, I imagine." Samuel Black moved a chair beside her and sat down. "I hope I am not disturbing you."

"Not at all." Sarah put her needle in her work and then folded it back into her bag. Samuel was looking across the room. She followed his gaze to Caroline.

"My brother is wise to marry," he said suddenly. "He needs a wife to help rebuild Caldern."

Sarah looked back at him, unsure how to respond. His eyes were half closed and his brow furrowed. "I am sure Caroline will do her best to help," she offered.

"Do you think so?" he asked musingly. "She is one of the most beautiful women I have ever met."

Sarah clasped her hands in her lap. Mr. Black's tone of voice had made his compliment sound insulting. "Do you object to her beauty?"

"Not at all." Samuel Black leaned back in his chair, stretching his legs out. "I just wonder at my brother's choice. He needs a strong woman. One who will support and understand him."

"Caroline will do her best."

Mr. Black glanced sideways at Sarah and grinned sheepishly. "I mean no insult to your cousin, but she does not strike me as a woman who would be willing to understand anyone except herself."

Sarah bit her lip and looked away. Mr. Black had seen through Caroline's beauty. "My cousin may seem a trifle selfish, but I am certain that will change once she settles down."

Samuel Black shook his head. "That has not been my experience with people. Your cousin needs a man who will adore and pamper her. Alex is not that man."

Sarah had the same doubt. "Perhaps that will change once they are married?" she suggested hesitantly.

"No." Samuel shifted in his chair and looked directly at her. "My brother needs a woman he can respect and rely on. He needs a wife he can love."

Sarah's heart began to beat rapidly at the intensity of Samuel Black's gaze. He seemed to be peering into her soul, delving into its innermost secrets. She cleared her throat and forced herself to speak. "Marriage is seldom about love."

"True, but that is what Alex needs."

"Then why is he willing to marry without it?"

"He is afraid. Our father enjoyed proving Alex wrong about women and love. Alex has become cynical, but underneath it all, he is still an idealistic boy longing for love."

"What about your childhood, Mr. Black?" Sarah asked softly, curious if this was the same reason he was still a bachelor. "Did your father sour your opinion of marriage?"

Samuel chuckled and turned his gaze back to Lady Caroline. "I never saw my father enough to be influenced by him."

"That must have made you angry."

Samuel looked over at her, his eyes wide with astonishment. "Quite the contrary," he exclaimed. "Being sent away from here was the best thing that could have happened to me."

Sarah had imagined that being forced out of his home at such a young age would have left Samuel bitter. "You did not feel abandoned?"

"The only thing I felt was relief," he admitted in a low voice. "My father was constantly pointing out the differences between us boys and belittling us. I suppose he thought it would make us more competitive and ambitious, but all he succeeded in doing was making our lives miserable."

Sarah's stomach knotted in revulsion at a father treating his children in such a manner. It was completely opposite of her own upbringing, where she had been surrounded by love. "How horrible."

Samuel nodded his head and sighed. "I escaped, but Douglas and Alex had no choice. They were forced to endure my father's cruelty."

"I did not realize the old Marquess was such a difficult man," Sarah said in a low voice. "I have only heard good of him from the tenants."

"My father was a man of many faces. I think he was jealous that one of his sons would inherit Caldern after he died. I know it sounds ridiculous." Samuel gave Sarah a wry smile. "One minute my father would be showing me the estate proudly and the next he would remind me that I would never own it. I was the eldest and he never let me forget the circumstances of my birth."

Sarah's chest tightened and tears welled up in her eyes as she felt the pain and disappointment young Samuel must have experienced. She reached over and clasped his hand, squeezing it reassuringly. "No child should have to endure that."

Samuel smiled. "Thank you for understanding, but I have forgiven him now. I was sent away young enough that it did not leave a lasting impression. At school I could separate myself from him. He no longer had the power to wound me."

"It must hurt to be back at Caldern."

Samuel shook his head and smiled. "Caldern holds no power over me and life has been very generous. I enjoy my vocation and my parishioners."

Sarah looked at Samuel intently for several seconds, seeing the truth of his words in his eyes. He was a man at peace with his life. "I almost envy you."

"Why?"

"You are not resentful or defeated by what has happened to you. You must be very courageous."

"No more than you, Mrs. Wellsley." Samuel raised

her hand to his mouth and gave it a light kiss before releasing it. "All you have to do is allow yourself to trust."

Sarah sighed heavily. "I think it is safer to trust no one. It is certainly less painful."

"And very lonely. I am here if you need someone to talk to."

Sarah glanced at Samuel sharply, but all she saw in his eyes was understanding and sympathy. "Thank you."

"Am I interrupting?"

Sarah jumped as the cold, detached voice of the Marquess sliced through the air. The blood rushed to her cheeks and her heart began to beat rapidly. She looked up and found herself impaled by his granite gray eyes. His mouth was clenched tightly and a pulse beat furiously at his temple. Her first instinct was to run. Instead, she straightened her shoulders and glared back at him.

"I see the two of you have become better acquainted. Fanny has asked for your services at the tea tray, Sarah." With a slight bow of his head, he turned on his heel and left.

"Do not be too hard on him," Samuel pleaded. "He was no more than a boy when he left to find his way in the world."

"That does not excuse rudeness." Sarah straightened her skirt and stood up. "There is no need to warn me about the Marquess, Mr. Black. We have come to an understanding."

"And what might that be?" Samuel asked with a raised eyebrow, standing up beside Sarah.

"I tend to his tenants' needs and he leaves me alone."

Samuel chuckled quietly. "From the way Alex has been glaring at you this evening, I believe he has other plans."

Sarah looked nervously over her shoulder, but the Marquess was speaking to Caroline. "He has given me his word."

"That does not stop him from trying."

Sarah looked up at Samuel and blushed at the implied meaning of his words. He was smiling down at her, his dark eyes warm with sympathy. "I have no intention of being persuaded."

"My brother has always been persistent when he wants something. Perhaps this time he will find what he needs," he mused. "For his sake, I hope you learn to trust again." Samuel Black bowed his head slightly and moved away to join Mr. Stanton at the fireplace.

Sarah took a deep breath and steadied her pounding heart before walking to the settee where Johnson had placed the tea tray. Lady Caldern motioned her to sit down.

"I do not expect to wait for you," she hissed in a low voice. "Your behavior this evening is inexcusable."

Sarah sat down. "What have I done?"

"No lady of breeding would willingly converse with a man such as Mr. Black."

Sarah stared at Lady Caldern in wonder. The woman's face was pinched in disapproval and her eyes narrowed in fury. Reasoning with her would be impossible. Instead, Sarah asked innocently, "You mean I should not speak to a vicar?"

"That is not what I mean," Lady Caldern spat at her furiously. "You would do better to mind your tongue. I am not blind to your character. If Alex had not insisted you be included at meals, I would have stopped your games."

"I have done nothing wrong," Sarah insisted. She turned away and started to pour tea. As she distributed the fine china cups of hot liquid, she focused

her mind on Mr. Black's words. His portrayal of
the old Marquess had been a shock. She knew the
man was a womanizer, but that was not unusual
among the aristocracy.

Her stomach clenched in sympathy for the
young boys who had grown up with such a father.
She glanced at the Marquess, who was still with
Caroline and her heart ached for him. The harsh-
ness of his childhood must have been difficult, but
that did not excuse his behavior toward her.

Her mind raced in confusion at all the different
sides she had seen of Alex. At one moment he was
taunting and the next reassuring. He had been
conversing with her openly this afternoon, but this
evening he had glared at her coldly, almost in
anger. She had befriended his brother and instead
of being grateful, he seemed to despise her.

Sarah handed out the last of the tea and leaned
back against the cushions. She had long given up
trying to understand men. Since meeting Alex,
her stomach was in a constant knot and everything
she did seemed to be wrong. Sarah rubbed the
side of her head and sighed. It was safer to bury
herself in her medicines.

"What ails you now?" Lady Caldern demanded.

Sarah forced herself to look at her hostess. "My
head aches. Would you mind if I retired for the
evening?"

"Not at all." Lady Caldern waved her hand at
Sarah to leave. "You will not be missed."

Sarah stood up and left the room without another look back. When the door had closed behind her, she leaned against it for a few seconds.
The ordeal of the evening was over. Wearily she
walked to the staircase and slowly climbed it. She
moved through the corridors of the old house
until she arrived at her room. Just as she reached

her hand for the doorknob, she was stopped by the voice of the Marquess.

"We need to talk."

Her heart leapt and then fell into a frantic beating. Sarah turned around slowly. His expression was stern and his eyes narrowed with purpose. "We have nothing to discuss." She forced herself to speak calmly.

"Do you flirt with every man you meet?" Alex spat out angrily.

Sarah frowned and rubbed her aching head with her hand. "What are you talking about?"

"You and Samuel."

Sarah looked at him blankly, searching her mind for something she had done to offend him. She shook her head. "I was not flirting with him."

"Then why were you holding his hand?" Alex put his arm on the door beside her. She hugged the wall to avoid him.

"I was not holding his hand," she denied loudly. "What right do you have to question what I do?"

"I am your host," Alex snarled at her. "I expect you to behave with decorum while you are under my roof."

"You are the one who insisted I get better acquainted with your brother. We were talking about his childhood."

"Is that why you held his hand?" Alex sneered.

"Yes," Sarah defended. "I was giving him sympathy."

"Sympathy," Alex repeated jeeringly. "And why was he kissing you?"

"He kissed my hand," Sarah cried indignantly. "How dare you suggest otherwise."

"Why would Samuel need your sympathy?"

Sarah sighed and shook her head. Alex's eyes

were still cold with disbelief, but his tone was calmer. "We were discussing your father."

Alex looked at her for a few seconds, then closed his eyes and turned his head away. "I am sorry for jumping to the wrong conclusion. Our past is not pleasant."

Sarah leaned her head against the wall and let out the breath she had been holding. Alex was still close to her, but his stance was no longer aggressive. "My actions were completely innocent. How could you think otherwise?"

"It was stupid," Alex admitted. He turned back to face her again. "If I had given myself time to think, I would have realized it."

"Your brother was kind and I wanted to show him that I understood his pain."

Alex nodded his head, but did not move away from Sarah. She forced herself to continue looking at him. His face had softened, his muscles relaxed and his mouth smiling slightly. His eyes remained hooded from her view, though. Sarah took a deep breath and inhaled the musky scent of him.

"Show me the same understanding," Alex whispered hoarsely.

Sarah's breath caught in her throat at the raw emotion she heard in his voice. Nervously she raised shaking fingers to his cheek and gently stroked it. He pushed his face into her hand, before turning his mouth to kiss it. Sarah's knees weakened and her mouth grew dry as his lips sent tingles of sensation up her arm.

Alex looked up at her, his eyes burning with intensity. "You give so much of yourself to others. Do not deny me."

Alex brushed his lips across hers and sent a

shiver of delight throughout her body. Sarah knew she should stop this before it went any further, but as she moved to escape Alex brought his other arm up to stop her.

"Stay," he pleaded. "You cannot ignore what is between us."

Sarah moistened her dry lips, her eyes shying away from the intensity of his gaze. Alex wanted her. There was no denying the attraction between them, but the risk was too high. Sarah could not afford to lose her freedom to any man, especially not the man who was going to wed her cousin.

"We should not be here like this," she whispered.

"It is too late." Alex moved his head closer and Sarah closed her eyes as his warm brandy-scented breath tickled her nose.

He captured her mouth slowly, gently nudging her lips apart and then easing his tongue in. An exquisite lethargy stole throughout her body. She surrendered to his kiss, allowing herself to be drawn into the web of pleasure he wove. Her lips clung to his and her body moved closer as he wrapped his arms around her.

Alex's gentle exploration eased her into a mindless state of bliss. His lips caressed hers, his teeth gently nipping and then his tongue soothing. Sarah followed where he led, letting him slowly build their passion. Her body throbbed with an aching need for fulfillment and she moved restlessly in his arms.

He held her close as the kiss spiraled out of control and his lips became more demanding. Sarah exulted in his fervor. Her body was on fire, burning with awareness of the man who held her. They were as one, connected in their rapture.

A slight movement of the head, a pause to catch

their breath and then the spell was broken. Sarah was bereft. Alex looked at her with smoldering eyes, his breathing ragged, his chest rising and falling rapidly. He shook his head and then eased his arms away from her.

Sarah sagged against the wall, her body too weak to stand on its own. Alex brushed a loose strand of hair away from her cheek and then ran his finger down to her mouth. He paused slightly before outlining its bruised fullness. A frown creased his forehead as his eyes searched her face.

"Forgive me," he whispered.

Sarah's eyes widened and she watched in disbelief as he walked away. Her body was still vibrating with the sensations he had created in her. Tears smarted in her eyes and she brushed them away. It was better this way. Alex was not free and she did not want any involvement with a man.

Chapter 13

"What took you so long?" Caroline's sharp voice was like a blast of cold air. Dawn was beginning to creep into the sky. "You must help Nellie fix this riding habit."

Sarah looked about Caroline's room and muffled a gasp. Everywhere there were clothes strewn and thrown about. "What are you doing?"

"Trying to dress for riding this morning," Caroline snapped. "You would think the Marquess would choose a more decent hour."

"He always goes this early," Sarah said automatically. She brushed back a loose strand of hair as she bent to pick up a blue morning dress and drape it over the back of a chair. Caroline's summons had caught her unprepared and she had thrown on an old brown work dress, a ripped cotton shawl for warmth, and secured her hair with a ribbon. She had been too rushed to find a cap to cover her head.

"I did not know you were so conversant with the Marquess's habits." Caroline glared at Sarah and then held up an emerald green dress. "This is the only decent riding habit I have and it has a rip in the hem."

Sarah walked to her cousin and fluffed out the gown. Yards of fabric fell in every direction. There was a large tear at the bottom and the hem was open on either side. It would take time to mend. "Where is the needle and thread?"

"Nellie," Caroline shouted impatiently.

Nellie appeared in the doorway of the dressing room. "I don't know why you won't wear the black one, my lady."

"It makes me look sallow. Just fix this one in a hurry," Caroline barked sharply.

"Surely the Marquess will wait for you," Sarah suggested.

"He does not know I intend to ride with him." Caroline threw the dress over her bed. "I have no intention of letting him find an excuse to go without me."

"He wouldn't do that, my lady." Nellie knotted her thread and started to sew the rip.

"He has avoided me for the past week," Caroline cried shrilly. "He has been here for over two weeks and still no hint of a proposal."

"He is very busy," Sarah soothed.

"He runs whenever he sees me." Caroline's eyes were narrow and her mouth thinned in determination. "I will not let him escape me this time, though."

Sarah shook her head and held the dress out for Nellie to sew. Caroline had not been exaggerating Alex's behavior over the past week. He had been absent from the house most days and in the evening closeted himself in his study after dinner. Alex was shunning Sarah also.

He still watched her, though. Sarah was not sure what he was suspicious of, but he was making her very uneasy. She only saw him at the dinner table in the evening, but whenever she looked up his eyes were on her. They were dark, almost smoldering in their intensity, sending shivers up her spine. That was the only contact she had had with him for over a week.

"I do not understand why Caldern is being so difficult." Caroline threw her hairbrush down on her vanity.

Sarah dropped the dress over Nellie's lap and went to her cousin. "Have you talked to him at all?"

Caroline shook her head and glared back at Sarah in the mirror. "He completely ignores me. I think there is something wrong with the man."

"Nonsense. There must be some way to approach him." She picked up the hairbrush and began to work on Caroline's curls.

"This is the only way." Caroline twisted the small ruby ring she wore on her baby finger. "The man will have to recognize me."

"I am sure he is waiting for the perfect time to talk with you."

"He better hurry, because I have written Father."

Sarah paused in her brushing. "Was that wise?"

"Who else should I have told?" Caroline heaved an exasperated sigh. "Honestly Sarah, sometimes I think you forget we are not without protection. Father will make the Marquess honor his promise to marry me."

"I did not know Lord Caldern had made such a promise."

Caroline frowned slightly, her eyes narrowing suspiciously. "Are you defending Caldern's actions?"

"I am only trying to be fair," Sarah explained. She arranged a section of ringlets in Caroline's hair and pinned them in place. "This visit was to allow the two of you to get acquainted. No definite engagement had been arranged."

"It was implied," Caroline snorted. "I would never have come this far north otherwise. The Marquess will live up to his word."

Sarah refrained from saying anything more on the subject. Alex had not agreed to anything, only his stepmother had made the promise. Still, Caroline did have expectations and Alex could not ignore that.

Sarah finished arranging her cousin's hair and then stood back to admire the result. Caroline was stunningly beautiful. Her pouting red lips and limpid blue eyes belied the fierce ambition that burned within her. Caroline was determined to be the Marchioness of Caldern and nothing would deter her. The thought of that marriage caused a stab of regret to pierce Sarah's chest, but she ignored it.

Caroline pushed the chair away from the vanity and started to pace around the room, kicking gowns out of the way as she walked. "Are you finished, Nellie?"

Sarah walked back to Nellie and shook her head. "It will take a while."

"The sun is already in the sky. There is no more time." Caroline moved back to the bed and grabbed the dress out of Nellie's hand. "Sarah, go down and stop the Marquess from leaving. I will wear the dress with pins in it."

Sarah hesitated. Her hair was falling out of its ribbon and her shawl was little more than a rag. Her heart began to beat frantically and she wondered that Caroline could not hear it.

"What are you waiting for?" Caroline demanded loudly. "Go."

Sarah nodded and ran out of the room. As

much as she hated speaking to Alex, she could not refuse her cousin's request. Caroline knew this would be the only time that she could surprise Caldern. Every other minute of the day, servants protected him. Good manners would demand that he wait for Caroline.

Sarah rushed down the empty hallway and stairs, the beauty of the panels and paintings a blur of color. She was out of breath by the time she reached the front door and paused a second before pulling it open. The glare of the rising sun blinded her momentarily, forcing her to stop on the stone landing.

When her eyes had adjusted, the first thing she saw was Alex. He was seated on his horse; his back turned away from her as he conversed with Mr. Stanton. Nathan Carter, who was trotting up the drive, was still some distance away. David Stanton raised an eyebrow when he noticed Sarah and motioned for Alex to look her way.

Sarah's mouth went dry and her breath caught in her throat when Alex turned around. His white cravat gleamed against the darkness of his apparel. His black riding coat and breeches were impeccably tailored to his muscular body. He tilted his head, his gray eyes darkening when they met hers. A tingle of electricity shot through Sarah's body and her knees felt weak. She wanted to run back into the house, but her legs refused to move.

"What can I do for you, Mrs. Wellsley?" His deep voice rang through the early morning silence, jolting her into awareness.

"If you please, my lord," she began haltingly. "I have a message for you from Lady Caroline."

"A message?" Alex moved away from David Stanton, walking his horse closer to her. Sarah watched his long, strong fingers gripping the reins.

Those same hands had held her close to him, she remembered with a shiver of delight.

When he was about ten feet away he stopped and leaned forward on his saddle. "What does your cousin want?"

Sarah looked down at her hands clasping the shawl around her shoulders and bit her lip. Already he seemed displeased with her intrusion and she doubted that he would welcome her message. Sarah glanced up, but avoided meeting Alex's eyes. "Caroline wishes for you to wait for her."

He stared at her for a few seconds and then laughed. "You are not serious, I hope?"

Sarah nodded her head. "I know this is unexpected, but Caroline is dressing to ride with you."

"We are intending to visit the outer farms this morning. This is not a pleasure ride."

"I know." Sarah straightened her shoulders, letting her shawl slip to her elbows. She looked at Alex directly. "She will only be a few more minutes."

"Why this morning?"

"She wants to spend time with you," Sarah explained quietly.

Alex sighed heavily and then looked over his shoulder. "Go on without me. I will join you shortly," he instructed. David Stanton nodded and then urged his horse forward to intercept the other riders. Fury pranced impatiently, but Alex held him steady until they were alone.

He looked back at her and then shook his head. "Dammit, Sarah. I am doing my best." He spurred Fury forward suddenly, almost reaching Sarah when a deafening crash exploded all around them.

The world filled with dirt and flying shards of stone. Sarah covered her eyes and felt something rip into her forehead. Her ears rang from the thundering noise all around her. Fury whinnied and she heard his hooves on the stone walkway, clamoring and kicking.

"Whoa." Alex's stern voice rang out over the horse's objections, trying to calm the animal down, but with little success.

"What the hell happened?" David Stanton shouted above the ruckus. His horse was galloping back to them.

Alex coughed. "Something's fallen from the roof. Keep the horses away."

"Right." Sarah heard Stanton's horse stop and then move away; seconds later, footsteps came pounding toward them.

Sarah's hands felt wet and she took them away from her eyes. The world spun slightly as she stared at the sticky redness that met her eyes. She stumbled backwards, feeling the cold sharpness of stone behind her. She leaned back against the wall, letting the blood drip down her face. Her eyes stung and her mouth was gritty with the dust she had inhaled. She began coughing in protest.

The air was clearing and Sarah's eyes widened at the devastation in front of her. All around were chunks of red boulders. The stone pavement in front of the entranceway had huge holes in it. Debris was everywhere. Rock and flagstones tilted at odd angles, rubble littered every inch of the entrance drive and portico.

Slowly, feeling began to return and Sarah's concern turned to the others. She saw Fury being led away by David Stanton. The horse seemed to be favoring his left rear leg. Her thoughts immediately turned to Alex. Was he hurt also? She pushed away from the wall, but a hand restrained her.

"Stay put," Alex ordered. He was beside her, leaning against the wall. "Are you hurt?"

Sarah shook her head, vaguely wondering when Alex had joined her. Her mind seemed to be full of wool batting. Her ears still had a ringing in them and there was a dull ache in her forehead. She put her hand to the side of her head, pressing against its dampness. She let out a slight groan as pain shot through her skull.

"What's wrong?" Alex demanded. He moved in front of her, blocking her view of the rock debris. He pulled her hand away from her head and swore. "You are hurt."

"It is only a scratch." Sarah's voice sounded weak and unsure. She did not have the energy to fight Alex as he pulled her shawl from around her shoulders. He bunched it up and pressed it against her head.

"Hold this in place."

Sarah took hold of the makeshift bandage and then looked more closely at the Marquess. He was covered in red dust. His hat was gone and his face and hair sparkled with bits of stone. "Did you get hurt?"

He shook his head. "Fury's rear leg has a large gash in it, but I think it should mend fine. The stone landed where I had been standing talking to you. Thank God I moved Fury forward when I did."

Sarah began to shiver uncontrollably. Alex had almost died. She had almost lost him. Her teeth began to chatter and she closed her eyes to stop her tears from falling.

"Shush," Alex pleaded in a whisper. He gathered her close to him, rubbing her back reassuringly. "Everything will be fine."

"You could have been killed," Sarah choked out. There was no stopping the tears now and she lowered her head against his shoulder. He held her close, rubbing his cheek against her hair as she sobbed uncontrollably. Sarah was unsure of how long she remained sheltered in his arms, but gradually she calmed down. The warmth of Alex's body began to seep into her. Her shivering stopped.

"Thank you," she gurgled with a hiccup.

"Better now?" Alex smiled at her crookedly, his eyes a soft gray. Sarah felt as if she were drowning in the secret promises of those eyes. Her breath caught in her throat and her heart began to beat frantically as he glanced down at her lips and then moved his head closer to her.

"I am ready now," a cheerful voice announced from the doorway.

Sarah jumped out of Alex's arms and stared into the cold condemning eyes of Caroline.

Chapter 14

Alex turned and looked at Caroline. She was the picture of outraged dignity. Her mouth was set in a tight grimace and her eyes were narrowed, condemning Sarah with a hateful glare. Alex's chest tightened in anger, his fist clenched, ready to do battle. He took a calming breath and forced himself to relax.

"We will not be riding this morning," he announced coldly.

Caroline turned her fury on him. "How can you refuse me? Have you no concept of how a gentleman should behave?"

Alex raised an eyebrow and stared at the beauty in front of him. Her green riding habit fit her like a glove, accentuating every curve of her perfect figure. Even in her anger she maintained a regal, almost haughty attitude, perfect for a future Marchioness.

A chill ran up his spine at the thought of making her his bride. She was incapable of giving warmth. He had always hoped to love his wife. He had been struggling with this decision all week and was still no nearer to a solution. As much as he knew he needed to marry, he could not bring himself to propose to Lady Caroline.

"It is manners that dictate we cancel our ride this morning," he answered calmly. "Perhaps it has escaped your notice that Mrs. Wellsley is injured?"

"What does that have to do with us?" Caroline tossed her head and picked up the skirt of her riding habit with one hand. "Sarah is perfectly capable of taking care of herself."

"Even if that were true," Alex said between gritted teeth, "We would not be riding this morning. The front drive has been destroyed."

Caroline looked over Alex's shoulder and her mouth opened in a gasp. "What happened?"

Alex felt Sarah begin to shiver next to him. He turned to her and saw that her face had become very pale. "Later," he snapped. "Right now we need to care for your cousin."

Sarah swayed suddenly. "Damn." He grabbed her up in his arms. "Open the door," he ordered.

Caroline stared at him openmouthed for a few seconds before heaving an indignant sigh and following his request. Alex shifted Sarah's weight in his arms and gathered her closer to him. She nudged her head into his shoulder and his breath caught in his chest. Nothing had ever felt so right as carrying Sarah in his arms.

Johnson, the butler, rushed into the hallway just as he entered. "What has happened, my lord?" he asked as he opened the drawing room door. "I hope Mrs. Wellsley is not seriously injured."

"She will be fine," Alex reassured. "We need water and some bandages."

Johnson nodded and left for the kitchen. Alex walked to the nearest settee and gently placed Sarah on it. He pushed a pillow behind her head and then took the blood-soaked shawl from around her head.

"How bad is it?" David Stanton asked, walking into the room.

Alex shook his head and sat down beside Sarah. "I think it is only a small cut, but there is so much blood it is hard to see. How is Fury?"

"Jacobs is taking good care of him. You will not be riding him for a while, though." David moved to the settee and now stood over Alex's shoulder. "Should it be bleeding that badly?"

"The forehead always bleeds a lot."

"She is probably faking it." Caroline's petulant voice announced from a chair in the corner.

Alex looked up and shook his head in disgust. "You could make yourself useful," he suggested curtly.

Before Lady Caroline could reply, Johnson arrived with the supplies. Alex took a cloth and wiped the blood away from Sarah's head. The cut was just beyond her hairline, high on the forehead. It was several inches long, but not too deep.

With deft fingers, he formed a pad from the cloth Johnson had brought and then secured it to Sarah's head with a bandage. "It should heal fine," he pronounced.

Sarah's eyes fluttered briefly, but did not open. A stab of fear shot through Alex's stomach. He had mended a lot of injured sailors during the war, but never had their outcome affected him in such a manner.

"Sarah," he urged. "Open your eyes."

She shook her head and grimaced before slowly opening her lids. She stared up at him and smiled. Alex's insides melted at the sweetness of that smile. There was nothing guarded about her at that moment. Only trust shone from her eyes.

"I must have fainted. How did I get here?"

"I carried you." Alex put the remaining cloths on the table. "Do you feel better?"

"Yes." Sarah struggled to sit up and Alex stood so she could swing her legs onto the floor. She put a hand up to her injury and winced.

"The pain should lessen."

Sarah nodded. "What happened?"

"That is what I want to know." Caroline got up from her chair and marched over to them. "All I wanted was a ride this morning and instead you have ruined everything."

"That is unfair," David Stanton interjected. "Mrs. Wellsley was an innocent bystander. It was a lucky thing she came down before you or you might have been hurt, too."

Caroline seemed to digest this information for several seconds before calming down and sitting beside Sarah. "Explain."

At that moment, Nathan Carter entered the drawing room. "The horses are stabled and I roped off the front entranceway until it can be repaired."

Alex stepped away from the settee. "I will set the work crew on the drive immediately."

"I am still waiting for someone to tell me what happened," Caroline interjected loudly, moving forward in her seat.

Alex turned back to Caroline. "Mrs. Wellsley was giving me your message when a part of the roof fell onto the drive beside us. It was lucky no one was beneath it."

Caroline glanced quickly at the men in the room and then at Sarah. "How horrible."

"Exactly," Nathan Carter agreed dryly. "I think we should take a look at the roof."

"Agreed." Alex glanced at Sarah. Her face was less pale, but he felt uncomfortable leaving her alone. "First we need to get Mrs. Wellsley to her room."

"I am fine," Sarah protested.

"Nonsense," Alex interrupted. "I will carry you. It is on the way to the roof anyway."

Sarah shook her head in denial and started to struggle to get herself off the settee, but Alex was too quick for her. He bent and picked her up in his arms. He noticed the faint color of red that suffused her cheeks and winked. He grinned as the red deepened in intensity.

He started to the door, but hesitated to look back at Caroline. "Are you coming?"

Caroline's eyes widened in surprise. "Whatever for?"

"To take care of her." Alex stared at his intended coldly, forcing his voice to remain civil. "She should not be left on her own."

Caroline shrugged her shoulders indifferently. "I will send for Nellie."

Alex did not trust his voice. Instead he nodded his head and left the room. He heard Nathan and David's footsteps behind him.

He reached Sarah's room quickly and put her down on her bed. "Are you going to be okay until Nellie gets here?"

"Of course." Sarah nodded, her eyes refusing to meet his. "Thank you for your help."

"I do not want your thanks."

Sarah looked up at him sharply. He cursed silently at the look of doubt that crossed her features.

"Do not look at me so," he said in a low voice. "I want nothing from you."

Sarah's face again suffused in color and she glanced down at her hands. "I am sorry," she whispered.

Alex almost asked her why, but thought it best to leave her in peace. If Nathan and David had not been waiting at the doorway, he would have sat down and taken Sarah into his arms until he had chased her doubts away.

Ruefully, he acknowledged that was exactly what she was afraid of. It pained him to see her in such discomfort. He did not know exactly what he expected of Sarah, but he had no intentions of dishonoring his vow to keep his distance.

The memory of the kiss they had shared over a week ago was still fresh in his mind. Never had he experienced anything so beautiful and it frightened him. All of his dreams as a boy had come flooding back at that moment. Then he had dreamt of love, a family, and sharing his life with a woman—a woman like Sarah.

David Stanton cleared his throat. "Is everything alright?"

Alex glanced over his shoulder and nodded before turning back to Sarah. "I must go now."

Sarah refused to look up at him. He hesitated a few more seconds and then heaved a heavy sigh. There was nothing more he could do. He turned to leave the room just as Nellie bustled in. He heard her clucking concern and felt the knot in his stomach lessen. Sarah would be in capable, caring hands now.

Once in the hallway, he led the way to the end of the wing and then they climbed the stairs to the roof. This portion of the house was seldom used nowadays, most of its rooms shrouded in white cloth. It was one of the things that he hoped to repair in the coming months.

The stairs ended at a door that opened onto the roof. It was one of the original towers of the old castle, employed to defend Caldern from its enemies in centuries past. Now it was only used when the roof needed repair.

Sunlight greeted them when they opened the door. All three men walked out onto the roof, pausing as they took in the view.

"I had forgotten how beautiful it was up here," Nathan exclaimed.

Alex nodded his head. "I have not been up here since I left nineteen years ago."

"If it's been neglected like the rest of the house, no wonder you have things falling from it." David Stanton shook his head in disgust. "This wing is a disaster waiting to happen."

Alex silently agreed with his friend's assessment, but there was nothing he could do about it now. Eventually all of Caldern would be restored to its former glory, including the roof. "Let's see where the stone fell from."

They walked to the front of the roof, stepping over debris and rubble as they went. When they were close to the front edge Alex noticed that the area seemed to be cleaner, almost as if it were swept or raked. His eyes followed the area back to another tower door on the east side of Caldern. He frowned and then looked back to where the stone had fallen.

There was a huge gaping hole in the crenellations. It was at least ten feet wide. The weight of that much stone was enormous, plus the force of it falling over four stories. It was a wonder there was not more destruction below, Alex thought grimly.

David Stanton shook his head in disbelief. "It is a miracle you moved away in time."

Alex nodded his head; the miracle had been Sarah. He had been irresistibly drawn to her. She had looked so forlorn standing on the top stair, clutching her shawl protectively. The wind had blown tendrils of her dark hair about her face, giving her the appearance of a lost waif. All he had wanted to do was gather her in his arms. That was the miracle that had moved him.

"I cannot believe the extent of the disrepair." Alex walked up to the jagged stones, running his hand over the edge of a portion of the hole. "Is it usual for so much to fall at once?"

David rubbed his nose. "I imagine if it were ready to topple, nothing could stop it."

"But was it ready?"

Alex snapped his head around to his brother. "What are you suggesting?"

"Look at how little stone there is on the roof." Nathan crouched down and pointed to the area under the missing wall. "If the stone had been ready to fall, would not some of it have fallen on the roof?"

"You should be thankful it fell the other way," David advised with a shrug of his shoulder. "I imagine the impact of that weight would have sent the rocks right through the roof and the floors below."

Alex exchanged a silent glance with his brother. David did not know of the shot Alex had taken in the arm a couple of weeks before. This accident was probably a coincidence, but Nathan had pointed out a different possibility.

Again Alex glanced to the swept area of the roof and then looked down and felt the mortar seams of the stone blocks that were left standing. The wall stood about five feet above the roof. There was the odd flaking and holes in the joints, but for the most part they were in good repair. It was possible that the fallen section had escaped repair, Alex reasoned.

He knelt on one knee, feeling the roof for any

signs of fallen mortar. There was a small amount scattered, but not enough to cause a whole wall of blocks to fall outward.

He stood up and brushed off his pants. Nathan was watching him silently. Alex guessed what his brother suspected, but he did not want to speak about it in front of David. It was better that no one else knew.

If someone had been up on the roof, why had he or she not mentioned it needed repair? Then again, it might have been someone coming to look at the spectacular view. Alex looked out over the ramparts. Everything for miles around was part of Caldern, all the hills and valleys, the tenant farms and the vast expanse of woods, his heritage.

Alex's heart filled with pride as he looked out at the estate. Since returning home, he had not allowed himself to embrace what it meant to be the Marquess of Caldern. He had been too busy trying to repair the damage Fanny had done. Now looking out at his land, he felt overwhelmed with humility.

Caldern was his. It was something he had never thought possible, not even in his wildest dreams. Never would he have to leave it again. Alex took a deep breath and looked down at the disaster below. His stomach clenched in anger. It would take weeks to repair the damage. That was minor in comparison to the possibility that someone had deliberately tried to kill him.

"We should go down." Alex motioned for David and Nathan to follow him. "There is nothing more to learn here."

David went first and Alex started to follow, but Nathan held him back.

"I hope you intend to look at this seriously."

"I take all my responsibilities seriously."

"You know what I mean," Nathan hissed. "I do not think this was an accident."

"You may be right," Alex agreed, "But we can do nothing about it right now."

"Find out who was up here."

"Somehow I do not think it will be quite that easy." Alex started down the stairs to the floor below.

"I intend to keep my eyes open," Nathan advised quietly.

"As do I," Alex whispered under his breath. He had no desire to become the late Marquess of Caldern.

Chapter 15

Sarah slid her bonnet back and touched her forehead gingerly. It had been five days since the roof had collapsed and her wound was almost healed. Today she had rushed to the village to tend to a sick child and had left the house without breakfast.

As she walked past The Hickory House, the local village inn, her stomach started to rumble. The smell of freshly baked bread was drifting toward her. Sarah hesitated for only a few seconds before turning back to the inn. She would get something she could eat along the way.

She entered the somber, dark inn and stood at the common room entranceway. She had only been here once before to fetch ale for one of her bed-ridden patients. The kitchen door opened suddenly and a large curvaceous woman came into the room.

"Mrs. Wellsley," she said in surprise, brushing a strand of gray hair behind her ear. "I didn't realize anyone had come in."

"I just arrived, Mrs. Weaver," Sarah explained. "I

wonder if I might get some bread and cheese to take with me."

"Of course." The innkeeper pushed open the door behind her and issued the order before turning back to Sarah. "Would you like to go into the private room to wait?"

Sarah looked about the room, which had a number of long trestle tables with benches on either side. There were also a couple of smaller, more private eating nooks near the windows. The room looked clean, but the air smelled of stale ale and wine.

Sarah shook her head and smiled. "I will wait here."

"As you wish." Mrs. Weaver pushed a small chair forward for Sarah. "I've been hearing good things about the work you do. It's about time someone took an interest in the people hereabouts."

"It is the least I can do." Sarah had never really spoken to Mrs. Weaver before. She had heard that the woman had married her husband almost twenty years ago and when he had died soon after, she had taken over the running of the inn.

"Well, it is appreciated. Lord knows when his lordship will do anything to help the situation."

Sarah's stomach tightened and indignation rose in her throat. "The Marquess is doing his best," she defended.

"I try," a deep voice interrupted from the doorway.

Sarah turned quickly and watched as the Marquess sauntered into the common room. Her heart began to beat frantically. This was the first time she had seen him since the morning of the accident. Alex had gone to Carlisle on business the afternoon of the roof collapse.

"What a surprise this is." Mrs. Weaver put a

hand on her hip and nodded at Alex. "It's been many a year since I last saw you."

"At least nineteen," Alex agreed dryly. "I see you have been comfortable, Rachael."

"More than comfortable, but you knew that."

"I knew you had accepted money from my father, but not what you had done with it."

"Old Tom was needing a bit of coin for the business, and we came to an agreement."

"Marriage, you mean."

Rachael chuckled, causing her voluptuous frame to shake slightly. "I hear you would be knowing a thing or two about that yourself."

Alex inclined his head. "A man in my position needs to be concerned about family."

"Who would have thought you'd be a Marquess one day. I should have taken my chances when you offered."

"I do recall insisting you would regret it one day."

"I'm happy enough with my inn. It looks as if you got along fine without me." Rachael's head tilted sideways and her eyes scanned the Marquess from head to toe.

Sarah's eyes widened at Rachael's remark, but when she looked at Alex, his face was impassive. He stared at Mrs. Weaver through half-closed eyes and then turned to look at Sarah.

"Why are you here?"

"I have been with the Dodd's baby all morning. Mrs. Weaver is getting me some bread and cheese."

"I will escort you. Come."

Sarah shook her head. "It is not necessary."

Alex sighed heavily. "You have been keeping to your room since the accident. That suggests you are still not well."

Sarah felt her cheeks redden. Since Alex had been at Carlisle, she had used her injury as an excuse to avoid the others. The atmosphere at Caldern was uncomfortable and Caroline's comments hurtful. Isolation was preferable.

"It was your choice to be isolated," Alex guessed.

"It was easiest," Sarah agreed. "Please do not discuss it." She looked over at Mrs. Weaver who was listening to every word of their conversation with interest.

"Don't mind me," the innkeeper said with a wave of her hand. "I already know everything that goes on at the big house."

"Is that right?" Alex tapped his riding crop against one of the tables. "Enlighten me."

"Behaving all lord and mighty now, are you?" Rachael folded her arms under her massive bosom. "There's very little that happens in these parts that I don't hear about. Like that little mishap you had."

Alex lifted one of his eyebrows disdainfully. "I am sure everyone heard about that minutes after it occurred. You forget, Rachael, I grew up at Caldern. I know how gossip travels."

"I wouldn't forget you, honey," Rachael said with a broad wink. "You've grown into a fine man. I'd be happy to listen to your woes like I did in the old days."

"I never give a woman a second chance," Alex stated coldly. "If that is all you have to say, then this conversation is finished."

He walked a couple of steps into the room and Sarah held her breath when she saw the granite expression on his face. She stood up quickly to block his way to Rachael, but instead of reaching for Rachael, he took her arm.

"This is not a proper place for a lady to be," he said as he led her out of the room.

Sarah tried to pull her arm free, but his grip was too tight. She winced at Rachael's laughter coming from the doorway and felt her chest tighten with anger. How dare he treat her like this.

"Let me go," she demanded through gritted teeth.

He marched to his horse and turned her about. "I do not want you near that woman."

Sarah's fists clenched and she glared back at Alex's implacable expression. "Why?"

"Because I insist."

"You insist?" Sarah could not believe what she was hearing. "You have no control over me."

"I am your host."

"That does not make it right. I have already told you I will not let any man tell me what I can do."

Alex heaved a heavy sigh and then leaned an arm against his horse. "Please do this, Sarah."

Just then Mrs. Weaver called. "Do you still want your lunch?"

Sarah nodded and went back to the inn. Mrs. Weaver handed her a bundle neatly wrapped in linen. "Thank you."

"Age hasn't improved him," Rachael commented with a nod toward Alex. "He's grown to be just like his father. A colder man you'd never want to meet."

Sarah's jaw tightened. There was no point in defending the Marquess to this woman. Sarah handed Mrs. Weaver a few coins and wondered at her animosity. She was the first person at Caldern that had criticized Alex.

She went back to Alex who was still waiting by his horse. "Are you finished?" he asked curtly.

Sarah nodded and then walked past him. She opened the small bundle and raised the fresh, buttered bread to her nose. She inhaled deeply, savoring its aroma before taking a large bite.

"You act as if you are starved."

Sarah jumped at the sound of Alex's voice beside her. She had not expected him to follow. "I am. I left without eating this morning."

"I will walk with you." Alex turned away too quickly for Sarah to protest. She watched him gather his horse's reins, urging the animal to follow.

"I do not need your assistance," Sarah protested.

"I asked you to take a footman with you," Alex reminded softly. "Where is he?"

Sarah turned her face away and sighed. "I did not want to bother anyone."

"Fine." Alex coaxed his horse to walk behind him. "I will take care of it."

"It is not necessary."

"Then why was Rachael treating you as if you were one of the laborers in the fields?"

"That is uncalled for," Sarah spluttered indignantly. "She was being friendly."

"I think I know her better than you." Alex looked down at Sarah with a twisted grin. "Believe me, she was not being friendly. She was trying to get information from you."

Sarah took a piece of cheese and munched on it as she considered Alex's words. Rachael had seemed friendlier than the last time she had seen her, but that still was no reason to be so critical. Small villages were cesspools of gossip.

"What if she was?"

Sarah offered Alex some of her lunch. He glanced over and shook his head. "She is not to be trusted."

"Neither of you like each other," Sarah frowned up at Alex's impassive face. "Why?"

"It is a boring and sordid story."

Sarah shrugged her shoulders. "We have a long walk ahead of us."

Alex squinted his eyes up at the sun. "It was nineteen years ago. It means nothing now."

Sarah shook her head. "You are still very angry with her. That was obvious at the inn."

Alex laughed harshly. "I said nothing to suggest that."

"It was your actions," Sarah explained. "You treated her with disdain. I have not seen you do that with anyone else at Caldern. The hurt must go very deep."

Alex gave Sarah a twisted smile. "You are very perceptive."

"Is she the reason you left Caldern?"

"Part of the reason," Alex agreed after a moment's silence. "I would have left soon anyway."

"You were planning to join the navy then?" Sarah finished her lunch and wiped her hands on her napkin before tucking it away in her basket.

Alex shook his head. "I never planned on the navy."

Sarah frowned. "What were your plans?"

"Originally, I thought I would go to Oxford and from there into the diplomatic corps. I had several relatives on my mother's side who were willing to give me a start."

"Then why the navy?"

"I had no choice. My mother's great uncle was an admiral and when I left Caldern I sought him out. I was too young for the government, so my only option was the navy."

Sarah glanced at Alex's impassive face. "Are they not two very different careers?"

Alex shrugged his shoulders. "Not really. Both are looking after the country's interest."

"One involves socializing and the other fighting. I would not call them the same thing," Sarah stated quietly. "You must have felt you had no choice but to leave Caldern."

Alex sighed heavily before looking down at her. "Do we really have to talk about this?"

Sarah nodded her head. "If you want me to stay away from Rachael Weaver, then I must have a reason."

Alex suddenly stopped walking, halting his horse with a stay of his hand. He kicked at the gravel beneath his feet and then stomped the foot down decisively. "Alright."

He threw his head back and looked up at the sky. "I fell in love with Rachael shortly after my sixteenth birthday. She was older than me, but I did not care. She was everything I wanted in a woman—beautiful, full of laughter, and caring. At least that was what I thought."

Sarah's chest tightened at Alex's words and the pain she heard in his voice. She regretted forcing him to speak about his past, but she was curious. "What changed your mind?"

"My father."

Sarah digested that for a few seconds. "He did not approve?" she guessed cautiously.

Alex laughed bitterly. "That is an understatement. He told me to bed the girl and have done with it. I stupidly told him that I wanted to marry her."

Sarah found it hard to believe that a Marquess's son would want to marry a woman like Rachael, but then he had been little more than a boy at the time. "What did your father do?"

"He proved me wrong, of course." Alex's tone was full of self-condemnation and derision. Sarah longed to comfort him, but his tense stance and stiff back warned her away. He did not want anyone to see his pain, least of all another woman.

"No comment?" Alex asked suddenly, turning his head to look at her.

Sarah shook her head. "I can see that whatever he did was extremely painful for you."

Alex kicked a stone across the road. "My loving father approached Rachael, offering money to stay away from his precious son. Then he bedded her himself, making sure that I would arrive at her house in time to witness the whole thing."

Sarah gasped at the cruelty of Alex's father. To have Alex's love betrayed in such a manner by the two people he should have been able to trust would have been devastating to anyone, but even more so for a boy. Her heart ached for him. Sarah reached out and touched his arm.

Alex pushed her away. "Do not feel sorry for me. My father's lesson has stayed with me to this day. I will not be fool enough to allow a woman into my heart. All they want is money."

"That is not true," Sarah defended.

Alex raised his eyebrow mockingly. "Can you say that your cousin is not interested in my money and position? If I were still the poor second son, do you think she would be trying to attract my interest?"

Sarah's mouth went dry and she could only stare at him. He was not wrong. Caroline had only one interest in the Marquess. "Then why marry her?" she asked quietly.

"I need a wife," he retorted loudly. "At least with Lady Caroline I know what she is interested in. She has been honest about her motives, not like Rachael."

Sarah shook her head sadly. "You are wrong about women."

"Then I suppose we are the same."

Sarah frowned. "How?"

"You refuse to see men any differently than your husband, and I will never see women as anything other than schemers like Rachael."

Sarah stopped walking and stared up at Alex. How on earth could he compare their situations? Her marriage was not the same as Rachael's betrayal, but a tiny voice inside her head disagreed. They had both been betrayed by love and were afraid to trust it again.

"Enough of this walking." Alex said suddenly, placing his hands around her waist and lifting her onto his horse before she had a chance to protest. "Arrange you leg around the pommel. That should make it easier.

Without another word, he grabbed the reins and then hoisted himself up. "Are you comfortable?"

Sarah nodded, clutching her basket close to her chest. This was highly improper behavior.

"How will we explain if anyone sees us?"

"Tell them you have a sprained ankle." Alex tightened his hold on Sarah and then coaxed the horse to turn back to the road. "It is too hot to remain in the sun much longer."

Sarah tried to remain upright on the horse, but the constant motion and her aching muscles forced her to lean back into Alex. The nearness of him was wreaking havoc on her nerves. Her ragged breathing caught in her chest as she tried to still her pounding heart. She prayed that they would reach the house quickly.

"Relax," he growled. "At this rate you will never make it back."

"You can leave me at the gatehouse." Sarah tried to turn to speak to Alex, but her shifting weight caused her to lose balance. Instinctively she reached for his arm, but he was quicker. He pulled her tightly into his body, leaving one hand around her waist while the other held the reins.

"Are you nervous?" Alex whispered, tickling her ear with the nearness of his mouth.

"I am not comfortable on horses," Sarah admitted defensively. It was partially the truth.

"Ah," Alex sighed. "I was hoping it was me and that you were having second thoughts about my proposition."

Sarah frowned. She was concentrating so hard on trying to relax that Alex's words made no sense. "What are you talking about?"

"You and me, together," he elaborated, his lips touching her neck softly.

Sarah's stomach fluttered nervously, the meaning of his words clear. She found herself struggling to deny him. Already she felt herself weaken as his arms tightened around her. She took a deep breath and forced herself to push away from him.

"You gave me your word," she reminded him.

"True," Alex chuckled. "I made you forget your fear, though."

"What fear?" Sarah asked in confusion. Alex was making no sense.

"Of horses," he answered smoothly, pulling up to a stop. "We are at Caldern."

Sarah looked up in surprise, the red stone stables directly in front of them. She had been so busy trying to ignore Alex that she had not noticed when they turned into the drive.

"I wanted to visit Bates," she protested mildly.

"You have done enough for today." Alex swung down from the horse and then reached for her. He lowered her to the ground gently, but kept his hands around her waist. Sarah's breath caught in her throat at the intensity of his gaze.

The sun glinted off his dark hair, highlighting a few strands of silver at his temples. His eyes crinkled at the corners and he smiled at her seductively. "I am always available, if you change your mind."

Sarah shook her head decisively. "It would not be fair to Caroline."

Alex raised an eyebrow. "Has she been fair to you?"

Sarah lowered her eyes and pushed away from him. "I do not want an affair." Sarah turned away and started to walk back to the house.

"What do you want?" Alex demanded.

Sarah stopped and looked back at him. His hands were braced on his hips, his eyes narrowed, and his jaw tightly clenched. Sarah sensed his frustration and hesitated before answering. Suddenly she was weary of their flirtation.

"When I was young, I wanted love," she admitted quietly. "Now I just want to forget."

"Let me help you." Alex walked over to her. "You cannot hide forever."

Sarah smiled softly. "I am protecting myself from men."

"You mean love," Alex corrected dryly.

Sarah sighed. "I suppose it is the same." She turned and began walking to the house. From behind her she could hear Alex kicking the stones in frustration.

"I expect to see you at dinner tonight," he barked. "And at the picnic tomorrow."

Sarah's heart sank at the mention of the picnic. She had forgotten about it. She had the rest of the day to prepare, but nothing would help her quell her uncertainty at spending another day with the Marquess.

Chapter 16

Alex turned away from the lake and looked back at his family and friends. It was one of those rare, perfect summer afternoons. The sky was blue without a cloud in sight and there was a slight breeze, which kept it from being overly hot. Alex inhaled deeply, letting his tensions from the past few days drain away.

"Wonderful idea, Lady Caroline had," David Stanton commented cheerfully. "Daylight becomes the fair lady."

Alex grinned at his friend. "Everything becomes the lady and she knows it."

David shrugged his shoulder slightly. "Perhaps, but that does not prevent us from appreciating her beauty."

Alex chuckled appreciatively. "I would recommend enjoying it from a distance."

"She is just high strung," David defended. "She has been on her best behavior since you returned from Carlisle."

Alex nodded and then scanned the scene in front of him. Multicolored blankets littered the lawn, their corners held in place with rocks. The servants were carrying food in large hampers and setting out the meal on boards covered with white linen. Soon luncheon would begin.

"We should probably join the others." Alex smoothed the lapels of his blue riding coat. "The servants are ready with the food."

They sauntered back and Alex found himself searching for one face. Sarah had come down for dinner the previous night, but when the men had joined the ladies, she had already excused herself. He was not sure she would appear this afternoon.

He finally saw her sitting against a large oak tree, half hidden from the others by brambles. Her brown dress and cap helped her fade into the scenery. Alex almost groaned aloud at the horrible attire. It completely hid her beauty.

Sarah must have sensed his look because she glanced up from her book and looked straight at him. Alex's breath caught in his throat and his heart started beating frantically. Time, place, and reason all scattered with one look from Sarah.

Before he could walk to her, his sister Julianna stepped in front of him. "Mother wants you to sit with her."

Alex looked down and smiled. "I think not."

"What do you mean? She is expecting you."

"I am sure someone else will be more than willing to take my place. Perhaps you?"

"She wants you," Julianna insisted. "Lady Caroline will be there."

"Now I understand the urgency." Alex turned to David. "Do me a favor."

"Of course."

"Keep Lady Caroline amused for me." Alex nodded and then walked away. He kept his eyes trained on Sarah.

The woman was driving him insane. He had been fighting with himself for weeks and he was determined to put an end to it. No more games or sleepless nights.

When he reached Sarah, she had stood up and was brushing the grass from her dress. "Good day, my lord."

"You should have brought a blanket over," Alex said as he held out his arm for her.

Sarah shook her head and smiled up at him. "The servants had arranged everything so nicely. I could not disturb it."

"That is why we brought them." Alex felt the muscle in his jaw tighten. She was the most frustrating woman he had ever met, never thinking of herself first.

"I am sorry. I did not mean to anger you." Sarah looked at him warily, her voice wavering in uncertainty.

Alex closed his eyes and silently cursed himself. He did not want Sarah to be defensive. "I just do not like to see you ruining your gown," he explained.

Sarah looked down at the drab brown dress and started to laugh. "I will remember that the next time."

Alex tried to maintain a straight face, but it was impossible. He was behaving like a fool. "Forget it." He placed her hand on his arm. "Luncheon is ready."

"There is no need for you to escort me." Sarah's eyes darted nervously to the others and then back to him. "It is senseless to annoy our families."

Alex slowed his pace. "There is no need for you to hide yourself. You are not a servant."

"It is best."

"Why?" Alex felt his stomach clench and he took a deep breath. He was finding it hard to contain his outrage at how Sarah was being treated.

Sarah glanced up at him and smiled slightly. "Caroline arranged this picnic to spend time with you. It would be wrong to disappoint her."

"I have always done as I please," Alex explained quietly. "I am not about to start living by the rules now."

Sarah sighed and shook her head. "As you wish."

Alex smiled inwardly at his victory. Sarah was a complicated woman; he had known that from the beginning. He could no longer ignore the attraction between them and somehow he must convince her to stop resisting him.

When they arrived at the picnic, Alex chose a blanket away from the others. Sarah looked up at him with a raised eyebrow, but he merely smiled. She would have to get used to being next to him. He had no intention of hiding her in the back corners of his life.

"This is crazy," Sarah whispered as she sat down and spread her skirt around her ankles. "You are deliberately trying to irritate Caroline."

Alex sat on the edge of the blanket, an arm thrown around his raised knee. "That is not my intention. If she is upset, it is not my fault."

"How can you say that?" Sarah turned to him, her dark blue eyes glaring at him indignantly. "You are to be married."

Alex stared at Sarah for several seconds, letting her essence surround and enthrall him. It was a new and heady experience for him. "You should not believe everything you hear."

Sarah frowned. "What do you mean?"

"My marriage is in no way certain."

Sarah opened her mouth to speak, but before she could say anything, Lady Caroline's voice shattered their privacy.

"Why are you sitting here?" she demanded.

Alex looked up at the enraged beauty, tilting his head away from the sun. "Is there a problem?"

"You should be sitting with me."

"Really?" Alex pushed himself up from the blanket, straightening his coat as he stood up. "I was not aware this was a formal picnic."

"That is not what I mean," Caroline hissed. "You are making a spectacle of yourself."

Alex narrowed his eyes, trying hard to contain his rising temper. "You are the one yelling and drawing attention."

Caroline stamped her foot. "You are deliberately trying to anger me."

"No," Alex denied smoothly, "but your behavior is trying my patience. Enough nonsense. You are welcome to sit with us."

Alex extended a hand to Lady Caroline. She stood glaring at him for several seconds before she thrust out her arm. He led her to a corner of the blanket and watched with amusement as she arranged herself. Her back was rigid and she avoided looking in Sarah's direction.

"Such a pleasant afternoon," he quipped, sitting down beside Sarah. He leaned his body back on his elbow, almost brushing Sarah's arm. He breathed deeply, letting her lavender scent envelop him. Awareness and desire surged through his veins.

"I do not think Sarah's presence is necessary," Lady Caroline sneered. "We hardly need a chaperon."

"Not as a chaperon," Alex agreed, "but I certainly feel a need for her."

Alex heard Sarah's quiet groan and glanced at her sideways. She was glaring at him, her blue eyes flashing her indignation. He winked back. The afternoon was proving to be more entertaining than he had hoped for.

"Are you trying to insult me?" Caroline demanded in a shrill voice.

"I would never insult a lady," Alex murmured, sitting up as one of the servants brought a plate of food.

An uncomfortable silence existed while the food was handed out and plates and utensils balanced on laps. The delicacies of honey-cured ham, cheese, fresh bread, and an assortment of side dishes captured their attention for several minutes.

"I never realized how hungry an outdoor dalliance could make one." Alex wiped his mouth with his napkin. "Obviously, you were well aware of it, Lady Caroline. My thanks to your vast experience."

Lady Caroline gasped loudly. "You are insufferable."

Alex raised an eyebrow. "You do not like my conversation?"

"Not at all." Caroline snapped her napkin down on her plate. "I can see that Lady Caldern was correct when she said that you had forgotten the ways of society."

"I wonder that you insist on my company then?"

Caroline pushed herself up from the ground. Alex stood and offered his hand, but she slapped it away. "Soon you will be forced to bear my presence," Caroline threatened with a glare. "I should imagine that even a man such as you understands he must do the honorable thing."

Caroline threw her head back and turned to walk away, but stopped to look down at Sarah. "I will deal with your behavior later."

"I would advise against it," Alex snapped coldly. "Mrs. Wellsley is in no way responsible for my actions."

Lady Caroline glared at him defiantly. "This is none of your business."

"I have made it my concern." A chill of foreboding skittered down his spine. He was in no position to protect Sarah from Caroline's cruelty. The only thing at his disposal was to threaten her. "I will not countenance a wife who I cannot respect. You would be well advised to tread lightly."

Caroline's eyes shot down to Sarah and back to him. Alex returned her questioning look with a cold stare. He did not want her to doubt his determination. After a few seconds her eyes shifted away and she turned and left them. He released the breath he had been holding.

Sarah cleared her throat and Alex looked down at her. "Was that wise?"

"What else would you have me do?" Alex threw his napkin down on the blanket and offered Sarah his hand.

"I am used to handling her." Sarah stood up and shook out her gown. "She was upset, but she would have calmed down."

"You see your cousin with blinders on."

"I have known her longer than you," Sarah insisted. "Surely you can see some good in her?"

Alex shook his head. "I see a spoiled, vindictive, self-centered shrew, who is fast on her way to becoming a spinster. No man in his right mind would take her."

"You are honor bound to do so, though."

Alex felt his stomach tighten in reaction to Sarah's words. She was right. He had allowed his stepmother to arrange a marriage for him and even though he had not offered for Lady Caroline, she had the expectation of a proposal. Honor demanded that he marry her.

He clenched his jaw at his own stupidity. For the first time in his life he knew exactly what he wanted and he was not free. He was in an untenable position, one that it would take skill to maneuver out of, but he would succeed. It was a battle he would win.

Alex forced himself to smile. "I will marry the woman of my choice."

Sarah frowned, but before she could reply, his stepbrother Bryan hailed him from another blanket. "Are you still game to accept my challenge?"

Alex looked up at Bryan, noticing the smug grin on his face. His brother had been hounding him ever since the gardeners had cleared the west lawn.

"What is he talking about?" Sarah asked.

"A race." Alex rubbed the back of his neck with his hand and sighed. "My brother wants to prove he is still the best horseman in the county."

"You are not going to accept, I hope." Sarah's hands fluttered nervously at her waist.

"There is no need for concern," Alex reassured. "It is only fair I let him try and best me. He has had a hard adjustment since I returned to Caldern."

"But a race?"

Alex shrugged his shoulders. "What harm can it do?"

Lord Bryan joined them, his brown hair windblown and his eyes sparkling with excitement. "The horses are standing ready."

"You are determined to do this," Alex observed dryly. "Where shall we race to?"

"The large oak." Lord Bryan pointed to a distant tree that stood on the outskirts of the western lawn.

Alex nodded his head. "There are several fences in between."

"Are you afraid?" Bryan taunted.

Alex grinned. "I am worried for you. I would hate to see you injured."

"Unlikely," Bryan boasted. "You forget I am familiar with this area."

"True," Alex admitted. "You also have your favorite horse, while I must do with second best until Fury has recovered."

"Is that a problem?"

"Not at all. Bring the horses over." Alex watched Bryan sprint off to the willow where their horses were tied. He then turned to glance at Sarah. She was standing to one side nervously twisting her hands together.

"Nothing can go wrong," he reassured.

Sarah smiled slightly. "It is silly, but I cannot forget the other two accidents."

Alex felt a surge of joy race through his body at her concern. He wanted to grab her close and reassure her, but instead he only touched her shoulder. "This is not the same."

Sarah nodded. "I know. Be careful."

"Done. We had best join the others." Alex led Sarah over to the fence where the race would begin. Everyone was gathering to watch.

David came up to him and put an arm around his shoulder. "It is cruel to lead your brother on in this way."

"Bryan is the one who wants the race, not I." Alex took the reins of his horse. "I will go easy on him."

Alex mounted and then walked over to the starting point. Bryan was already there before him, struggling to keep his horse under control. Alex looked back over his shoulder, hoping to reassure Sarah.

His stepmother and his sister Julianna were

standing to one side of the fence. Fanny glared at him with narrowed eyes, her disapproval very evident. Lady Caroline stood in the shade with her arms crossed and head turned away. David Stanton was beside her.

His eyes searched for Sarah until he spied her sitting on a large rock away from the others. Her eyes were trained on the racecourse. His horse stomped its feet impatiently, forcing Alex to turn around.

"Are you ready?" Bryan asked.

Alex nodded, walking his horse up beside Bryan. "Whenever you say the word."

Bryan leaned forward on his horse, gathering his reins tightly. "On the count of three. One. Two. Three."

Alex gave the horse its head and it leapt away from the starting point. The race began in earnest, each rider urging his horse to faster and faster speeds. The wind blew through Alex's hair, his hat falling off seconds after their start.

Exhilaration surged through his blood as he became one with his horse, his heart beating in unison with the pounding hooves beneath him. His body moved with the animal, both determined to be victorious as the ground sped by them. The first fence loomed close when Alex felt a shift in his saddle.

He pulled on the reins, but it was too late. The horse had already begun his jump. Alex held on with his knees, hoping to avoid disaster, but when his horse lunged forward his saddle slid sideways, taking Alex with it.

The reins were jerked from his hands and he sailed weightlessly through the air. His shoulder hit the ground first, pain ripping through his body as the breath was knocked out of him. His legs crashed against some rocks and he winced at the sharp tearing of his skin. He clenched his teeth together tightly, leaning his head back on the ground. He closed his eyes against the spinning world, focusing on the sounds of the horses' hooves and Bryan's shouts.

He felt a nudge at his shoulder, the cold nose of his horse checking his inert body. He pushed himself upright, gasping as the air rushed back into his lungs. His eyes blurred, but he forced himself to roll over and ease himself up.

Pain shot through his leg and he grabbed his thigh. His hand slid on the sticky wetness that had soaked through his riding breeches. Instantly he was alert, noting the blood and pressing his hand against the jagged wound.

Chapter 17

Sarah's stomach plunged as she watched Alex fall from his horse. The sound of his body hitting the ground echoed through her body. She started running, gulping air as she raced across the freshly mowed field.

When she reached him, he was sitting up, clasping his right thigh with both hands. There was blood everywhere. Sarah knelt beside him.

"How bad is it?"

Alex shook his head. "I think it is only my thigh."

Sarah pushed his hands away and ripped his pant leg. There was too much blood for her to see the wound clearly, so she lifted her gown and tore a strip of cloth from her chemise and started to clean away the blood.

Lord Bryan raced to her side and watched over her shoulder. "It is deep."

"Too deep to heal on its own," Sarah agreed. "A doctor should be called."

"Nonsense," Alex argued. "Surely you can deal with it."

"It needs stitches. I would prefer the doctor to do it."

"Do what you can." Alex gritted his teeth and let her wrap more of her chemise around his leg.

"That should hold until you get back to the house." Sarah wiped her hand across her damp brow.

David Stanton arrived just then, panting and gasping for air. "What the hell happened?" he demanded.

"The damn saddle loosened." Alex struggled to stand.

Sarah put his arm around her shoulder, easing him upright. "Can you walk?"

"Go and get the horses," David Stanton ordered Lord Bryan.

"I am fine," Alex insisted. "Find the saddle."

David nodded and searched the tall grass near the stone fence. He moved the grass with his feet until he bent and picked up the dark leather saddle, its straps dangling on the ground as he brought it over for Alex.

Sarah frowned. One strap was shorter than the other, ripped near the seat of the saddle. Even though Sarah was several feet away, she could see that the cut was smooth, as if done by a knife.

Alex grabbed the saddle and touched the cut strap. "Unusual wear pattern," he commented dryly.

"I do not understand." David turned the saddle over. "This was deliberate."

"I am afraid so." Alex turned to Sarah. "Tell no one about this."

"You cannot ignore it," Sarah insisted in a low voice.

"I will take care of it, but I need your promise of silence."

Sarah stared at Alex's ashen face and knew she could not deny him. He looked as if he would fall over at any minute, but his eyes shone with strength and determination. She lowered her eyes and nodded. She would trust him to deal with it.

Bryan brought the horses up at that moment and Alex leaned on David, who helped him mount Bryan's horse. Once he was astride and had the reins in hand, he pointed the horse in the direction of the house.

"Can you bring my horse back to the stables, Bryan?"

"Of course." Bryan grabbed the reins and started to walk across the field.

Alex watched him walk away and then looked down at David. "I'm going up to the house. Will you take Mrs. Wellsley back to the others?"

"You need a doctor," Sarah reminded.

Alex nodded and then headed off in the direction of Caldern. Sarah watched him go, swallowing back her tears. He had almost been killed. She closed her eyes briefly, reliving his fall from the horse.

David cleared his throat. "He has survived worse," he reassured.

Sarah nodded and straightened her bonnet before taking his outstretched arm. The others were already starting to gather at the barouche by the time they crossed the field.

"What happened?" Lady Caldern demanded as Mr. Stanton handed Sarah into the open-aired vehicle.

"Lord Caldern took a tumble from his horse." Mr. Stanton spoke before Sarah had a chance to reply. "Foolish of him, but it looks as if he may need some stitches."

"Is that all?" Lady Caroline snorted. "I thought he was dead the way you two ran over there."

Sarah eyed her cousin silently, biting her lower lip to prevent her from saying anything. Caroline held her parasol above her head, smiling through her lashes at David Stanton.

"Luckily his injury was not fatal." David Stanton bowed low and then moved away. "I will meet you back at the house."

Caroline watched him move toward his horse silently, but as soon as the carriage started to move she turned to Sarah. "How could you behave in such a hoyden manner?"

"No lady of breeding would consider running like you did," Lady Caldern added.

"He needed help," Sarah defended.

"He was well enough to mount his horse and ride back to the house." Caroline glared at Sarah with narrowed eyes. "Do you think you are the only person who can help?"

"No," Sarah sighed.

"You did not even have your medicines with you," Caroline continued. "We all saw you use the skirt of your chemise. It was unpardonable."

"I only meant to help."

"Your help is not needed," Lady Caldern insisted coldly.

Sarah nodded her head and then looked away. When she had seen the Marquess fall, she had not stopped to think about her actions, but she had not expected Caroline and Lady Caldern's outrage. His safety had been her only concern.

Sarah kept her eyes on the landscape during the ride back to the house. She knew that Caroline continued to glare at her, but she did not have the energy to deal with her cousin's temper. Sarah had reacted instinctively.

When the wheels of the coach clattered onto the paving stones of the newly repaired front entranceway, Sarah turned to face the others. Lady Julianna smiled at her timidly. The others ignored her. She was the last to descend the barouche and when they entered the house, Johnson approached her.

"His lordship requests you attend him in his chambers."

"Impossible," Lady Caroline screeched.

Sarah ignored her cousin's outburst. "Has the wound worsened?"

Johnson nodded. "We cannot stop the bleeding and the doctor will be at least an hour arriving. I took the liberty of carrying your medicine basket to his room."

Sarah nodded and started to ascend the stairs. Caroline followed closely behind her. "I will not allow you to be alone in that man's room."

"He is a patient," Sarah explained calmly.

"I am going with you."

"As you wish." Sarah shrugged her shoulders indifferently. "I will not be able to help you if you faint, though."

"I never faint," Caroline denied shrilly. "You are not the only one in the family who can take care of the sick. I have . . ."

Caroline stopped abruptly when they reached the Marquess's door. Sarah took a deep breath and knocked. Hobson, his valet, opened it immediately and ushered them in with a slight bow.

"How bad is it?"

"I have slowed the bleeding, but he insisted that you be called."

Sarah walked into the room. Her stomach fluttered nervously and her heart started to pound rapidly when she saw Alex. He was sitting on the bed. Her cheeks flooded with color when he patted it suggestively.

Before Sarah could do anything, Caroline pushed past her and rushed to the Marquess's side, picking up one of his hands. "How horrible," she gushed sweetly. "You might have been killed."

"Hardly," Alex denied dryly. He pulled his hand out of Caroline's grasp. "I want your cousin to look at the wound."

"I think you should wait for the doctor," Caroline insisted sweetly.

"Gladly," Alex shifted on the bed, pushing back the blanket that was covering his thigh. "After Mrs. Wellsley has stopped the bleeding."

Caroline gasped loudly, putting her hand to her mouth and backing away from the bed. "That is horrible."

Sarah moved around her and removed the blood-soaked bandage. "You should not have ridden home," she scolded.

"It was the quickest way."

"Not for your recovery," Sarah admonished. "If you lose much more blood, you will be too weak to leave your room."

"Does that bother you?" Alex teased in a low voice.

Sarah looked up at him sharply and then glanced quickly at her cousin. Caroline was standing near the window, arms crossed tapping her foot impatiently. She was too far away to hear their conversation.

"You would be wise to mind your tongue." Sarah soaked a cloth in the water basin and wrung it out. She cleaned away the blood and then put a fresh bandage over the jagged three-inch wound.

"Put your hand over this," she instructed Alex. "I will get another cloth to tie it down."

Alex shifted on the bed and leaned his hand

onto the new dressing. Sarah took a long strip of clean linen and wrapped it around Alex's leg, securing it in place with a tight knot.

"That should stop the bleeding for a while," she murmured to herself. "Now we need to elevate the leg."

She reached over Alex and took one of his pillows, bunching the feathers up before placing it under the injured leg.

"I appreciate your help." Alex smiled and Sarah's stomach fluttered in response.

"Are you finished now?" Caroline's abrasive voice broke the spell.

"The doctor should be here soon," Sarah explained. "I think we can leave now."

"What if I need you again?" Alex asked as he leaned back against his pillows. "Surely you can wait until Dr. Caruthers arrives?"

"Of course we will," Caroline agreed. She looked around the room and pointed at a chair beside a desk. "Bring that over here," she ordered Hobson.

When it arrived, she sat down and arranged her gown. The sunlight streamed through the western window, bouncing its rays off her golden hair. She seemed to glow with brilliance. Sarah straightened her cap and moved to go sit near the window when Alex grabbed her arm.

"Stay here."

Caroline leaned forward and was about to object when a knock sounded on the door. Hobson opened it immediately. It was Dr. Caruthers.

"Good afternoon, my lord," he greeted as he entered the room carrying a small black bag. His riding boots and pants were spattered with mud and his gray coat was slightly wrinkled. He looked to be in his mid-thirties, of medium build with light brown hair already graying at the temples. Sarah had never met the man before, but the people in the area spoke very highly of him.

"I came as soon as I heard." He walked over to the bed and Sarah moved aside. "Rather unpleasant circumstances to meet, my lord."

"Not at all," Alex reassured. "I have always found that the more unusual the situation, the more lasting the friendship." Alex looked across at Sarah and winked.

The doctor looked up from his bag and smiled. "I like that philosophy. Especially because I am sure we will meet again."

"Count on it." Alex heaved a heavy sigh and leaned further into his pillows. "I intend to keep very close to Caldern."

"You cannot be serious," Caroline hissed.

"Very." Alex looked over at Caroline, his eyes unwavering until she paled slightly and turned away.

Dr. Caruthers cleared his throat, glancing from Alex to Caroline quickly before turning his attention to his patient's leg. "What happened?"

"It was a riding accident." Alex crossed his arms over his chest. "Careless of me, actually."

Sarah inhaled her breath sharply and was about to speak when Alex caught her eye. His look was intent, almost hypnotic. For whatever reason, he did not want her to deny his story. Sarah closed her mouth and looked away from the bed. If the Marquess wished to keep secrets, that was fine. She did not have to be a party to it, though.

The doctor removed the bandage. "I can see you've had excellent care, my lord. Your wound has been cleaned nicely and the bleeding has almost stopped."

"I did not want to bother you," Alex explained wryly. "A bandage would have been fine."

The doctor looked up from his work. "Is that what happened to your face?"

Alex stared at the man coldly, finally smiling when the doctor refused to be intimidated. "Our doctor died during the battle aboard ship that day. I was one of the lucky ones." Alex rubbed his hand down the scar. "A small price to pay."

The doctor nodded. "A doctor is available now and this cut needs stitches. You were wise to contact me."

"Not me," Alex denied quietly. "You will have to credit Mrs. Wellsley's judgment."

The doctor looked up from his work. "Is she here?"

"Behind you."

Sarah clasped her hands tightly, forcing herself to meet the doctor's eyes. Her experience with medical men was usually unpleasant. They did not approve of her "meddling in matters that were not her concern." Dr. Caruthers was smiling, though.

"A pleasure, Mrs. Wellsley." He bowed his head slightly and Sarah curtsied in return. "I have heard a lot about you."

"I have tried to help," Sarah defended.

Dr. Caruthers waved his hands at her dismissively. "I have no argument with your work, quite the opposite. I am far too busy a man to tend to all of the needs in this area."

"Then you are not upset?" Sarah breathed a small sigh of relief.

"I know that most medical men would feel threatened by you, but I am not one of them." The doctor turned back to the bed, pulling out some instruments from his bag. "I hope Lord Caldern realizes how lucky he is to have you here."

"I am a very lucky man." Alex grinned widely at the doctor. "More so than I ever imagined."

Sarah felt her cheeks redden at the unexpected praise from the two men. A glare from Caroline ended her euphoria. Caroline stood up from her chair, almost tipping it over in her haste.

"I think it is time you went back to your work, Sarah."

"She stays," Alex snapped coldly. "I am sure the doctor could use her help."

Caroline took a deep breath and then sat back in her chair. "As you wish."

Sarah's eyes widened at her cousin's acquiescence. She had expected a scene. Perhaps the Marquess's injuries had really upset Caroline.

"Could you help?" the doctor asked over his shoulder.

Sarah walked over to the bed and took the old bandage away. The doctor had set out a needle and thread and was now washing the wound with some clean water that Hobson had left.

"I will need you to hold down his leg while I stitch." The doctor threw the cloth into the basin. "Can you do that?"

Sarah nodded and walked around the doctor. She held Alex's thigh steady, watching carefully as Dr. Caruthers threaded his needle and then pushed the edges of the cut together before he began.

"Brace yourself," he ordered.

The needle plunged into Alex's skin and his leg jumped beneath her hands. She held on tighter, but Alex did not move again. She glanced over her shoulder at him, noting the perspiration forming on his forehead. He tried to smile back through his tightly clamped jaw, but only succeeded in a grimace. Fighting an urge to kiss away his pain, Sarah turned back to the doctor.

He was tying the knot in his last stitch. "That

should do it." He snipped the thread with his scissors. "I need a clean bandage now."

Sarah moved away from the bed and took the linen Hobson handed her. She folded it several times, until it was a thick pad the length of the cut. When she had finished she handed it to the doctor.

"No strenuous exercise or riding for a couple of days, but other than watching for infection I think you should be fine."

"When do the stitches come out?" Alex leaned back against the pillows.

"A week should do it." The doctor packed his things up in his black bag and then shut it sharply. "Change the bandage twice a day and if there is any problem, call me."

"Thank you, Dr. Caruthers. Hobson will see you out."

The doctor bowed his head slightly and then followed Hobson from the room. When he had left, there was a heavy silence, and Sarah held her breath, waiting for Caroline's outburst.

"I do not want you correcting me in public," Caroline began through clenched teeth.

Alex sighed heavily. "There would be no need if you behaved civilly."

Caroline's mouth gaped open in astonishment. "How dare you?" she spluttered.

"I dare because it is the truth." Alex sat up and gingerly moved his leg to the edge of the bed. "We have nothing further to discuss. Kindly leave."

Caroline stood up and pushed the chair back. "Come, Sarah."

Sarah stood indecisively for a few seconds, noting the gleam of amusement sparkling in Alex's eyes. He was enjoying Caroline's anger. She turned and followed her cousin out of the bedchamber, looking back at Alex's grinning face. She did not understand what he hoped to accomplish. He certainly did not want a peaceful relationship with Caroline.

Chapter 18

Sarah stood at the open window, watching the stars flicker in the night sky. The cool breeze was refreshing after a day spent in the upper-floor sewing room. She closed her eyes and breathed deeply. The air was filled with the fragrance of roses.

She pulled the pins from her hair, shaking her head so that her brown tresses fell down her back and shoulders. She picked up her brush and ran it through her curls in a rhythmic motion, releasing the tensions of the day.

Suddenly the door opened and she turned around in surprise. Her breath caught in her throat and the frantic pounding of her heart echoed in her ears as she watched Alex walk into her room.

"Surprised?" he asked, shutting the door behind him. He turned the key in the lock before looking back at Sarah.

"What are you doing here?" Sarah stammered. Alex was still dressed in black evening attire, but the top button of his shirt was open and his cravat was missing.

"You have been avoiding me since yesterday," Alex explained, walking into the room. The candlelight cast shadows across his face. "I thought now would be a good time to talk."

"Now?" Sarah repeated. Her mouth had gone dry and her mind was refusing to function.

"Yes." Alex looked over at her bed, the burgundy covers turned back to expose the stark whiteness of the sheets beneath. "I see I came just in time."

Sarah glanced at the bed, feeling her cheeks burn with embarrassment. "We can talk tomorrow."

Alex shrugged. "I agree. Why waste our time on words?"

Sarah gasped and then felt anger surge through her veins. "Get out," she spat.

Alex leaned his head to one side and stared at her for a few seconds. "You look tired." He walked over to her and took the brush from her hands, before leading her to the bed. "Sit."

Sarah found herself pushed onto the mattress. She moved to stand, but Alex stopped her with a hand on her shoulder. He lifted her hair and pulled the brush through it.

Tingles of sensation shimmered through her scalp. Sarah closed her eyes and relaxed, letting Alex continue his gentle ministration. She luxuriated in the feel of his hands easing the tension from her body.

"Does that help?" he murmured after several minutes of silence.

"Hmmm," Sarah agreed. "It has been years since someone brushed my hair for me."

"If I had known, I would have done it sooner."

"You should not be doing it now." Sarah pushed off the bed and stood up. "Thank you."

"Now can we talk?" Alex caught her hand. He

sat on the bed and patted the space beside him. Sarah hesitated for a second and then sat on the edge.

Alex clasped his hands behind his head and leaned back against the bed poster, leaving his feet to dangle over the edge. "I am sorry about your cousin. I should not have antagonized her."

Sarah sighed and looked away. "Caroline has been very troubled. She is anxious about you."

"Have you been worried?"

Sarah had been terrified, constantly thinking about Alex and wondering if he would become victim to another accident. She did not want to admit the extent of her fear, so instead, she said, "Is there something to be concerned about?"

Alex grinned. "You are upset with me, otherwise you would have insisted on seeing the wound. Is it because I have kept silent over the saddle?"

"I assume you know what you are doing." Sarah forced herself to keep her face passive.

Alex nodded, his face suddenly serious. "I do."

"This is the third time an accident has happened." Sarah's hands moved restlessly in her lap. "It cannot be a coincidence."

Alex shook his head. "No. That does not mean it was deliberate, though."

Sarah looked down at her lap. Her stomach tightened as the image of Alex's bloodied and torn skin flashed before her eyes. If these attempts were planned, how soon before they succeeded in injuring him fatally?

"Do you intend to let them keep trying?"

"Of course not." Alex cleared his throat. "I do not think Bryan meant to hurt me."

Sarah looked at Alex. He stared back unblinkingly. "Should I wait until you are dead?"

"It will not come to that," Alex reassured. He

leaned forward. "Bryan only intended to wound my pride. To prove he was the best."

"What if it was not Bryan?"

"Who else?" Alex looked down at the floor and sighed heavily. "I do not want you to be anxious."

Sarah shut her eyes. She could not stop worrying. Alex had been on her mind since she had met him. Telling herself to stop caring did not work.

Sarah straightened her shoulders. "You are right. There is nothing you can do now."

"Bryan achieved what he wanted." Alex smiled ruefully. "I am sure the whole county knows about my ignoble toss."

"That is not fair," Sarah blurted out indignantly.

"I know it was not my skill at fault. That is all that is important to me." Alex's hand touched her arm, gently stroking it with a finger. "We have wasted enough time discussing this."

Sarah inhaled sharply as a shiver of desire passed through her body. Never had she experienced such a sharp yearning before. She bit her lower lip and moved her arm away.

"It is time for you to leave."

Alex shook his head. "The conversation is just about to become interesting."

Sarah eased away from Alex, but he held onto her hand. He turned it over, tracing a finger down her palm before raising it to his mouth. His lips barely touched her, but tingles of sensation raced up her spine.

"Do not hide from me." Alex took her other hand and kissed it, letting his lips glide over each finger. He looked at her, his eyes smoldering in their intensity. Sarah felt her resistance weaken at the unrestrained passion she saw in his eyes.

"I want you, desperately." Alex's emotional plea curled deep inside her. Her own body echoed the same need and unconsciously she leaned toward him.

He gathered her into his arms and eased her back onto the bed. His body draped over her, protecting and secure in its warmth. She inhaled his musky scent, enjoying his nearness. His eyes caressed her face and Sarah's body responded with answering warmth. Her chest constricted and her breath caught in her throat in anticipation of his kiss.

Slowly his lips captured hers. His tongue stroked until she opened her mouth, allowing him to explore. Sarah sighed as an exquisite lethargy stole throughout her body. She closed her eyes and savored the sensations Alex was creating within her. He continued his sweet onslaught until her body throbbed with desire.

Gradually his lips became more demanding, searing in their intensity, but Sarah was equal to his fervor. His hands began to explore her body and Sarah moaned as a jolt of piercing pleasure cut through her. Alex undid the ties of her robe, exposing her thin white nightgown beneath.

His lips moved away and she opened her eyes. He was gazing at her, his eyes half closed, slumberous with passion. "You are the most beautiful woman I have ever met," he whispered hoarsely. "I have never needed anyone like this before."

Sarah's heart melted. She could not deny how she felt for Alex. It had been with her since she had first met him and yet only now could she see clearly. He was a man who frightened her with his intensity and assurance, yet she longed to be with him. He was in her thoughts constantly, making her question everything about the life she had chosen. The truth had been with her long before this evening. She loved him.

She looked up into his dark fiery eyes and smiled. He may only think of her as another conquest, but right now he wanted and needed her. She might never have another chance. Tonight would last her a lifetime.

A part of Sarah knew she should deny him, but she was beyond reason. Her body craved his touch. She nodded her head and felt tears come to her eyes at the look of joy that washed over Alex's face. Whatever regrets she might have in the morning, she could only think of how right it felt now.

With shaking hands, Alex undid the small blue ribbons that held her nightgown together. He eased it off her shoulder and when she would have turned her head away shyly, his hand stopped her. "Do not look away. Your body gives me great pleasure. Share in my delight."

Sarah was mesmerized by Alex's voice. A slow burning ache, deep within her womb began to spread throughout her body as she watched him remove her gown. His breathing became more ragged with each inch of skin that was exposed. His passion and anticipation filled the air between them, fanning the flames of Sarah's own excitement.

He groaned when her breasts were fully exposed, closing his eyes briefly, before lowering his head. His tongue lightly stroked one of her nipples. Sarah cried out in surprise, her back arching upward at the sudden intense pleasure. Every nerve of her body pulsated with awareness.

Slowly, he lathed her nipple, stirring her mounting passion to a fevered pitch. When she thought she could bear no more, he captured it in his mouth. He suckled and caressed until she thought she would die. Her hands clutched at the sheets and her body moved restlessly, desperately urging him to end this sweet torture, but Alex refused.

When he had finished with the one breast, he moved to the other. Again he took his time, fondling and suckling, building her mounting passion to a screaming point. Sarah twisted and turned, urging his body closer with her hands.

Instead, he left her breast and his lips began to explore lower. He licked and nipped her skin, sending shivers of delight throughout her.

Alex looked up at her, his mouth hovering above her stomach. "I have dreamt of seeing you like this since the first moment we met. Am I moving too fast?"

Sarah shook her head. "No," she denied breathlessly. "I do not think I can take much more."

Alex grinned with satisfaction. "I have only begun. We have the whole night and I intend to spend every moment of it loving you. You will be mine totally."

Sarah was past the point of reason. Her body hummed with a passion she was powerless to deny. Alex stroked her with his hands, moving her nightgown lower over her body until he had drawn it off her. He threw it onto the floor and then began his gentle torment again. His lips moved softly at first, almost featherlike in their touch.

He roamed lower until he reached her pulsating inner core. His lips caressed around it, teasing her with a promise of fulfillment. He lifted one leg with his hand, circling it with kisses. She was on fire now, her body beyond her control as moans escaped her lips. He nuzzled her toes, licking her skin and then blowing on it lightly. Sarah's whole body shivered with sensation.

Alex moved to her other foot and repeated his caresses. He moved up her leg with an agonizing slowness. Sarah panted with need, her body stretched to a breaking point. She could handle no more.

When Alex finished he moved between her legs, spreading her body wide before he lowered his head to her engorged inner center. His tongue fluttered against her and Sarah shuddered with the spiraling sensations that spread throughout her. Alex's caress intensified and she felt her body split apart as waves and waves of ecstasy shook her.

She cried out at the utter beauty of her climax, tears trickling down her closed eyes as she was awash in the total rapture of the moment. Never had she dreamed such pleasure was possible. Nothing in her marriage had ever hinted at such delights.

Slowly, she came back to awareness. Her body felt totally depleted and satiated. She yawned and then felt an urge to giggle.

Alex had moved up beside her, his hands gently stroking her face. "That was only the beginning." His voice was husky, his eyes still burning with desire.

Sarah knew that Alex had unselfishly put aside his needs to show her the secrets of her own body. Whenever Stephen had taken her, his urges had been too great to even wait for her acquiescence.

She brushed his cheek with her finger, savoring the shiver that ran through Alex's body. Tonight he was hers. "If that was the beginning, show me the rest," she whispered.

Alex left her breathless as he captured her mouth. His lips were insistent, demanding total surrender. Willingly, she allowed him to lead her on another journey of discovery. She lost all sense of time and place, becoming part of a world that held only her and Alex. This time they would find fulfillment together.

Sarah's hands tugged at Alex's shirt. Her fingers pulled at the buttons until they had exposed his chest beneath. He groaned when she stroked his skin, her fingers twirling the curling dark hair around his nipples. She wiggled beneath him and he answered her with a thrust of his hips.

She felt his hardened penis through his pants, but before she could react, Alex grasped her close and flipped them around. She was now on top of him, looking down at his body.

"Undress me," he demanded hoarsely.

Sarah shivered at the surge of excitement that rushed through her. She remembered Alex's words about her own body and suddenly realized that seeing him nude would give her the same delight. With shaking hands she reached for the buttons on his pants.

The first button came away easily. Sarah's heart was beating rapidly and she licked her dry lips. Alex groaned and she looked up at him inquiringly.

"You are teasing me," he insisted.

Sarah shook her head. "I am doing what you asked."

Alex shuddered and closed his eyes briefly. "You have no idea what seeing you does to me. I can wait no longer."

Alex made swift work of the remaining buttons and lifted his hips to remove his pants. Together they pushed away the last obstacle to their union.

Sarah's eyes widened as Alex's manhood was finally freed. It was huge. She hesitated for a second before looking back at him.

"It will be fine," he reassured. He brought her down beside him. "I would never hurt you."

He kissed her gently and she felt herself relax. She would trust him to show her. She clasped her hands around his neck, her fingers smoothing his silky hair. Alex's kisses left her breathless and weak with desire. He built their passion again until they were both taut with need.

A loud bang pulled Sarah from her haze of pleasure. Their lips separated and they looked at each other, both panting for breath.

"Did you hear that?" Sarah whispered.

Alex tilted his head, but no sound came. He shrugged his shoulders and lowered his head to her, but before his lips reached hers, another bang. Someone was outside her door.

"Sarah, are you in there?"

"Nellie!" Sarah exclaimed.

"Sarah," Nellie answered back. "You must come immediately. Lady Caroline needs you."

"Can it wait till morning?" Sarah moved away from Alex's arms and shivered.

"She is insisting. I wouldn't disturb you otherwise."

Sarah heaved a heavy sigh. She looked down at Alex and almost laughed at his expression of dismay. Nellie's timing could not have been worse. Still, Sarah had no choice but to go, or risk Caroline coming down to her room.

"I'll get dressed." Alex groaned into her pillow.

"Thanks." Sarah could hear Nellie turn and shuffle away from the door. Silence filled her room.

"Does she do this often?"

She shook her head. "Seldom."

"Should I wait?"

Sarah was tempted to tell him to stay, but she knew from experience that she would probably be up the rest of the night with Caroline. When her cousin could not sleep, everyone else was expected to share in her problem.

"I will be late." Sarah slid off the bed and padded over to her wardrobe. She pulled out a dull gray gown and her chemise. Quickly she pulled the chemise and gown over her head.

Alex continued to lie on the bed, watching her dress through half-closed eyes. His head rested high against the headboard. Sarah felt his unspoken desire from across the room, a desire that echoed in her.

"This is not the end," Alex assured.

Sarah shook her head. She pulled her hair back in a ribbon, grabbed her shawl and quickly left the room. She leaned against the wall beside her door and closed her eyes. Images of Alex filled her mind.

No matter what society thought or expected, she could not deny him. Even with a wall between them, she felt his pull on her. It might be wrong, but she intended to steal what little time she had with Alex. It would have to be enough to last her a lifetime.

Chapter 19

Alex paced around the library. He should have been doing estate work, but he could not concentrate. Last night was fresh in his mind and all he could think of was Sarah.

Images of the candlelight reflecting off her deep brown hair and the shadows of their lovemaking dancing on the walls had kept his body taut all day. He did not know if he could wait until tonight to see her again.

There was a quick knock at the door and then it opened unceremoniously. David Stanton walked in. Alex's brother Nathan followed and shut the door behind him.

Alex raised an eyebrow. Both men looked serious. "Why the interruption?"

"We need to talk." David pulled out a chair by the desk and sat down.

"Now." Nathan perched on the edge of his desk.

Alex shrugged and walked over to them. He sat down in the chair opposite David and leaned back with his hands behind his head. "About what?"

"The saddle," David began. "I spoke to Nathan

and he seems to think it was more than an accident."

"Does he?" Alex glanced over at his brother. He was sitting with his arms crossed over his chest, his face scowling back at him.

"You know it is." Nathan uncrossed his arms, grasping the edge of the desk with his hands. "You must tell David about the gunshot."

"What gun?" David sat up in his chair and stared at Alex openmouthed.

"It was a poacher, nothing more than an accident," Alex explained calmly. "There is no connection to the saddle."

"David says the saddle was cut." Nathan leaned forward. "Was that an accident too?"

Alex sighed heavily and shook his head. "No. It was deliberate."

"That is definitely something to be concerned about."

"No harm was done. Let me handle this in my own way," Alex insisted.

Nathan cleared his throat and looked toward the door. There was silence in the room except the sound of his finger tapping on the desk. Alex looked at his brother and frowned. Even though he had not seen him in years, he knew when Nathan was upset.

"What is the problem?" he asked quietly.

"It is Douglas's death," Nathan admitted hesitantly.

"He died in a riding accident. What is mysterious about that?"

"My mother says there was some gossip about his saddle. She says that the locals thought it was put on wrong."

Alex snorted. "Douglas was probably too drunk to notice how he saddled the horse."

Nathan shook his head. "Mother says he took

his responsibilities at Caldern seriously. He was only here two months, but he was in the process of overhauling the farms."

"I have seen no evidence of it." Alex frowned and looked out the window. He had always thought his elder brother had the same love for Caldern as he did, so he had found it strange that he had done nothing to improve it while he was the Marquess.

"Once he died, Lady Caldern reversed all of his decisions. She said that there was not enough money to do the work."

"That is a lie." Alex sat forward. "There is plenty of money."

"Did you also know that Douglas was engaged to be married?"

"No." Alex felt his head whirl at this piece of news. His stepmother had told him that Douglas had neglected Caldern horribly; refusing to even consider what was best for the estate. His brother's engagement proved otherwise. He had always sworn that he would only marry for the sake of an heir.

"He was engaged to Lila Tremayne, Andrew's younger sister. She was just a babe when you left Caldern."

Alex remembered Andrew Tremayne vaguely. He was the only son of Viscount Tremayne, who owned a large estate on the other side of the county. The two families had not been close, but were often together at the same social events, such as hunting parties and balls.

"I heard nothing about an engagement. When was it announced?" Alex asked with a frown.

"Apparently there was no formal announcement." Nathan rubbed his neck. "Mother says that Douglas had just returned to Caldern when he began visiting Lila. The two had come to an understanding the night of his accident."

"How does your mother know this?" David asked with a snort. "Sounds like gossip."

"Douglas stopped on his way home from the Tremaynes'. He was bursting with the news and he wanted to tell someone who would be happy for him."

Alex looked out the window behind his desk. There were a few clouds in the sky, billowy and white. A gentle whiff of cut cedar reached his nose. The gardeners were tackling the overgrown maze today, he remembered abstractedly. With a heavy sigh, he turned back to the room and concentrated on the problem of Douglas.

Douglas had been close to Mary Carter, too. All three boys had spent most of their time together in the summer months. Both he and Douglas needed to escape a house dominated by Fanny. Douglas may have tried to bully his younger brothers, but Alex still had fond memories of him. It made sense that he would tell Mary his plans first.

"Where is Lila now?"

"She moved away shortly after Douglas's death. She is staying at a small house the family owns in Wales."

Alex frowned. "That is quite a distance."

Nathan nodded. "The family says her health is poor, but Mother thinks it is because of Douglas's death. Apparently Lila had refused quite a few proposals before accepting our brother."

"Does Mary remember anything about Douglas's accident?"

Nathan gripped the edge of the desk tighter, his knuckles turning white in the effort. "Lady Caldern said Douglas had been drinking heavily that night and insisted on riding. They found him in the morning, dead. Apparently he had tried to jump a fence and fallen from his horse."

"No mention of a saddle problem?"

Nathan shook his head. "The horse returned to the stables that night, with the saddle slipping off its back. They decided to wait until morning to look for Douglas."

"The saddle could have been moved in the fall."

"Anything is possible." Nathan stood up suddenly and walked behind the desk. He looked out the window for a few minutes before speaking. "I think you should look at these accidents more carefully."

Alex sighed and leaned back in his chair. "It is just speculation right now."

"Mother insists that Douglas had not been drinking since he returned to Caldern."

"So you think Lady Caldern lied."

"Yes."

David cleared his throat and waited for the two men to look at him before speaking. "Whatever the truth about your brother, Alex, you need to look at what has happened to you more seriously."

"I agree." Nathan sat in the chair behind the desk. "Your saddle was definitely cut."

"That was Bryan trying to prove he was a better horseman."

"Was Bryan also trying to prove that when you were shot off your horse?" Nathan snapped back. "And I suppose the roof falling was another attempt to unseat you?"

"The whole house is in disrepair. The roof was probably ready to fall."

"With you conveniently beneath it," Nathan added sarcastically.

Alex rubbed his eyes. It was impossible to deny the strange coincidences that had happened to him lately. They were all accidents, except the saddle. He had not been seriously injured in any of them, but the potential for death had been there.

"What would you like me to do?" he asked in resignation. "I cannot hide away in this house."

David shifted in his chair. "I think it would be best if you had someone accompany you everywhere."

Alex gaped at his friend in surprise. "That is impossible."

"Not really," David insisted. "I am here with you at the house and Nathan will help."

"I would hate it." Alex stood up from his chair and walked to the fireplace. He kicked at the corner of the brick hearth. "What good would it do?"

"We would be there if something happened." Nathan leaned on the desktop. "If someone tries something obvious, we can stop him or her."

Alex shook his head. "No."

"You are not thinking clearly." Nathan pushed back from the desk and walked toward his brother. "Especially now that you are almost engaged."

"What does my engagement have to do with it?"

"Douglas died after he announced his engagement."

"The family has known about my likely betrothal since my arrival at Caldern."

"And the accidents started happening one week later," Nathan reminded.

Alex frowned and leaned his shoulders against the mantle. "Fanny arranged the meeting with Lady Caroline. Why would she do that if she did not want me to marry?"

Nathan seemed to ponder his words for a few seconds before he shrugged. "I have no answer. I still think you need to be careful."

"I will be more cautious," Alex agreed. "Following me around is out of the question, though."

David stood up from his chair and walked to the middle of the room. "I understand how you feel about your privacy, but you may regret your decision. Think about it."

"I will." Alex knew David was only concerned about his safety, but Alex still did not want to be followed.

David shook his head and walked to the door. "I hope you know what you are doing," he said before leaving the room.

Nathan continued to stare at him for several seconds after David left. "What is the real reason you are refusing our help?" he asked finally.

"I already told you."

Nathan shook his head. "You have been preoccupied lately. Are you having second thoughts about marriage?"

Alex shook his head. His brother was almost uncanny in his perception. "No. That is the one thing I am certain about."

Nathan grinned at him lopsidedly. "I would never have thought you would have been happy with someone like Lady Caroline. You have my best wishes for your happiness."

"You are premature in your congratulations." Alex felt a twinge of regret in not being honest with his brother, but he needed time. "I have not asked the lady yet."

"You will, though. I can see it in your eyes. You have made a decision."

Alex glanced down at his feet, seeing the reflection of his dishonesty in the shine of his Hessian boots. Alex sighed and looked up at his brother. "I hope my choice will not disappoint you."

Nathan shook his head. "I only want you to be happy. Choose wisely."

Alex grinned. "I have done so." At least in this

he was truthful with Nathan. "No more worrying over my safety, though."

"I will still look out for you when I can." Nathan gripped his shoulder and looked at him seriously. "Do not fail me in this."

Alex returned his brother's somber look. "I will not."

Without further discussion, Nathan turned from Alex and left the room, leaving an almost deathly silence in his wake. Alex heaved a sigh of regret and shook his head. He had wanted to tell Nathan everything that was in his heart, but he knew that he needed secrecy now. If he was somehow going to succeed in his goal, he must not let anyone guess his true intentions.

He walked over to the window and looked out across the terrace to the formal gardens below. Caldern was beginning to come alive again. His men had worked wonders in a few short weeks, and soon his eyes would see order and neatness. He wished that he could do the same with his life.

Things were more complicated than he had expected. Alex rubbed his eyes and turned away from the window. He sat down in his desk chair and leaned back. When he had left London for Caldern, it had seemed so easy. He would take his place as the Marquess, marry, produce an heir, and maintain the lands he had loved.

He should never have agreed to let Fanny choose his bride. Ruefully, he admitted it would have worked if he had never met Sarah. Now it was impossible. His plan to make Lady Caroline beg off had not worked. She was impervious to his insults. Somehow he had to honorably extricate himself from a situation that promised only misery.

Now he had been presented with another problem, Douglas's possible murder and the likelihood of his own. He could not deny that some strange accidents had happened, but he could only prove one had been deliberate. Alex shut his account books with a loud bang and stood up. There was something even more pressing than Bryan on his mind. Sarah. Nothing else mattered until he had settled things with her. His body hardened in anticipation.

The afternoon sun was already setting in the sky, and soon it would be dinner. He would be able to feast his eyes on her once more. It would have to satisfy him until he could hold her in his arms.

Chapter 20

The soft, warm glow of the full July moon was Sarah's only guide to the lake, and now her only companion. With the swiftness of need, she stripped off her clothes and dove into the water, swimming until her breath would hold no longer. When she surfaced, she threw her hair from her face and laughed in exultation. She could not remember the last time she had felt so ecstatic at flaunting society's rules.

Sarah sank into the cooling water and let it soothe her tired and hot body. After a night catering to Caroline's needs, she had spent the rest of the day in the sewing room. The heat had been unbearable. She had tried to sleep, but had given up the effort after an hour and in desperation headed for the lake.

Sarah felt her muscles relax as the water's silken ripples moved gently against her skin. Her worries slipped away. Leaning her head back, she floated across its moon-dappled surface. She let her mind wander back to the events of the previous night.

She could still feel the warm glow Alex's lovemaking had given her.

Suddenly the silence of the evening was broken by the loud crack of a branch. Sarah held her breath and looked warily toward the shoreline. As if her thoughts had conjured him up, Alex was standing beside her abandoned clothes. She felt herself blush as the intensity of his searching eyes burned their way through her body. Somehow he had found her.

She sighed at the inevitability of it. She could not fight this man any longer. He had broken through her barriers. She could not trust any man completely, but she knew Alex would not hurt her.

"Why were you not at dinner?" Alex asked sharply.

"I was too tired," Sarah explained hesitantly.

"Not too tired to come here."

Sarah leaned her head back in the water. "It was too hot in my room. I could not resist."

"Neither can I." Alex smiled crookedly at her before reaching his hand up to his cravat. His fingers loosened the white linen and pulled it from his neck.

Alex held her gaze. He leisurely removed his jacket and threw it on the ground. Sarah's breath caught in her throat and she watched in nervous anticipation. He bent to remove his boots before capturing her eyes again.

"What are you doing?" she asked breathlessly.

"Joining you," Alex answered huskily. He threw his waistcoat on top of his jacket.

Next he undid his shirt buttons, pulled the shirt from his pants and shrugged it from his shoulders. Sarah's eyes widened at the perfect symmetry of his muscular chest. She licked her dry lips, her eyes never wavering from his hands. They descended to his pantaloons. With slow and deliberate movements, he unfastened them and pulled his legs free. He stood before her naked.

She had only a few seconds to register the strength and beauty of his well-honed body before he dove into the water. Her heart beat frantically as heated excitement unfurled in her stomach. Sarah had never felt such a fierce need to touch a man before and the intensity of it frightened her.

Alex surfaced a few feet away from her. With easy strokes he swam to her side. "You were not in your room, so I took a chance you would be here," he whispered, reaching out to her.

Sarah hesitated a moment before giving him her hand. "We should not be here."

"There is no need to be afraid," he reassured. "Everyone at the house has been in bed for hours."

"What if someone finds us together?" Sarah bit her lower lip nervously. "It would be disastrous."

Alex turned Sarah to face him. "I will protect you. There is no reason to be afraid."

Sarah melted. Alex's eyes reflected the moon's light and his desire. She floated into his arms willingly. This man was her destiny now and despite all the difficulties, she could not deny him. Her body desired his touch and her soul craved his love.

Slowly he brought his lips to hers. She was suspended in time, luxuriating in the heated flow of pleasure that ran through her body. Sighing with the blissful release of her fears, she finally surrendered. There was nothing left for her to fight. No need to control the wantonness she felt in his arms. She was finally set free.

Alex's lips touched her gently, his tongue teasing her with its slow exploration. She was wrapped in a sea of delicious sensations as she relaxed into Alex's embrace. She brought her arms up around his shoulders, sinking her fingers into his cool, damp hair, stroking and kneading his scalp.

Within minutes his lips demanded more. Eagerly she opened her mouth, welcoming Alex's sweet invasion. Their tongues met and joined in an erotic mating dance. Shivers of pleasure spread throughout her body, heightened by the silky coolness of the water that surrounded her. Every nerve ending tingled with awareness. She kissed him with wild abandon, oblivious to the world around them. The water, the cool night air and the noises of the night creatures were forgotten. Nothing existed beyond the two of them.

Alex suddenly tightened his grip on her, lifting her body closer to his. She gasped at the rush of electricity that ran through her as she was clasped high to him. She felt their hearts beating frantically in unison, their chests rising and falling rapidly. Their lips parted, and she gazed directly into his eyes.

"God forgive me," Alex groaned. "Nothing can make me leave you tonight."

"Promise?"

"Are you certain?"

Sarah clasped Alex's head and brought his lips to hers. She poured all of her love into her kiss, showing him how great her need was. He accepted her gift. Tonight would be theirs.

Alex continued to hold her to him with one hand, while his other roamed down her back, lightly caressing her until she thought she could stand the tension no more. Her body was taut with desire. Alex's hand moved lower, caressing her buttocks. He brought her tightly against him, allowing her to feel the extent of his arousal.

For a moment she stiffened, but Alex gentled his touch, coaxing her to relax. He continued to allow his hand to skim across her back, sending shivers of delight throughout her body.

Slowly her inner turmoil eased, and the fear that clutched her chest subsided. Closing her eyes, she savored the sensation of being gradually filled by Alex. His penetration was unhurried and gentle, allowing her body to accommodate him fully. They were truly one now, both spiritually and physically.

They remained joined, without movement for several moments. Alex continued to coax her with his lips and his hands, deliberately guiding her legs, until she had clasped them about his waist. His lips left her mouth, moving in a leisurely descent to her neck. She clung to his shoulders, flinging her head back to give him greater access. He was arousing her to a fevered pitch.

Suddenly Alex's lips left her neck and captured one of her breasts. Sarah jumped at the jolt of pleasure that went through her. Alex tenderly eased her back into his arms. He continued his slow perusal of her breast, his tongue teasing her nipple before he finally captured it with his lips.

Sarah moaned as the sharp edge of desire began to build in her. She allowed the water to support her weight and leaned back to give Alex greater access to her body. He did not disappoint her. His lips moved to her other breast eagerly.

Sarah's body was on fire. She began to tremble with the mounting urgency Alex was awakening. She could no longer control her actions. With panting breath, she sat up and felt Alex surge deep within her. That was her undoing.

Frantic with need, she captured his lips and began to move her body. Alex grabbed her hips and guided her motions until they were lost in each other. The water surrounded and held them, but it could not put out the fire they had created. With a startled cry, Sarah reached the summit and the world exploded with blinding brilliance. Seconds later she felt Alex's body shudder in release.

Gradually she descended back to reality, and to Alex. She clung to him as her body shook in the aftermath of their lovemaking. They floated in the water's coolness, content to drift together. It was not until she turned her head against Alex's shoulder that she felt her tears. Alex looked down at her tenderly and wiped her cheek.

"Did I hurt you?" he asked quietly.

Sarah shook her head. "It was beautiful."

"Only when there is love." Alex kissed her gently. "I love you, Sarah. I think I knew the morning we first met, but I was too stubborn to admit it."

"You could not have known so soon," Sarah denied as she raised her head to look at him. Her heart quickened at the sincerity in his eyes.

"The attraction was immediate." Alex gave her a crooked smile. "If you had not spent so much time fighting me, you would have realized it also."

Sarah gazed at Alex intently. She had felt drawn to him that morning at the lake, but fear had sent her running. When she had seen him wounded, her first response had been panic and then a sense of loss. Looking back at the past few weeks, she realized that she had only been alive when Alex was in the room. The darkness of her life had lifted since she had met him.

"You are right." Sarah felt as if her soul had been freed from a horrible bondage. "It was love from the beginning."

Alex smiled joyously at Sarah's words, lifting her into his arms, holding her high against his chest. Water dripped from her body as he carried her to the shore. He lowered her when they reached their clothes, allowing her to slide slowly down his half-aroused body before reaching down for a drying sheet. He wrapped the sheet about her and then pulled her into his arms, capturing her lips in a playful nibble.

"I knew you would eventually realize the truth," he whispered hoarsely."

"You were more certain of it than I."

"Not certain," Alex denied. "More determined."

Sarah laughed softly as she considered just how determined he had been in his pursuit. She never really had a chance of escaping him. At this moment, though, she was happy he had been so stubborn. He had wiped away her memory of the past and replaced it with the beauty of the love they had shared. She would never regret this stolen night together.

Alex's eyes began to darken with renewed passion. She allowed him to pull her down to the ground before he lay beside her. In his arms, she again felt the renewal of their passion, not yet quenched from their first joining. Within moments, all thought of the next day and their problems were forgotten as she lost herself in Alex's expert caresses.

It was not until the early morning light filtered through the tree branches that Sarah stirred in Alex's arms. Raising her hand to brush away her hair from her face, she shivered with the cold and damp. Every muscle in her body ached, yet within her was a sense of peace and contentment. She smiled at the remembrance of the love she had shared with Alex throughout the night.

He had been a considerate and demanding lover. There had been no inhibitions between them and Alex had driven Sarah to ecstasy more than once. Her passion equaled his and they had made love several more times before sleep finally claimed them. Alex had been insatiable, but so had she, Sarah admitted ruefully.

Sarah squinted her eyes at the sun's bright light reflecting off the water in the lake. The world was fresh and new. The birds were singing wildly in the surrounding trees, echoing Sarah's own joy. She threw her head back and inhaled the pungent perfume of the lady's mantle that grew wild around the lake's shore. Soon it would be ready to harvest.

With a sigh, Sarah rose slowly from the ground, careful not to disturb Alex. Their time together was at an end. She rubbed her arms, already missing the warmth of Alex's body. With a determined shake of her head, she looked for her discarded clothing. She found it on a nearby rock and scrambled to dress.

She had just finished when Alex began to stir under the sheet. He raised himself up on his elbows and surveyed the world through half-closed eyes before his gaze turned to her.

"Morning already?" he asked in a sleep-filled voice.

Sarah bent to retrieve his clothes, handing them to him with a smile. His face was relaxed in the morning light as if he had no cares in the world. She gazed at him intently, memorizing this moment.

"Why did you dress so soon?" Alex asked standing up and stretching his long lean body. "I was hoping for an early morning swim."

"It is late," Sarah explained. "The servants are already working in the house and soon others will be on the grounds."

"You are right," Alex mumbled, bending to pull on his pantaloons. He straightened up and reached for his shirt. "I am too old for sleeping on the ground. Next time we make love, it will be on a bed."

"Next time?"

"And every time after that," Alex agreed with a grin. "I want to see you surrounded with silk and satin bed sheets, in the comfort of my room. At least we will not be scrambling to avoid others."

"I will not be your mistress, Alex," Sarah said in a tight voice. "Especially when you are to marry Caroline. I cannot do that to her."

"Mistress?" Alex repeated incredulously. "I love you, Sarah. Surely you must know I want you for my wife?"

Sarah looked at him blankly and felt her stomach clench. The thought of another marriage was enough to make her body tremble. She took a deep breath to control her shaking. She had vowed she would never allow another man to have control over her life again. As much as she loved Alex, she did not intend to break that vow. No man would control her destiny.

"I cannot marry you," Sarah answered in a tight voice, before turning away from Alex.

Chapter 21

Alex reeled with shock. Sarah's rejection cut deeper than the knife that had sliced the side of his face. After days of battling with himself over his marriage, the last thing he had expected was to fight Sarah. He forced himself to breathe, taking several seconds to find his voice. "What do you mean?" he asked through gritted teeth.

"Just what I said." Sarah remained turned away from him, but he noticed a slight waver in her voice. A glimmer of hope began to glow in his heart.

"You must have a reason," Alex insisted calmly.

Sarah straightened her shoulders. "I will not put myself in that situation again."

"I am not Stephen," Alex reminded her.

"I know." Sarah turned to face Alex. He forced himself to look at her calmly, but his jaw was clenched tightly.

"I vowed I would never marry again. You must understand," she pleaded. "Besides, you are to marry Caroline."

"I would never marry Caroline when I love you," Alex snapped. Sarah took a step away from him and he put out his hand to stop her, drawing her closer to him. "What kind of man do you think I am?"

"An honorable one," Sarah whispered, looking up at him with a sparkle of tears in her eyes. "That is why I know you cannot contemplate marrying anyone but Caroline."

"My stepmother and your family may think so, but I have not declared myself. Neither have I given her any reason to think that I will," Alex explained in a tight voice.

Sarah shook her head. "It is not that simple."

"You are the only woman I will ever make my wife. Let there be no misunderstanding about my feelings."

She stared at him wide-eyed for several seconds. "I cannot risk it." She picked up her skirts, turned, and ran.

"Sarah, come back," Alex demanded, but it was no use.

She had disappeared into the woods. He threw his shirt down in exasperation. Never had he felt so unprepared or vulnerable. He had given Sarah his heart and she had thrown it back at him.

Alex sighed and picked his shirt up. Silently he cursed his stupidity. He knew Sarah was still hurting from her marriage, but he had arrogantly thought that his love would be enough to overcome her objections. What a fool he had been.

Last night had been the most fantastic and spiritual experience of his whole life. Sarah had been so responsive, so loving. She had come to him eagerly, without fear or inhibitions. He had tried to show her that not all men were like Stephen and he thought he had succeeded.

This morning she was determined to push him out of her life, though. Alex sat down and pulled on his boots. The woman loved him, and yet she was unable to trust him. Somehow he would have to make her see that he would never knowingly hurt her.

When Alex had his boots on, he picked up his discarded jacket, waistcoat, and cravat. He tried looking for a sign of Sarah, but there was none. She had disappeared into the woods and was probably back at the house.

He decided to give her time to calm down. Then he would ask her again. He gave the lake one last, lingering look before picking up the drying sheet and walking back to the house. He went straight to his room and changed into riding clothes before heading to the stables.

He stomped his feet impatiently as he watched Jacobs saddle his horse. A good ride was what he needed to clear his head and plan his next step. He was determined to make Sarah see reason. They loved each other. They should be together and that meant marriage.

When the horse was ready, he jumped onto its back and urged it to trot until the open fields were reached. Then he loosened his grip on the reins and the two raced across the freshly cut field. When they had both worked up a sweat, Alex slowed their pace.

He stopped on one of the hillcrests and surveyed the land around him. For the whole of his life this had been the most important thing to him. Caldern. When he had banished himself from it, he had felt a hollowness within that had never healed. He had thought nothing could equal it. He was wrong.

"Damn," he swore beneath his breath.

He could not imagine life without Sarah. Somehow he would prove to her that they were meant to be together. He would do whatever was necessary.

They loved each other and he would not stop until he had made her his wife. Eventually she would see that he was right and accept him as her husband.

With a renewed sense of purpose, Alex turned the horse back to the house. The next time he saw Sarah, he would silence her fears. They would be married. Then she would realize that he would care for and protect her. All he needed was the chance to prove it.

When he arrived at the house he ordered his carriage to be brought around. It was still early enough that he could ride into Carlisle today and be back before dinner. He was not going to give Sarah a chance to change her mind once he had convinced her to marry him.

It was late afternoon before his carriage returned to Caldern. He had spent the day on the road and was exhausted. Despite his physical weariness, he felt a sense of joy when he jumped down from his carriage. Soon he would have everything he wanted.

When he entered the front door, Johnson greeted him immediately. "There is a gentleman to see you, my lord."

Alex handed Johnson his hat and gloves. "Who?"

"Viscount Henley, Lady Caroline's brother. I placed him in the library."

"You should have shown him a guest room." Alex spoke sharply. Johnson was not usually so slack.

"He insisted on seeing you first," Johnson explained with a slight sniff of distaste. "I told him you might be several more hours, but that did not dissuade him."

"How long has he been waiting?"

"An hour, my lord."

Alex gave Johnson a nod and then went to the library. Lord Henley was looking out the window behind the desk. He was tall, with the same golden blond hair as his sister. When the Viscount turned around, Alex was struck by the piercing blue of his eyes. He judged him to be in his late twenties, although the seriousness of his demeanor made him appear older.

"Henley," Alex greeted with a slight bow. "An unexpected pleasure."

"My apologies for coming unannounced, but my father insisted."

"Indeed?" Alex walked into the room and pulled out a chair, motioning for Henley to sit. Alex took the chair opposite. "How may I be of help?"

Henley cleared his throat and looked at Alex apologetically. "My father wishes to know why there is no news of a betrothal."

Alex leaned back in his chair and sighed. He had expected Lady Caroline's family to be curious in the outcome of her visit, but not impatient.

"I know this is awkward," Lord Henley interjected hastily. "I tried to convince my father to wait, but there was no dissuading him. My sister wrote him a very disturbing letter and he felt I should come in person."

Alex frowned slightly. "What did Lady Caroline say?"

Lord Henley tugged at his cravat nervously. He took a deep breath and then looked at Alex directly. "Caroline felt that she was being neglected. In particular, she felt that your behavior . . ." Lord Henley paused for a few seconds as if trying to find the right words before continuing. "She felt that you were not serious in your intentions."

Alex winced at the implied condemnation. Lady Caroline had probably been much more abusive in her missive home. "I can understand your father's concern," Alex agreed mildly.

"It has been over two months now." The Viscount shifted in his chair.

"I only arrived at Caldern three weeks ago."

Lord Henley stared at Alex silently, tapping his finger on the arm of the chair. "My father believed that everything was settled before you arrived. The announcement was only a formality."

"Then your father was misinformed." Alex straightened up in his chair and leaned forward. "I made no such arrangement."

"Lady Caldern and my father had an agreement," Henley insisted.

"My stepmother does not speak for me." Alex pushed himself away from the chair. He walked to his desk and flipped open a book abstractedly. "I only agreed to meet Lady Caroline."

"I understand." Henley rubbed his eyes. "When can we expect a formal announcement?"

Alex looked up at the ceiling, noting how peaceful the painted cherubs looked. He had been expecting to deal with the problem of Lady Caroline, but had hoped for more time. There was no solution to his predicament except the truth. He slammed the book shut.

"There has been a slight change in plans," Alex stated. "I am prepared to make a formal request for marriage, but not the one your father is expecting."

The Viscount shook his head. "What do you mean?"

"Everything will be clear in a few minutes." Alex rang for Johnson. The butler responded almost immediately.

"Kindly ask Mrs. Wellsley to join us."

Johnson bowed and left the room. Alex turned back to the Viscount, noting the slight frown that marred his otherwise perfect features. "I will explain everything once Mrs. Wellsley has joined us. Would you care for some brandy?"

Alex walked to a small cabinet next to his desk and brought out two glasses and a brandy decanter. He filled them and brought one over to the Viscount before sipping his own. Alex savored the sensation of the burning liquid sliding down his throat. He needed the added fortification it would give him when dealing with Sarah.

She would not be pleased with his manipulations, but she had left him no other choice. He was determined to make her his wife, despite her fears. It was what they both wanted.

Sarah stood outside the library door, her hand raised hesitantly. She had dismissed Johnson, insisting she would announce herself. She took a deep breath and tried to calm her shaking nerves. She had spent the whole day hiding in the sewing room, trying to forget how stricken Alex had looked when she had told him she would not marry him.

Nothing had worked. Instead, the memory of his lovemaking had been with her all day, making her doubt her decision. Alex's request for her to come to the library had seemed inevitable. She had known that he would not accept her refusal easily. Still, her stomach clenched with misgivings.

With a deep breath, she straightened her shoulders and knocked on the door. Alex's calm voice bade her to enter. Sarah opened the door and walked hesitantly into the room. The sun was low in the sky and its reflection through the windows blinded her for a few seconds.

"At last," Alex welcomed. He moved toward her,

blocking her view of the room. His eyes seemed to devour her and Sarah felt her resolve wither. Somehow she must resist him.

"I do not understand why you summoned me. We have nothing further to discuss." Sarah stood stiffly at the door, holding onto the doorknob tightly. Her heart was racing and she knew she could not trust herself with this man.

Alex motioned for her to enter the room, but she shook her head and turned to go. A muffled cough stopped her. With a frown, she glanced around the room until her eyes rested on its other occupant. She felt a jolt of surprise and delight when she recognized her cousin.

"Jack," she exclaimed with a smile. "What are you doing here?"

Jack grinned sheepishly. "Father sent me."

Sarah ran forward and hugged him. "It is wonderful to see you." Sarah stood back and noted his appearance. He was still in his travel clothes. "Have you just arrived?"

Jack cleared his throat and shook his head. "I have been waiting for the Marquess to arrive home."

Sarah looked back at Alex in surprise. "You have been gone?"

Alex nodded. "I just returned home from Carlisle. Your cousin has some rather urgent news from your uncle."

Panic gripped Sarah. "Is everyone well?" she asked quickly.

Jack held up his hand reassuringly. "There is nothing wrong at Hartford. My business concerns Caroline."

Sarah exhaled the breath she had been holding. "It is about her letter."

"Father thought I should come in person. The letter sounded hysterical."

"She only told me that she had written, not what it was about."

Jack glanced down at his feet and then looked back up at her. "I have told the Marquess that Father is concerned about the delay in an engagement."

Sarah clasped her hands together and forced herself to look at Jack directly. She heard Alex close the door and move into the room behind her. Now was the moment she had known would come. Alex had no other choice, but to formally declare his intentions to Caroline.

"The Marquess insisted that you be called down to clear up some confusion in this matter." Jack took her hand and led her to a chair by the desk.

Sarah glanced at Alex sideways, but his expression gave her no clue as to his thoughts. She had told him that he was honor-bound to wed her cousin, but he had ignored her. Now Caroline's letter home had taken the choice away from him.

Sarah sat down, her hands tightly clasped in her lap. "I know that Caroline has been feeling anxious," she began diplomatically. "I do not see how I can help, though."

"You have the answer to all of our problems," Alex stated firmly. He sat down on the edge of his desk.

Jack looked at Alex with a slight frown. "How can Sarah help?"

"It is simple actually." The Marquess tilted his head toward Sarah. "I have no desire to marry your sister Caroline."

Sarah's stomach dropped and her eyes widened at Alex's directness. She looked at Jack who sat staring at him with his mouth open. It was several seconds before he spoke.

"My father will not accept this."

"Perhaps when he hears my reasons, he will think differently." Alex crossed his feet in front of him.

Jack looked at him with narrowed eyes. "And that is?"

"I am not in love with her."

Sarah had been holding her breath, but relaxed with Alex's words. For a few agonizing minutes, she had thought he was about to tell Jack about them.

"What does love have to do with marriage?" Jack asked in a raised voice. "If you had wanted love, you would not have agreed to the arrangements your stepmother and my father made."

"I only agreed to consider it," Alex reminded gently. "I must confess I did not think about love then."

"What changed your mind?"

"I fell in love with Sarah."

Sarah gasped in surprise. Jack turned to her, his face incredulous. She stared at Alex, stunned by his words. He had just placed her in the middle of his fight with her uncle and he dared to look as if it did not matter.

Jack turned back to Alex. "What do you intend to do about it?"

"I have already asked Sarah to marry me," Alex informed him quietly. "She has refused."

Jack turned back to her with a raised eyebrow. "Is this true?"

Sarah nodded her head. "I have no wish to marry."

"That is unacceptable," Alex interrupted in a steely voice. "I thought that once you had some time to reflect, you would be more rational."

"My answer is final." Sarah pushed away from the chair and stood up.

Jack held up his hand. "I am confused. If Sarah does not wish to marry you, why will you not accept her answer?"

Alex looked down at Jack and then up at Sarah. His eyes sent shivers through her body. "Please reconsider, Sarah."

She shook her head. "No," she whispered. She could not risk marriage.

"Do not make me force the issue," Alex threatened in a low voice.

Jack stood up. "You are making this difficult, Caldern. Sarah has already given her answer." Jack took Sarah's arm and started to lead her away from the desk. She almost sagged against him in relief. The worst was over.

From behind them she heard Alex sigh heavily. "So I am not good enough to be your husband, only your lover."

Sarah stumbled as Jack jerked to a stop. She closed her eyes, hearing Alex's words echo in her head. For a second she thought she would faint, but Jack's arm supported her. Her feet refused to move, her mind numb with the realization that her world had been ripped apart.

Chapter 22

Alex's stomach sank as he watched Sarah turn around to face him. It had been a risk declaring their relationship in such a blunt fashion, but she had given him no choice. Somehow he had to convince her that they were meant to be together.

Sarah's eyes accused him and he cringed inwardly. She was right. He had betrayed her and to her, that was a crime worse than murder. Still, he did not regret it. He was certain that her cousin would not let the matter rest now.

Henley tilted his head, his narrowed eyes looking directly at him. "You cannot mean to insult Sarah in such a fashion. I am honor-bound to protect her."

"It was no insult. I was merely stating the truth."

"Explain yourself," Henley said in a menacing voice.

Sarah put her hand up and stepped between the two men. "Please do not do this," she begged.

Henley moved around her and stood about a foot away from Alex. "I am waiting."

"Sarah loves me," Alex explained quietly. "She is not thinking clearly right now."

Jack turned and looked at Sarah. "Is this true?"

Alex clenched his hands, his body taut as he waited for Sarah's reply. She seemed to be staring blankly at the window, but after a few seconds of silence she nodded her head slightly. Alex let out the breath he had been holding. She had not failed him.

"Then marriage is the only answer," Jack stated firmly. "As soon as it can be arranged."

"I already have a license." Alex patted his coat pocket. "That is what I was doing in Carlisle today."

"You seem to be very certain of yourself," Jack observed dryly.

"No." Alex shook his head. "The only thing I am sure of is my love for Sarah."

Alex glanced over at her. She was shaking uncontrollably. Alex's chest constricted with guilt and he quickly stepped around Henley and moved to Sarah's side. He put his arm around her shoulders and guided her back to her chair.

"There is nothing to fear," he reassured her. "Everything will be fine."

"You are no better than Uncle John," Sarah accused through clenched teeth. "How could you force me into this situation?"

Alex knelt down beside her and clasped her cold hands. "You have forgotten the possibility of a child."

Sarah's face paled and Alex's resolve almost melted. He hated scaring her like this, but somehow he must make her see that they were meant to be together.

Sarah pulled away from him and stood up. "I should never have allowed myself to believe a man."

"If you truly trusted me, you would marry me." Alex stood, brushing the knees of his pantaloons.

"You cannot force me."

Alex clasped his hands tightly behind his back. "You have left me no other option. We will be married this evening."

Sarah gasped loudly and then shook her head in denial. She looked at her cousin Jack. "You cannot allow this."

Jack looked down at the floor and sighed. "I am afraid it is necessary."

Sarah stood silent for a minute. She stared at both of them in disbelief and then turned and ran from the room. The slam of the door reverberated throughout the library.

Alex felt the energy drain from him. He sat down, sagging against the chair's back. He had not wanted to hurt Sarah, only to make her see that marriage was the best option. Instead, she was even more afraid and distrustful of him than before.

"You better know what you are doing," Henley muttered.

Alex leaned his head back and stared at Sarah's cousin. "She left me no other choice."

"Sarah's a woman who has had few choices in life," Henley explained hesitantly. "I think the decision not to marry again was the first thing she ever insisted upon."

"What about her herbs?"

Henley shook his head. "That was something her mother taught her. She helped her father with the parish work and when she came to live with us, she continued."

"Until your father insisted she marry."

Henley looked at him steadily before nodding his head. "It was a poor choice of husband for

Sarah. I have no idea what happened during the marriage, but I do know that Sarah was a different person when she returned home."

"How?"

"I remember her full of life and laughter before she was married." Henley sat down on the desk edge and looked at his crossed feet. "Do you know about her marriage?"

"I know she was unhappy and that her husband was a fool."

"Then you know more than me. She refuses to speak of it."

Alex sat up in the chair. "Never?"

Henley sighed. "She also refuses to marry. My father has pointed out that she will never have children, but even that does not change her resolve."

Alex knew Sarah's pain and fear were centered on the cruelty of her marriage. He had not thought about how much she was willing to sacrifice to maintain her freedom. He waited patiently for his guest to continue.

"Sarah always wanted children," Henley explained. "When she came to live with us, she was ecstatic because there were other children. She used to tell us stories about all the babies she would have when she was older."

Alex digested this information slowly. If Sarah had wanted children so desperately, her fear of marriage must be deeply ingrained. For a few seconds he doubted the action he had taken, but shook it off. Once they were married, he would make her happy.

With a sigh, he heaved himself off the chair and walked to the door. "I will go and make the arrangements for the wedding."

Henley followed. "I will change. Someone is

going to have to deal with Caroline. She will not be happy about this turn of events."

"She might take it better than you think," Alex suggested with a slight grin.

"You have not seen Caroline when she is angry." Henley opened the door.

"Let me make the announcement," Alex suggested. "I want to be certain that Sarah is my wife before I tell anyone."

"I will leave everything in your hands."

Alex watched Johnson escort his guest up the stairs before turning back to the library. He stood in the middle of the room for a few seconds before ringing the bell. He had much to accomplish. The first thing was to find his brother Samuel.

Sarah ran into her room, slamming the door behind her and flinging herself onto her bed. How could this be happening to her again? The first time she had been too naïve to understand what marriage entailed, but now she shook with fear.

Once she was legally married, she lost all her freedom. She was no longer her own person, but whatever Alex decided he wanted. For a split second she contemplated ending everything, but reason pushed that thought away. There was still time to change Alex's mind.

Sarah pushed away from her bed and walked to the window. The sun was already setting in the sky and soon she would have to get ready for dinner. There would be no escaping after that. Her mind refused to concentrate on a solution, though.

A knock on the door drew her attention away from the window. Before she could ask who was there, Nellie rushed in carrying a large box. Behind her, servants carried a bath and jugs of water.

Sarah stood silently by the window until the bath was full and the servants were gone.

Nellie was the first to speak. "Seems you've been busy."

"I have done nothing," Sarah defended, surprised at Nellie's disapproval.

"The Marquess has ordered a bath and your presence an hour before dinner."

Sarah frowned. "Why should that upset you?"

"Master Jack spoke to me."

Sarah's stomach sank. If Jack had spoken to Caroline, then there was no hope of escaping the marriage. "What did he say?" she asked faintly.

"Seems that Lord Hart sent your cousin to Caldern to arrange a marriage with the Marquess. He has been successful, except the marriage will not be with Lady Caroline." Nellie eyed Sarah sternly for a few seconds before putting the box on the bed. "Time for you to get ready for dinner."

Sarah walked over to the bath as if in a dream. There was nothing she could do to stop Alex now. Things were beyond her control. She felt as if her world was spinning away, leaving her cold and unprotected.

Nellie undid her dress and led her to the bath. Without protest, Sarah sank into the soothing hot water and let it cleanse her body. If only it could quiet the fears and doubts that raced through her mind, she thought as she scrubbed her body with soap.

Nellie helped her out of the bath and led her to the small vanity. When Sarah was seated, Nellie began to brush out the braids.

"You need to have your hair styled properly, but for now I'll just arrange it in a knot at the top of your head and let some curls hang loose."

"There is nothing wrong with my hair," Sarah

protested. Alex might be able to force her to marry him, but she did not mean to change her appearance for him.

"You have beautiful hair," Nellie agreed. "That is why it is senseless to continue to hide it. You will have to get used to your appearance."

"Nellie, do not force me," Sarah begged, looking at Nellie in the mirror. "I do not wish to be dressed in this manner."

"Nonsense," Nellie comforted in a softer tone. "You have nothing to fear. The Marquess will make certain that you are protected."

"I have no wish to be put on display."

"Is that what you think the man is doing?" Nellie stood back with a hand on her hip. "He's a sight smarter than I gave him credit for."

"Why?" Sarah asked sullenly. "Because he was able to force Jack to consent to this marriage."

"No." Nellie began to brush Sarah's hair again. "He picked you over Caroline."

"Caroline would have made a better Marchioness," Sarah objected. "She knows the ways of society."

"True," Nellie agreed. "You will make a better wife, though. The Marquess was able to see that despite your caps and drab dresses."

Sarah digested this information quietly while Nellie fixed her hair in a style that flattered her delicate features. Dark ringlets fell from the top-knot with wild abandon and Sarah shook her head at the difference they made in her appearance. Despite Nellie's efforts, her dark blue eyes looked too big for her face and her cheeks were pale.

"You look beautiful," Nellie assured her with a slight nod, pinching Sarah's cheeks slightly to bring up the color. "You have no reason to fear anyone making unkind comparisons."

Nellie walked to the bed and held up a gorgeous ball gown. It was sapphire blue with an overdress of silver filigree lace that sparkled with reflected candlelight. The silk of the dress rustled as Nellie shook out its folds. Sarah could only stare at it in wonder. She had never worn anything so beautiful before.

"It is lovely," Sarah whispered.

"The Marquess said he picked it out special for you." Nellie held the dress open so that Sarah could step into it. When Nellie had finished fastening it, Sarah smoothed her hand over its luxurious material before walking to the mirror.

She bit her lip when she saw her reflection. Even in her anger over Alex's high-handedness, she had to admit the gown was perfect. It brought out the highlights in her dark hair and made her eyes sparkle. She twirled around the mirror slowly, admiring the vision before her.

"You look perfect." Nellie started to pick up the box on the bed, but a knock at the door stopped her. She walked over and opened it. "Lord Henley is here," she announced.

Jack walked into the room. "I would like to speak to Sarah alone."

"I was just finishing up." Nellie curtsied and left the room, closing the door behind her.

Sarah turned to her cousin and smiled. Despite his refusal to stop the marriage, he had always been her only friend in her uncle's house.

"You look lovely," Jack admired as he walked into the room. "I had forgotten what a beautiful woman you are."

Sarah gave a mock curtsey. "Thank you, my lord." When she stood up, she looked at him seriously. "Is there any hope of you changing your mind?"

"No. Marriage is the only solution." Jack let out a loud sigh. "What were you thinking of to become involved with the Marquess?"

Sarah shook her head and turned toward the window. "It was not something I had planned," she confessed. "It just happened."

"You are too careful to allow that." Jack came up behind her and clasped her shoulders. He squeezed them affectionately. "You must have feelings for him."

Sarah considered denying her love, but she knew that Jack would not change his mind. Numbly she nodded her head and turned to face Jack. "I love him."

Jack looked at her quietly, sympathy and understanding in his eyes. "I thought as much. You would never have allowed him to get close otherwise."

Tears began to well up in Sarah's eyes and she brushed them away defiantly. "That does not mean I want to marry."

"The Marquess loves you, too. That is more than most people have when they wed."

"I do not want a man to control me."

"Caldern does not strike me as a man who would do that."

Sarah gripped her hands tightly and moved away from Jack. "That is exactly what he has done by forcing me to wed him."

Jack shook his head. "Caldern is looking out for your best interests. He is offering you the protection of his name."

"I do not want it."

Jack put his hands on his hips. "It is best. You love him. You made your decision long ago."

"Not to marriage," Sarah denied with a sob.

"That is the only option open for a woman of your position," Jack explained gently. He lifted her chin with his hand and looked into her eyes. "I can almost guarantee that the risk you take today will bring you a lifetime of happiness."

"I wish I could be certain."

"You will have to trust Caldern." Jack went to the door and opened it. "Come. It is time."

Sarah gathered her reticule and followed Jack from the room. She knew that he had been trying to comfort her, but that still did not make her feel any better. Her stomach was in a tight knot and it was an effort to breathe. Sarah straightened her shoulders. There would be plenty of time to speak to Alex before the ceremony.

Chapter 23

Alex stood at the bottom of the stairs, pacing. There was still an hour before dinner. He had made arrangements with Samuel to marry them, but he had not announced it to the rest of the family yet. He wanted Sarah to be his wife and by his side when he told them.

He took his watch from his waistcoat and snapped it open. Two minutes had passed since the last time he had checked. Sarah was late. He grabbed the banister and was about to ascend when he was stopped by Sarah's appearance.

He stared at her in wonder, his breath caught in his throat. He moved away from the stairs and waited for her to reach him, his eyes never leaving her face. He smiled at the faint blush that appeared in her cheeks. He had never been so certain of his love than at this moment.

"You look wonderful." Alex's voice was husky. "More gorgeous than any bride I have ever seen."

Jack chuckled softly. "Every groom should have eyes only for his bride, but I agree. Sarah is a beautiful bride."

Sarah stood rigidly beside her cousin and Alex's heart started to beat frantically. He sensed that she wanted to run away, so he took her arm and slipped it through his. He could not risk losing her now.

"Everything is ready." Alex led her past the library and toward the west wing.

"For what?" Sarah asked in a small voice.

"The wedding," Alex explained. "Samuel has agreed to marry us now."

Sarah stopped walking. "We are to be married now? You said this evening."

Alex looked back at Jack with a raised eyebrow. "I thought Jack told you."

Terror rose from deep within, paralyzing in its grip. One thought kept repeating itself. Marriage. Sarah had thought she had time to convince Alex to forget about marrying her, to let her go free. She had not realized he had meant them to wed so soon. Sarah took a deep breath and started walking again.

"There is no need to wait," Alex explained.

"I thought we would have time to discuss it." Sarah's voice sounded hollow even to her own ears.

Alex gently touched her hand that rested on his arm. "You must trust me."

"How can I trust a man who would force me to marry him?"

Alex sighed deeply and removed his hand. "I am sorry you see it that way. In time you will realize that I am doing what is best."

They walked in silence until they reached the small ancient chapel in the oldest wing of the house. Solid double oak doors usually protected the sanctuary, but now they stood open.

"This is the chapel the first Lord Caldern built for his wife." Alex stopped in front of the doorway. "Legend says that anyone married here will be blessed with a happy and long marriage."

"Most brides are not forced to the altar."

"His was."

Sarah glanced at Alex, noting the soft glow in his eyes. "How is that possible?"

"The king granted the first baron this tract of land and one of the wealthiest women in the kingdom to be his bride. Her father had other plans though, and forced her twin sister to be married to the baron," Alex explained.

"How horrible," Sarah cried.

Alex shrugged. "In the end they were both happy and that explains the superstition about the chapel." Alex cleared his throat and started into the sanctuary.

Sarah let Alex lead her into the chapel, noting the faint odor of mildew that mixed with the freshly cut roses and lilies that filled the room.

Samuel Black stood at the front. Behind him was a small, ornately carved wood altar. Also waiting for them were Nathan Carter and Lady Julianna. All three were smiling back at them.

"I have asked Nathan and Julianna to stand up for us," Alex explained in a low voice. "Jack will give you away, of course."

Sarah merely nodded her head. Everything was happening too fast for her to grasp it. She had expected time to plan an escape, not to be part of a hurried, secretive affair. She should have expected it from Alex. He was a man used to making things happen.

Alex raised her hand to his mouth and kissed it lightly before looking deeply into her eyes. "Trust in our love." He nodded to Jack and then walked up the aisle to the altar.

Jack clasped her hand. "This is the right thing to do."

"I wish I could believe you," Sarah whispered.

Jack started to walk them up the aisle and Sarah forced herself to follow. Her body was shaking and her teeth chattering, but she held her head high. She focused on the picture behind the altar. Christ on the cross.

Their footsteps echoed loudly on the stone floor. It was the only music to accompany her. Sarah smiled inwardly at the comparison to her first wedding, when the church had been full of well-wishers and song. Tears came to her eyes as she remembered the naïve young girl she had been, blindly trusting in her new husband.

She was not so foolish now. Years and experience had left her wise. Now she only prayed that there would still be some way to escape. Even her love for Alex was not enough to convince her that it might be different.

Jack stopped when they reached Alex's side and bowed slightly as he passed Sarah to the Marquess. Alex placed his own hand over hers to stop its uncontrollable trembling. This was the moment of truth, the moment when she could deny her intention to be married.

Alex leaned over. "Do not refuse me," he whispered. "It is the only choice. I promise you will never regret marrying me."

Sarah gasped at Alex's words. How could he have known what she was planning? Her stomach sank as his words penetrated her mind. Her uncle would never allow her to live at Hartford again. She could not remain at Caldern either. Her only choice was marriage.

Sarah turned away from Alex and looked at Samuel. He was dressed in the black garb of a minister and held a small prayer book in his hand. He looked at her questioningly and Sarah smiled faintly. There was no point in delaying the inevitable, she reasoned.

"My brother has requested that the ceremony be brief, so I will begin with your intentions. Do you John Alexander Norward take Sarah Jane Wellsley to be your wife?"

"I do," Alex stated firmly.

"Do you Sarah Jane Wellsley take John Alexander Norward to be your husband?"

Seconds seemed to pass as Sarah forced the words from her mouth. "I do," she whispered.

The rest of the ceremony passed in a blur. She could not focus on anything other than the fact that she had actually agreed to marry Alex. Nothing seemed to matter beyond that.

As if from a deep fog, she saw Samuel raise his hand in a blessing. "I now pronounce you man and wife. You may kiss your bride."

Sarah closed her eyes, holding back the tears that threatened to overwhelm her. Once again, someone else had decided her fate. Her thoughts scattered as she found herself drawn into Alex's strong arms. She opened her eyes in surprise, her heart stopping at the tenderness and love shining in his eyes. He clasped her head and brought it toward him, brushing his lips across hers.

Her body tingled with awareness, pulsing with warmth that spread throughout her body. Unconsciously she relaxed and leaned toward Alex, her lips softening as he deepened the kiss. The world spun out of control, but Alex held her safely within his strong, protective arms.

A small voice in her mind whispered that this was what she wanted, to be held and loved by Alex.

All she needed was to stop fighting and trust in their love, but she brushed the thought aside.

Alex ended the kiss, moving his head back and gazing at her with a smile. "You are safe now."

Sarah frowned. Everything about marriage made her shake with fear. "How can you say that?"

"I will never hurt you," he promised in a low voice. "You are my wife and I love you."

Samuel Black cleared his throat, forcing Sarah to turn and look at him. He was smiling broadly and his arms were outstretched. "I wish you both happiness."

Alex shook his brother's hand. "Thank you, Samuel. You have been a great help."

"It was a pleasure," he reassured. He bent forward and kissed Sarah on the cheek. "It is seldom I marry two people who are truly in love."

Jack came up to her side and hugged her. "It is for the best, Sarah. I know you will be very happy."

Sarah glanced up at Jack, surprised by the conviction in his voice. Before she could reply, Lady Julianna came up to her side. "What a wonderfully romantic wedding," she gushed shyly.

Jack stepped back from Sarah and looked at Alex's sister with admiration. "Your brother could not have chosen a better setting. I am certain that many a happy marriage began here."

Julianna nodded. "The chapel was built in the fourteenth century," she said reverently. "It was used for many years before my grandfather insisted the family go to the village church."

"Are you telling the family secrets?" Alex asked as he put his arm around Sarah's waist.

Julianna shook her head. "Just how much I love the chapel."

Alex looked up at the vaulted ceiling and sighed.

"It is a shame to see it abandoned. It is one of the loveliest rooms in Caldern."

"Did you tell Sarah about the legend?" Nathan Carter asked.

"Yes. That is why I chose to be married here," Alex explained with a grin. "Sarah and I will be happy, but it does not hurt to honor the family's superstitions."

"I agree," Nathan stated firmly. "You have chosen your bride wisely."

Sarah felt Nathan's penetrating gaze and glanced up at him. "Thank you," she murmured.

"I was afraid my brother would not see reason." Nathan clasped Alex's shoulder. "I knew you were struggling over matters of the heart. I am happy for both of you."

Alex drew her closer to him and Sarah felt her heart beat quicken. No matter how angry she was with him, her body betrayed her. Somehow she must stay firm in her decision.

"Sarah and I both thank you for being here at this special occasion." Alex turned them toward the door. "Now it is time to announce our marriage to the rest of the family."

Nathan chuckled. "This is when I bow out. I will be in Carlisle for the next few days. Good luck." With a slight wave he left the chapel. Sarah looked after his departing figure longingly. She wished that she had the same freedom to leave.

Alex leaned over and whispered in her ear. "I would prefer to make the announcement with you by my side, but if you want to leave, you are free to go straight to your room."

Sarah looked up at him with a frown. "Why would I do that?"

"It is written all over your face," Alex explained in a low voice. "If you do not want to speak to the family tonight, that is fine. I will make the announcement and order supper to be served in our bedchamber."

Sarah inhaled sharply and her mouth went dry as she realized what Alex was suggesting. He thought she was anxious for the wedding night to begin. "No," Sarah denied quickly. "I will come with you."

"As you wish." Alex winked at her and straightened up. "Let us go and give the others our good news."

Lady Julianna and Samuel Black left the chapel first, followed by Jack. Sarah took a deep breath and straightened her shoulders. Somehow she would have to face her cousin and Lady Caldern. Neither one would be happy at the news of the wedding.

Alex led her through the large doors before stopping and closing them behind him. Together they continued in silence until they reached the drawing room. The others had already entered and the doors were closed. Johnson was waiting for them.

"If I might be so bold, my lord," he intoned somberly. "The staff and myself would like to wish you and Lady Caldern every happiness."

Alex grinned. "Thank you, Johnson. It does not surprise me that the staff knows our news before the rest of the family."

Johnson bowed his head slightly and then opened the drawing room door. Sarah tightened her grip on Alex's arm as a sea of surprised faces turned in their direction when they entered the room.

"Why have you kept us waiting?" Lady Caldern demanded in a querulous voice. "And who is that woman with you?"

"It is Sarah." Caroline's eyes narrowed as she looked at Sarah closely. "Wherever did you get such a gown?"

"I would like to introduce you to my wife," Alex announced with a broad smile. "We have just come from the chapel."

"What!" Caroline shrieked loudly.

"This is outrageous," Lady Caldern shouted. "Why would you marry such a creature?"

"You have upset Mother. That is unforgivable." Lord Bryan sneered before turning his back on them.

Sarah felt her stomach sink. She knew the news would come as a shock, but she had not been prepared for such venom. She moved as if to run, but Alex strengthened his hold on her hand, moving further into the room.

David Stanton whistled. "I cannot believe you married without telling me." He walked up to Alex and patted him on the shoulder. "Congratulations."

Sarah's taut muscles eased slightly when Mr. Stanton took her hand and kissed it. "I can see Alex has chosen wisely," he said with a smile.

"Thank you," she murmured. Her chest relaxed enough for her to take a deep breath.

"I do not believe you," Lady Caldern interrupted loudly. "It is not possible for you to arrange a marriage so quickly."

"I assure you it is true," Alex informed her in a cold voice. "I already had a special license and Samuel agreed to wed us."

"A special license," Caroline repeated hysterically. She pounded her own chest angrily. "That was meant for me."

Sarah cringed with remorse at the pain she was causing her cousin. "I never meant for it to happen. You must believe me," Sarah pleaded.

Caroline walked up to Sarah, stopping when she was an arm's length away. Sarah reached out her hand, hoping that Caroline would be reasonable.

Instead Caroline pushed her hand away and raised her own to slap her.

Sarah jumped back defensively, but it was unnecessary. Alex grabbed Caroline's wrist. He held her hand inches away from Sarah.

"Enough."

"You are the most ungrateful person I have ever known." Caroline glared at Sarah, her eyes piercing in their intense hatred.

Chapter 24

Sarah stood in the middle of her new bedroom and shook her head in disbelief. It was absolutely magnificent, all light blue with gold gilt moldings. The furniture was dark rosewood, intricately carved with cupids and flowers. Everything was delicate and feminine. It was so unlike anything that Lady Caldern would have chosen, that Sarah thought she was in the wrong room.

She walked over to the dressing table and picked up a sterling silver comb that was arranged beside her own. The glare of the candlelight reflecting off its surface was almost blinding, no comparison to her own wooden one.

Sarah put the comb down and sighed, her fingers trailing over the vanity distractedly. The whole evening had felt like a dream, so why should this be any different, she reasoned. After dinner she had gone to her old room, only to find herself redirected to the suite of rooms beside the Marquess.

"Is there anything I can get you, my lady?" a timid voice asked.

Sarah turned around and smiled. Mary was one of the upstairs maids, probably forced into waiting on her until a proper lady's maid could be found. "I can manage," she reassured her.

Mary bobbed a curtsey and left the room. Sarah sat down in a chair by the window. It had been an exhausting day and the worst was yet to come. Somehow she must convince Alex to annul the marriage. Sarah dropped her head in her hand and groaned.

"Do not get too comfortable," a voice warned from the doorway. "Lady Caldern had this room specially decorated for me, the Marquess's intended bride."

Sarah looked up in surprise, rising out of her chair when she saw her cousin. "What are you doing here?"

"I would have thought that was obvious." Caroline closed the door behind her.

Sarah's stomach sank and she pressed her hand against it protectively. Caroline had refused to eat dinner and had gone to her room, but Sarah had known that she would eventually have to speak to her. She had hoped it would be after she had convinced Alex to set her free.

Sarah straightened her shoulders. "What can I do for you?"

"There is no need for the niceties now," Caroline sneered. "You have already shown yourself to be a conniving, deceitful witch."

"That is unfair," Sarah protested.

Caroline waved her arms around the room. "You are sitting in the room that should be mine."

"I know," Sarah agreed quietly. "I tried to dissuade Alex against the marriage, but he would not listen. Give me time to convince him."

"So now you think I am at your mercy?" Caroline put her hands on her hips, her face screwed up in outrage. "No man does what he did to me."

Sarah's chest constricted with fear. She had never seen Caroline in such a state before. "We never intended to hurt you."

"That is easy for you to say." Caroline walked over to the dressing table and picked up one of the crystal perfume bottles. "You have what you want now. My mistake was allowing Father to convince me to bring you."

"I did not want to come," Sarah reminded her cousin.

"You repay my generosity with lies and betrayal." Caroline turned away from the table, the perfume still in her hand. "I treated you as family and you steal my husband."

"That is not what happened." Sarah eyed the bottle in her cousin's hand warily. "We fell in love."

"Love," Caroline shouted. "What man could possibly love you?"

Sarah felt as if she had been slapped in the face. She clamped her mouth shut, refusing to give into the anger and doubt that clenched at her chest. "I understand you are hurt," she empathized calmly. "I tried to dissuade Alex."

"You were with the man constantly," Caroline spat out. "When he should have been with me, you were there."

"That is not how it was," Sarah denied. She moved toward Caroline, her hand outstretched for the perfume bottle. "Please believe me."

"I was a fool to leave you alone." Caroline raised her hand and threw the perfume at Sarah.

The bottle missed Sarah's head by inches and crashed into the wall behind her. Sarah turned, one hand on her mouth as she eyed the mess. The floral wall covering was soaked and the odor of roses filled the air.

"Was that necessary?"

"That is just the beginning of what I intend to do." Caroline threw her head back defiantly. "You have ruined my life and if you think I will sit back and watch you enjoy yourself, you are mistaken."

Sarah took a deep breath and started picking up the shattered bits of perfume bottle. There was no way to reason with Caroline when she was in this kind of mood. It was best to let her rant until she had worn herself out.

"Did you hear me?" Caroline's voice was raised in frustration.

"I imagine the whole household can hear you," a calm male voice suggested from the doorway.

Sarah turned her head, eyes widening at the sight of Alex standing in the open door. With careful deliberation he shut the door behind him and walked into the room. Caroline stood looking at him with narrowed eyes, her arms crossed over her chest.

"Do not think you can scare me," she warned him.

"I have no intention of doing so." Alex stood a few feet away from her, his face devoid of expression. "I would like to know why you are in my wife's room, though."

"How can you ask such a question?" Caroline demanded. "Have you no honor?"

"I have done nothing to be ashamed of," Alex asserted dryly. "You, on the other hand, have behaved atrociously to my wife. That I will not allow."

"She is my cousin." Caroline straightened her shoulders, moving her hands to her hips. "What is said between us is not for an outsider."

"On the contrary," Alex insisted quietly. "What you say to Sarah, you say to me."

"Fine," Caroline spat. "I think the two of you are horrible."

Alex inclined his head slightly. "There was no formal agreement between you and me."

"It was understood. Do you think I would have come to this godforsaken place otherwise?"

"We would never have suited." Alex walked over to Sarah and offered her his hand. She took it gratefully, standing up with the glass in her hand. He took it from her before leading her to a chair. "Sit down, my love."

"How touching," Caroline sneered. "I suppose you would have me believe you love Sarah."

Alex dropped the glass shards in the ash bucket beside the fireplace. He turned and looked at Caroline. "Yes," he said quietly. "I do love Sarah."

"That is impossible," Caroline scoffed. "She is too old for marriage. You may have dressed her in a fine gown, but that will not last long. Sarah will never give you an heir or be a proper Marchioness."

Sarah looked down at her trembling hands and clasped them together. She feared that Caroline spoke the truth and as much as it hurt to hear, perhaps Alex would see sense.

"Sarah is exactly the wife I want," Alex stated firmly. "I am sorry that you are hurt by our marriage, but in time I am certain you will see that it is the best possible solution for all of us."

"How do you know what is best for me?" Caroline shrieked. "I did not ask you to interfere in my life."

"It was my life, too. I am sure you will make some lucky man a perfect wife, but not me." Alex clasped his hands behind his back and looked directly at Caroline. "I need a wife who loves Caldern, who wants to live here for the rest of her life, and help me rebuild the estate. Above all, I need someone I can love and who loves me. Sarah is that woman."

Caroline seemed to be at a loss of words and stood staring at him. When she had composed herself, she turned to Sarah. "You have not heard the last of this. Jack is here and he will stand by me."

"Your brother Jack demanded that Sarah and I marry," Alex informed her gently. "He gave Sarah away."

Caroline clenched her hands. "Jack always was on your side," she spat at Sarah.

"No one meant to hurt you. Please believe me," Sarah begged. She half rose from her chair, but sat back down when she saw the flash of venom in Caroline's eyes.

"You will not win," Caroline promised. She turned on her heel and flounced out. The deafening slam of the door echoed through the room.

"That went well," Alex muttered, turning back to Sarah. "I hope she was not too harsh with you before I came in."

Sarah felt numb. Caroline's tirade had been worse than she had expected, and yet she understood it. All of Caroline's plans had been ruined by her marriage. Guilt threatened to overwhelm her as Caroline's accusations repeated themselves in her head.

"You have not done her any harm," Alex said quietly.

"How can you say that?" Sarah retorted angrily. "I have robbed her of a husband."

"No," Alex insisted, taking quick strides to where she sat. "She will find another victim soon enough. Besides, I would never have married her."

Sarah shook her head and looked away. "You had every intention of marrying her only a few short weeks ago."

Alex sighed heavily. "I did not know you then."

"That does not make it right." Sarah leaned back

in the chair. "How could I have let such a thing happen?"

"You did not do it alone," Alex interjected ruefully.

"I should never have let you near me," Sarah continued. "I knew how Caroline felt and still I stole a few hours of pleasure for myself. I never dreamed it would end like this."

"You are not to blame." Alex sat down beside her and took her hand in his. "Once I realized I loved you, nothing could stop me."

"There is still time to correct it."

Alex tilted his head at her. "What are you suggesting?"

Sarah took a deep breath and straightened up in the chair. "We should annul the marriage."

"Why?" Alex's voice was devoid of emotion and Sarah shivered at its coldness.

"It would solve everything," she explained hesitantly. "Caroline would not create a scandal about being jilted and you would get the wife you need."

"And you would be free," Alex added.

Sarah nodded her head. Her stomach sank at the cold glare Alex gave her and she looked down at her hands. She knew that he would be angry, but she could not allow herself to be tied to a marriage.

Alex leaned back in his chair and crossed his legs. "Is it me, or marriage you fear?"

Sarah looked up quickly. "I cannot be married," she insisted. "I will not allow any man to have control over me. Not even you."

"So it has nothing to do with me personally," Alex surmised quietly.

"Try to understand," Sarah begged.

"I understand." Alex laughed bitterly and stood up. "You are unwilling to trust in our love."

"I cannot."

"Trust or love?" Alex asked mockingly.

Sarah's heart sank and she bit her lip. Alex's coldness was almost more than she could stand. She loved him desperately, but she could not give him what he asked. Every nerve in her body ached for him, but her head would not allow her to risk it.

"You cannot hide from life forever." Alex walked over to the window and pushed back the drape. "There is a whole world waiting for you. Hiding will not change that."

"I am not hiding," Sarah insisted.

"You are denying yourself your dreams," Alex countered. He let the curtain drop shut and walked over to her chair, leaning on the arms so that his face was inches away from her.

Sarah leaned back, but Alex followed. "What dreams?" she asked hesitantly.

"Children."

Sarah's heart stopped and then started beating furiously. The world seemed to spin for a split second and she put her hand to her head to steady it. How had he guessed? She had never admitted to anyone, let alone herself how much the loss of her baby had devastated her.

Alex's expression softened. "I know your secrets." Alex brushed her hair away from her face and kissed her on the forehead gently. "I love you."

"I have learned to live without children," she insisted.

"There is no need," Alex countered huskily. "Even as we speak you may have conceived our child. Do not condemn me to a life without children, a life without you. Let me take care of you."

Alex knelt down beside her and gathered her face in his hands. "Let me love you," he whispered.

His eyes had softened to a warm silver gray, hypnotic in their intensity. Before Sarah could protest, he had captured her lips.

Soft and inviting, Alex coaxed her body to melt as his tongue brushed the seam of her lips. Sarah could not resist his gentle onslaught. With the ease of taking a breath, she opened for him. Nothing was hurried about Alex's exploration. His tongue caressed hers with slow, seductive strokes, sending a flare of heat to every nerve.

A quiver of desire flooded Sarah, her body enthralled by Alex's touch. All thoughts of resistance were forgotten when his teeth nipped at her engorged lower lip before soothing it with his tongue. His fingers fluttered against her face as he pulled his lips away. Alex gazed down at her, his eyes burning with such intense love that it shook Sarah to her very core.

He waited, his breathing ragged, his eyes never wavering from hers. Sarah knew that she should move away, but her body refused. Desire pounded in her veins, she shuddered with a need for fulfillment. Instinctively she leaned closer.

Strong arms encircled her and pulled her from the chair. Alex held her high against his chest, his heart beating in unison with hers. The air was electric with excitement. Sarah's breath caught in her throat, her body pulsed in anticipation. With careful, deliberate movements, Alex let her slide down the full length of him, until her knees rested against the floor.

He captured her lips again, this time demanding and insistent. The touch and smell of Alex vibrated throughout her being. His lips devoured her hungrily. A surge of pleasure twisted deep within Sarah as she responded to his urgency. Her tongue dueled with his, feasting on the taste of him, delighting as each thrust of their tongues sent their passion spiraling higher.

Her body shook with need, moving restlessly against him. Alex's arms tightened, bringing her closer. She shivered as his hands moved across her back, massaging and kneading until every inch danced with awareness. Only then did he move lower, pressing her buttocks firmly against his hardened shaft.

His hips moved rhythmically against her, simulating the mating that their bodies craved. Alex began to rain feverish kisses across her neck. His lips and teeth pulled at her bodice until one of her breasts was freed. His hot, wet tongue washed across her nipple and Sarah gasped as a quiver of ecstasy cascaded through her.

Her body burned. The heat of their passion was all consuming. There was no room for thought, only feeling. Sarah surrendered, throwing her head back and giving Alex complete access. His tongue flicked across her hardened nipple, teasing and licking until she sobbed with need. Only then did Alex relent and capture it with his mouth.

Sarah clutched at Alex's arms, silently begging him to give her release. Instead he lifted his head. The cool air of the room on her exposed skin sent a shiver through her, but before she had a chance to move, Alex was nudging at her other breast. Once it was free from her bodice, he repeated his slow ravishment.

Sarah's body shook as tremor upon tremor of sensation washed over her. Alex was relentless, overwhelming her with his lovemaking. It was insanity, but she was helpless to stop him. Her body was weak with yearning as the sweet ache for Alex enveloped her. Suddenly, he lifted his head. Sarah struggled to pull him back, but he resisted.

"We are meant to be one." Alex's voice was husky, his words coming in gasps. "Do not deny me."

A shiver of warning raced up her spine. Sarah fought her way back from the fog of desire that clouded her head. Her body still craved Alex's touch, but her protective shell had been honed by years of experience and pain. She could not let Alex make her his wife.

Sarah shuddered and pushed away. Alex was too smooth. He had tried to seduce her with kisses when his words failed. How could she trust a man who had forced her into a marriage she did not want? Even her love could not blind her to his betrayal.

"No." Sarah stood up, grimacing as her legs wobbled. She took a deep breath and straightened her bodice. "This is not what I want."

Alex leaned back, his hands clenched, his face expressionless. "It is," he insisted wearily. "You love me. You cannot deny that."

"I did not ask for marriage," Sarah cried indignantly. "You had no right to force me."

"It was the only option you left me. You would not listen to reason or love."

"I do not want a man controlling my life." Sarah stumbled away from Alex. She needed distance to think. His nearness chased all rational thoughts away.

"No one plans this, Sarah." Alex ran his hand through his hair distractedly and stood up. "We have been given a gift. You cannot throw it away."

"I cannot allow you to consummate our marriage."

"Why?" Alex demanded incredulously, his eyes widening in astonishment.

"It is the only way," Sarah explained hesitantly. "For the marriage to be annulled."

Seconds of silence passed and Sarah clutched her fingers nervously. Alex stared at her in disbelief. "I do not want an annulment," he stated firmly, gazing at her with unblinking eyes. "You are my wife. I will give you time to become accustomed to your new role. Good evening."

Alex walked to the door that adjoined his bedchamber to hers. He opened the door and glanced back at her. "Understand that I am not a patient man," he bit out before slamming the door behind him.

Sarah stared at the closed door for several seconds before collapsing onto her bed in tears. Nothing was happening as she planned. She had hoped to convince Alex to release her from the marriage. Instead, she had angered and frustrated him.

His parting look had sent shivers of doubt throughout her. Despite his harsh tone, he had looked at her with love. Stephen would never have given her time to think. He would have insisted that she do what he asked, even if he had to use force.

Sarah moaned with indecision. What if Alex was right? Was she being a fool to throw away the gift of their love? Perhaps she could learn to trust him. Even though he had insisted that they marry, it was the honorable thing to do.

Sarah closed her eyes and remembered the previous night. She had felt safe in Alex's arms. Perhaps that was the answer she was searching for, but would Alex forgive her? Had she ruined any chance they had of being happy?

Sarah shook her head and sat up. There was no point in trying to reason right now. She had not slept the previous night and she was exhausted.

Her mind was fuzzy and nothing seemed to make
sense. She needed sleep. She quickly undressed
and climbed into bed. Morning was soon enough
to make a decision.

Chapter 25

Alex slammed the book shut and put his head in his hands. What a mess! With a moan, he rubbed his sleep-weary eyes with the heel of his hand. He had spent the night in the library and now that the sun was rising on the horizon, he still had no answers. Somehow he had to make Sarah see reason.

A loud knock at the door shook him from his reverie. He shouted, "Come."

David entered the room. He was dressed in a brown riding jacket and breeches, his riding crop and hat in his free hand. He quickly glanced around and then grinned at Alex. "I did not expect to find you here. You must be losing your touch."

Alex's lip twitched appreciatively. He could always count on David to bring him back to earth. With a sigh, Alex heaved himself from behind his desk. "Do not ask me to explain."

David raised his hand. "I would never think of it," he reassured. "I was on my way to the stables, hoping to catch an early morning ride before that brother of yours descends from his room."

"I assume you mean Bryan." David and Bryan

had been competing with each other in the past weeks, each daring the other to greater feats to impress Lady Caroline.

David nodded his head. "Lord Bryan has been persistent in his attempts to race me, both with the horses and the ladies."

"The field is clear now." Alex sat in one of the reading chairs by the fire. "I made certain of it."

David sat opposite him, putting his crop and hat on the table beside him. He looked down at his hands and then up at Alex. "You did surprise me with your announcement last night. I had no idea you were interested in Mrs. Wellsley."

Alex slanted his head at his friend and grinned sheepishly. "I was not certain myself until this week."

"She is a very beautiful woman," David commented quietly. "I had no idea."

"She takes my breath away," Alex admitted.

David nodded his head. "I do have a slight problem, though. I had always expected to attend your wedding."

"Everything happened so fast," Alex apologized. "I did not even think."

"Why the rush?"

Alex leaned back in his chair and looked at his friend through half-closed eyes. He had never had secrets from David before. He could trust him and right now he needed someone to talk to.

"I had to marry Sarah before she had a chance to run away."

David's eyes widened and he whistled softly. "That might make things a trifle difficult."

"Just slightly," Alex agreed dryly. "Sarah does not wish to be married."

David cleared his throat. "I have never known you to force a woman before."

Alex waved his hand dismissively. "The only thing I forced on her was marriage."

"Why?"

"Because I love her and before you ask, she loves me too."

David lifted his eyebrow. "Then what is the problem?"

Alex sighed. "She had a horrible first marriage and nothing I say or do can convince her that this time will be different."

"Maybe you remind her of her first husband," David reasoned.

Alex's chest tightened in anger. "I am nothing like that bastard. He was abusive and restrictive."

"What do you call compelling her to marry you?"

"It is not the same," Alex insisted vehemently. "I love her. I am not afraid to admit it, or to show it. Besides, marriage is necessary and if she would just trust me, she would see I am right."

"Sounds a bit forceful and controlling to me," David suggested gently. "Why not give her time to adjust to the thought of marriage."

Alex sighed. "Sarah thinks that a husband would treat her like his property, preventing her from continuing with her herbs and healing. The only way I can prove she is wrong is to marry her."

David rubbed his hand across his mouth, his eyes narrowing as he considered his friend. "Are you certain you will be able to give her that freedom?"

Alex inhaled deeply. "I have to."

"I wish you luck." David stood up. "I have never seen you this crazy before."

"I have never truly loved before," Alex confessed quietly. "I will give Sarah the time she needs to adjust to marriage."

David picked up his riding crop and gloves. "I am off, then."

"Wait." Alex stood. "I will walk out with you."

David raised one eyebrow questioningly. "Perhaps you should reassure your wife."

"She needs her sleep." Alex ushered David out. The slam of the library door and the clapping of their boots on the wooden hallway floor followed them out of the house.

"Are you riding?" David asked as he put his hat on.

Alex shook his head and glanced in the direction of the lake. "Bryan has been reminding me for days to check out the ice storage at the lake."

"What is wrong with it?"

Alex shrugged his shoulders. "The same as everything else on this estate. Neglect."

David chuckled. "Now is the time to repair it."

"That is what Bryan keeps reminding me," Alex explained dryly. "He is lost without his summer ices."

"Ride with me," David suggested suddenly. "We can look at the ice storage afterwards. I will wait while you change."

Alex considered David's invitation for a few seconds and then shook his head. "No. I need the time alone."

"I understand," David slapped Alex on the back before turning in the direction of the stables. "I will meet you at the lake after my ride."

Alex watched David until he disappeared around the corner and then he glanced at the sky, streaked with soft billowy clouds backlit by the rising sun. He inhaled deeply and started in the direction of the lake. The day promised to be hot. There was no better time to check on the underground ice storage than now.

The pathway to the lake had been pruned back by the gardeners and Alex walked through the dew-ladened grass quickly. He shook his head at the changed landscape. More than the appearance of Caldern had changed, Alex admitted wryly.

For the first time in years he had a sense of hope. Sarah had given him that. She had restored the dreams he had abandoned when he had left Caldern as a boy. With her by his side, he knew that he could face anything. A sharp stab of doubt gripped his gut and he almost stumbled.

What if Sarah refused to give him a chance to make her happy? The thought of living without her was unbearable. Somehow he must convince her. If that meant not consummating the marriage until she was ready, then he would live with that.

He came to an opening in the woods and beyond was the lake. It glistened, reflecting the reddish glow of the early morning sun. Memories of his time here with Sarah flooded him, almost paralyzing in their intensity. This was where he had first seen her, where she had captured his heart and given him back his life.

Alex clenched his jaw tightly. He must focus all of his energies on convincing her to stay. He would examine the ice storage quickly and then return to his wife's side.

With quick footsteps he walked around the outer edge of the lake, toward the far shore. This was where the underground ice storage had been built nearly a century earlier. In the winter months, ice was cut from the lake and moved underground, where it was stored. The insulation of straw and the coolness of the stone cavern usually kept the ice into the fall months.

Evergreen trees provided shade cover and hid the cavern entrance from view. Alex ducked under the lower branches of the trees and walked down a small stone wall, built into the hillside. The wall was now completely covered with dirt and moss.

When he reached the bottom there was a large hole in the side of the hill. Alex walked in a few feet and pulled open the heavy wooden door that guarded the entranceway. Darkness greeted him. He felt around on the shelf above the door for the candles, flint, and tinderbox. Nothing.

Silently Alex cursed and walked back outside. There was no point in looking without light. He would have to return to the house. He walked back up the small incline and out to the lake. He turned to the house when something caught his eye, the grass-covered domed roof of the underground ice storage.

There was a hatch in the dome that allowed the ice to be moved from the lake to the storage house easily. This opening would provide enough light for him to see inside, he reasoned happily. It would also save him the walk back to the house.

Alex started to walk up the side of the dome when a distant noise disturbed him. He paused and looked around, but saw nothing. He was within a foot of the hatch and had bent to reach it, when the noise came again. It was a shout.

Alex turned and this time he saw a familiar figure wave and then start running to him. It was Sarah. She seemed anxious and he straightened up, shifting his foot nearer the hatch. A strange cracking noise alerted him to danger. Before he had a chance to move, the earth gave way beneath his feet and he was falling.

Instinct, honed over years of battle, made Alex duck his head to his chest. The hard jolt of the ground crashing into his body reverberated through his shoulder before darkness and unconsciousness enveloped him.

Sarah threw her bedcovers back and grimaced at the glare of the sun. She had spent most of the night at the window seat, drapes pulled back to allow the moonlight to stream in. She still had no answers to her questions. With a groan, she rubbed the sleep from her eyes and pushed herself off the bed.

She walked to the window, reaching up to close the drape and shut out the offending light when she saw someone walking outside. Her window looked out on the southeast side of the house, giving her a view of the gardens and the path to the lake beyond.

Her breath caught in her throat when she realized that it was Alex. She held herself motionless as she watched him saunter through the garden and then head in the direction of the lake. Her heart began to beat furiously and she gripped the curtain tightly in her hand.

Memories of making love at the lake flooded her mind, causing her body to tighten with excitement. Everything had been so right that night. Was she wrong to deny what her body craved?

Sarah turned from the window, nervously biting her lower lip as she considered what to do. If she followed him, then she risked losing everything that she had fought so hard for. She would lose her independence.

After a night spent alone, she had realized that her need for Alex was stronger even than her freedom. Perhaps he was right and she should trust in him. Her only other option was to never see him again.

She shook her head and rushed to the wardrobe door. She pulled out a thin white cotton gown and put it on. With shaking fingers she fastened it and then pulled on some walking boots. She would follow Alex to the lake. Intuitively she knew that all of her questions would be answered there, the place that was special to them.

Sarah raced out of her room, down the stairs, and out the front door. She slowed her pace once she had reached the path to the lake. Doubts began to fill her mind, clutching at all of her old fears. As she neared the lake, her feet had slowed to a crawl.

Sarah clutched her hands at her side, regretting her decision to run after Alex. He would think her a fool. One minute she wanted him and the next she was afraid. Why could she not learn to trust, she wondered in frustration.

The lake was within view now and Sarah took a deep breath. She would face Alex as she had planned. This morning she would decide whether to fight the marriage or risk it. She could not bear another night of indecision.

She stopped at the water's edge and frowned. Alex was nowhere in sight. She raised her hand to her brow, blocking out the sun's bright light, and surveyed the shoreline. A slight movement at the distant edge of the lake made her pause. She squinted her eyes and made out the faint outline of a man.

"Alex," she shouted. He glanced back, but then turned around and walked up a slight hill.

Sarah cupped her hands around her mouth and yelled again. "Alex."

This time he stopped and turned around, looking straight at her. Sarah waved and then started to run toward him. He seemed to smile and then his eyes widened and looked down. He tilted forward, swinging his arms to regain his balance. She watched in horror as he fell backwards, disappearing from sight.

Sarah gasped, her heart pounding wildly as she watched her husband fall through the earth. "Alex," she screamed hysterically.

Silence. Sarah picked up the skirt of her gown and started to run around the lake. She was gasping for breath, sobbing Alex's name and praying for his safety all at once. When she reached the mound where he had stood, she saw a huge gaping hole with half of a wooden frame buried in the side of a mound.

Carefully she edged her way up the hill, noting the protruding stones beneath the surface grass. The ground felt unsteady beneath her feet, so she lay on her stomach and crawled to the opening. She peered over the side of the hole. Darkness greeted her.

"Alex?" she shouted, grimacing when all that came back was the echo of her own voice.

"Alex!" she screamed again, her voice shaking with panic.

Silence. Her stomach churned with fear and she forced back the nausea that threatened to overcome her. Somewhere in that deep cavern Alex lay wounded. He needed her help. She refused to consider the alternative, that he might be dead.

Chapter 26

Sarah backed down from the mound and started to run to Caldern. She needed help. The branches of the trees whipped across her face and hands, but she was oblivious to the pain. She stumbled a couple of times, the rough stones of the shoreline cutting her knees and ripping her gown. She picked herself up and continued.

When she had reached the beginning of the path that led to the house, she started to shout. Her voice was hoarse and she doubted that anyone could hear it between her sobs. Still, she had to try.

She rounded the last bend of the path where a large oak tree stood with a newly repaired bench under it. She paused for a few seconds, bent over, gasping for air. Her hand held her side where a stitch of pain ripped through her. Dazedly she looked up, wondering how she was going to make it to the house.

The sound of hoofbeats behind her gave her a burst of energy. She started shouting and waving her arms frantically in the air. The horse and rider were several hundred yards away, but turned in her direction. It was David Stanton.

"What is the problem?" David galloped to her, his eyes widening as he took in her appearance. "Has someone harmed you?"

Sarah shook her head. "It is Alex," she cried. "He has fallen into a large hole."

"The ice shed," he whispered, looking in the direction of the lake. "We must get help. Climb on."

Sarah took the arm he offered, pulling herself up behind Stanton. She held on tightly to his waist as he took off in the direction of the house.

"He is at the lake," she shouted.

"We will need help to get him out of there," David explained, reining the horse in at the front portico. "Johnson will get the necessary men."

Sarah nodded her understanding. Her body tensed at the delay, but she knew that Mr. Stanton was right. They could not carry Alex by themselves.

"Johnson," Stanton shouted, leaning over to bang the door with his riding crop.

Johnson opened the door almost immediately, his normally impassive face showing outrage. When he saw who was at the door, his expression changed to one of surprise.

"The Marquess has fallen into the underground cavern at the end of the lake. Round up some men and something to carry him on," he ordered curtly. Without waiting for Johnson's reply he hurled his horse away from the house and back toward the lake.

Sarah held on tightly, her head bent and her lips whispering the same words over and over. "Please let him be alive."

It took them a couple of minutes to reach the place where Alex had fallen. David jumped off the horse and reached up for Sarah. When her feet touched the ground she ran over to the large gaping hole in the side of the mound.

"Alex," she shouted again, her voice shaking with fear.

"Down here," came back a faint reply.

"He's alive." A surge of relief rushed through her. The tears she had been holding back flooded her eyes, running down her cheeks. She brought a hand up and wiped them away.

"How do we get in?" David asked impatiently. He had walked around the mound and was now back with his hands on his hips.

Sarah shook her head. "Where is the entrance?" she yelled down to Alex.

"By the evergreens."

Sarah looked up, her eyes scanning the area around them. To the right was a grove of tall fir trees. She pointed to it. "There."

Sarah followed David to the trees, stumbling down the small incline, clutching at the stones to regain her balance. David reached the entranceway first, opening the large door and running inside.

Sarah's eyes took several seconds to adjust to the darkness inside the large cavern. Her nose protested at the damp, musty odor, forcing her to take shallow breaths. The sound of melting ice trickling onto the floor echoed off the stone walls. A stream of light came from the hole in the roof and she followed it to where David was bent over Alex.

She rushed to him, her feet brushing against the damp straw that lay all about the stone floor. He was lying on what looked like a large mound of ice covered by straw. When Sarah knelt down beside him, she realized that most of the ice had already melted, leaving a pile of damp straw to soften his fall.

"How bad is he?" she asked in a wavering voice.

"I am fine," Alex retorted brusquely. He winced at his effort, though.

"I think you have dislocated your shoulder." David was feeling along Alex's body with his hands. "You may also have a few broken ribs."

"It sure as hell feels like it," Alex gasped. "Help me up."

"No." David put his hand on Alex's chest and held him down. "Johnson is sending some men to carry you back to the house."

"Nonsense," Alex protested. "I can walk."

"Not until a doctor sees you," Sarah insisted. "You cannot take a chance."

"I feel like an idiot." Alex struggled to get up, but David continued to restrain him.

"Please Alex," Sarah begged. "You fell almost thirty feet."

Alex looked at Sarah and lay back down. He reached a hand up to her head, brushing a tangled strand of hair away from her face. His thumb brushed her damp cheek. "There is no need to cry."

For some reason, Alex's concern only made Sarah weep more. She had almost lost him and he was worried about her. She struggled unsuccessfully to contain her tears, burying her face in her hands.

Alex drew her down to his side. "I promise not to move," he reassured.

"You could have died," she mumbled into his torn coat.

"But I did not."

"I have never been so frightened," Sarah sobbed. Now that the danger was over, she could not stop the onslaught of emotion.

"Shush," Alex crooned gently. "It is nothing more than a scratch."

Sarah listened to Alex's reassurances, her body relaxing with each passing second. He was safe. That was all that mattered. She gulped in the scent of him, hiccupping now that her tears had finished.

He started to chuckle, but groaned. "It hurts too much to laugh."

Sarah sat up, pushing her hair behind her head. She kissed Alex lightly on his lips and then took a good look at him. His right shoulder was at an odd angle. There were cuts on his face and hands, his clothing was torn and wet with blood and melting ice.

"Mr. Stanton is right," Sarah stated in a calm voice. She was now in control, the healer within taking over. "Your shoulder has been dislocated."

She felt along his side, noticing his wincing at the slight pressure of her hand. She looked up at Mr. Stanton. Their eyes met and he nodded slightly. The broken ribs could prove to be serious. She longed to look under his shirt to see if there was any bruising on his chest, but thought it best to wait until he was at home.

The sound of people coming into the cavern forced her to stop her examination. Johnson had sent about ten men and between them, they carried an old wooden door.

"Over here," Mr. Stanton motioned.

The Marquess's groom, Jacobs, led the men across the uneven floor. "What did you go and do now?" he asked with a shake of his head.

"Nothing to be worried about," Alex reassured. "I probably can get back on my own legs, but these two insisted I wait for you."

"Just as well, my lord. Nasty things, falls." Jacobs motioned to the men to lay down the door. "Easy does it, now."

Sarah stood up to allow the men to lift Alex onto the door. They moved quickly and carefully. Alex winced slightly at the pain, his jaw clenched tightly until he was positioned on the door.

"We'll go as easy as we can," Jacob assured. The men heaved the door up and then moved out of the cavern. Sarah and Mr. Stanton followed behind.

"We will ride ahead to make certain everything is ready," Stanton instructed the men.

He helped Sarah onto the horse and once they were both mounted, he rode back to the house swiftly. Johnson was waiting for them at the front door. They dismounted quickly.

"Has the doctor been sent for?" David handed the horse to a waiting groom.

"Yes, sir. Young Smith found him in the village, so he should be here shortly."

"Good." David escorted Sarah through the doorway. All the servants seemed to be waiting in the hallway.

"The family is in the drawing room. Perhaps you would like to join them, Lady Caldern," Johnson suggested.

It took Sarah a few seconds to realize that she was being addressed. She shook her head. "No. I will wait for the Marquess."

Johnson nodded and brought a chair forward for her to sit on. She sank back into its hard wooden frame gratefully. Her knees ached and when she looked at her hands resting in her lap she almost gasped aloud. They were covered with dirt and blood.

Self-consciously she hid them in the folds of her gown. She had not realized how her appearance must look to the servants. Her hair was falling down her back, her ribbon lost long ago. Her once-white gown was covered with mud and grass stains. It would never be the same.

The sound of a carriage approaching scattered all thoughts of herself from her mind. Within a couple of minutes, the doctor appeared in the doorway.

"Where is the patient?"

"The men are bringing him back from the lake," David Stanton explained. "He looks to have a dislocated shoulder and maybe some broken ribs."

"How the hell did he manage to fall?"

Stanton shook his head and turned to Sarah. "Lady Caldern was there."

Sarah felt her cheeks redden under the surprised glance the doctor gave her. Obviously the news of her marriage had not reached everyone in the village. She forced herself to look at him directly. "I shouted to him from the far side of the lake. He turned to look at me and then just disappeared."

The doctor and Mr. Stanton exchanged guarded looks. David Stanton cleared his throat. "I will check it out."

The doctor nodded and looked out the door. "Here comes my patient now."

Sarah rushed to the doorway and would have run to meet Alex, but David Stanton grabbed her arm. "It is best to wait here."

Sarah moved back into the hallway. Several minutes later the men brought Alex in. His face was set in a tight grimace and there was sweat on his brow. Sarah choked back her tears. It would not help Alex to see her crying.

She went to his side and held his hand. He opened his eyes, smiling faintly. "It would have been easier to walk."

"Nonsense," Dr. Caruthers disagreed briskly.

"Until I have seen what the damage is, you should not be moving."

"And the doctor is always right," Alex replied dryly.

Dr. Caruthers grinned. "Most times. Up to his room, lads."

Alex was led toward the stairs and Sarah was forced to move away to give the men space. She refused to leave Alex, though, and followed closely behind. Hobson was waiting in the room, the bed sheets pulled back and ready. Once Alex was settled the men left. The doctor took his coat off.

He turned to Hobson and Sarah. "If you would be good enough to leave."

"No," Alex panted from the bed. "My wife stays."

The doctor hesitated for a second before nodding his agreement. Hobson bowed himself out of the room, closing the door quietly behind him.

The doctor handed Sarah a small knife. "Please remove Lord Caldern's coat."

David Stanton had closed the door and was now standing by the doctor. "Will you need me?"

Dr. Caruthers nodded. "It will take both of us to put the shoulder back in place."

Sarah's breath caught in her throat and she had to force herself to breathe. She had been present at a number of cases involving a dislocated shoulder and she knew how painful it was. She gripped the knife in her hand tightly.

Alex must have sensed her distress, because he clasped her hand. "I will be fine."

Sarah bit her lip and nodded. The best way for her to help Alex was to be strong. She picked up the end of his jacket and started to cut it away from his body. Sarah winced when Alex's chest was exposed. There were cuts and bruises scattered all over his upper body.

The doctor examined Alex quickly, his hands moving expertly over his chest and back. Alex's jaw was clamped tight and his sharp inhale of breath was the only clue to the pain he was in.

The doctor stood back and opened his bag. He measured a few drops from a small bottle of laudanum and poured it into a glass of water. "For the pain, my lord."

Alex grunted and threw back the liquid. "Do it quickly," he ordered.

"You also have two broken ribs," the doctor explained. "I will bandage those after your shoulder is in place. Then it is just a matter of time until it heals." Dr. Caruthers turned to Sarah. "Lady Caldern, would you prepare some bandages?"

Sarah hesitated for a second, but Alex nodded for her to go, so she left the room. She found that most of the servants were waiting in the hall outside the room. Sarah saw Mrs. White, the housekeeper, and went to her.

"We need linen for bandages."

"Aye, my lady," she agreed. "I had Lucy go and fetch some. How is his lordship?"

Sarah sighed and leaned against the wall. "He has two broken ribs and a dislocated shoulder," she explained. "The doctor says he will be fine."

Sarah smiled at the murmur of relief from the servants. Alex's stay at Caldern had only strengthened their respect for him. They had expected him to take care of Caldern and he had not disappointed them. Sarah wished she could be as trusting.

"Thank goodness," Mrs. White declared in heartfelt relief. "Here is Lucy, now."

Sarah took the bandages and reentered the room. Alex was sitting up against his headboard with the doctor and Mr. Stanton on either side of him. His face was pale and his eyes closed, but when she entered, he opened them and smiled wearily.

"Bring the bandages here," the doctor commanded.

Sarah stood at the bed and watched as the doctor wrapped his ribs first and then secured Alex's arm to his side. "This should heal in a few weeks, but you need to have care with the wrappings."

Sarah took the excess cloth from the doctor and placed it on the table near the bed. She knew from past experience that Alex would be in pain for several weeks, but as long as there were no complications, he should heal totally.

"Now you need rest," the doctor insisted as he shrugged into his coat. "The laudanum should help you sleep. I will check in with you later this evening."

"Thank you," Alex murmured.

The doctor left the room, leaving an eerie silence in his wake. The laudanum had started to work on Alex. His eyes only flickered when Sarah eased him onto the pillows and pulled the covers up to his shoulder. She sank down onto the bed and brushed Alex's hair back from his forehead.

David Stanton, who had moved to the window, cleared his throat. "I must go and see Nathan," he announced. "We will have a closer look at the lake."

Sarah sighed and looked up from Alex. "Do you think that someone tampered with it?"

Stanton seemed to hesitate before he nodded his head. "There have been too many unexplained accidents."

"I know."

"It would be best if we restricted who visits Alex until he is better. With your permission I will discuss this with Hobson."

"Yes," Sarah agreed. She turned her attention

back to Alex, noting his steady even breathing. He would be in severe pain for a couple of days, but the worst was probably over now.

David Stanton walked over to the bed. "I have known Alex most of my life," he murmured. "I have trusted him with my life and he has never failed me."

Sarah closed her eyes briefly. "He has spoken to you," she guessed.

"Alex loves you. Everything he has done has been because of that."

"I know," Sarah whispered. "Loving each other is not the problem."

"Can you truly love without trust?" Stanton asked quietly. He did not wait for a reply, but turned and left the room.

Sarah felt the tears fill her eyes and this time she did not try to stop them. She had almost lost Alex. All of her doubts and distrust seemed foolish in comparison. She was deceiving herself if she believed that she would be able to walk away from him.

Today she had realized that she needed him, just as she needed air to breathe. He was vital to her very existence. She felt the wall she had built around her heart start to crack and the floodgates of her love break free. She lay her head in her hands and let the tears cleanse her fears.

When she had finished, she sat up and wiped her eyes. Alex was a man worth trusting. Her marriage would have struggles, but she would trust in their love to work through them. She embraced her newfound lightness, letting love fill her soul and set her free.

Chapter 27

"Anything interesting?" a familiar voice asked from the doorway.

Alex sighed and threw his book down on the bed. "It has been three days. When are you going to let me out of this room?"

"The doctor says that you can move around," David Stanton advised with a slight grin. "Is that not enough?"

Alex threw his covers back. "Very amusing." He pushed himself to the edge of the bed. "Have you ever been confined to a small space?"

"No, but you should be used to it after years in the navy."

"That is why I hate it." Alex walked over to the window.

"It is for your own good."

"That is what you and Hobson keep telling me, but somehow I doubt it. My shoulder feels fine."

"And the ribs?" David Stanton picked up the book Alex had thrown on the bed.

"They still hurt a bit, but nothing unexpected."

"*Gerard's Herbal?*" David asked with a raised eyebrow. "When did you become interested in herbs?"

"I found it here this morning." Alex turned away from the window. "Sarah must have left it behind. Reading it is probably the closest I am going to get to her."

"She is worried about you." David put the book on the table and pulled out a chair to sit on. "She relieves Hobson in the evenings when you are asleep."

"After the laudanum has taken effect," Alex murmured dryly, glancing at the connecting door between his and Sarah's rooms. "The sooner I can leave this room, the better."

"It is safer if you separate yourself from the family. Even Sarah agrees. That is why she has stayed away. She does not want anyone to think that you are well enough to have visitors."

"It is unnecessary." Alex started to pace the room, his hands clenched at his side.

"There have been too many accidents."

"Keeping me confined to quarters is not going to help."

A knock at the door prevented further conversation. David motioned for Alex to return to bed. He walked to the door and opened it hesitantly. With a slight chuckle, he opened it wide.

"Next time announce yourself." David ushered Nathan Carter into the room.

Alex leaned back on his pillows. "The prodigal returns."

"I have only been gone a couple of days," Nathan protested. "I expected to find you enjoying your newly married state, not confined to a sick bed."

"I can thank David's over-cautious nature for that." Alex threw back his covers and left the bed, walking to the window. "He seems to think someone means me harm."

"Perhaps they do," Nathan murmured quietly.

Alex, who had been looking out the window, felt his chest constrict at the seriousness of Nathan's tone. He turned around and looked at his brother, noting the grim look on his face.

"I went to Carlisle after your wedding," Nathan explained. "I met with the family solicitor, MacBain."

"Well?" Alex demanded impatiently.

"I will not bore you with my business discussion, but he did enlighten me about Douglas." Nathan paused for a second, his eyes scanning past David and resting on his brother. "Douglas had decided to marry Miss Tremayne before he returned to Caldern."

"That does not prove foul play." Alex tried to relax the tension that held his body in a vice. He sensed that Nathan had further news.

"Douglas had also given up drinking." Nathan moved into the room and leaned back against the bedpost, his arms crossed over his chest. "His marriage was to be a love match. Apparently he had met Lila Tremayne in London several years ago. She had insisted that until he changed his lifestyle she would not commit to him."

Alex shut his eyes and took a deep breath. As much as he loved Caldern he would not have wanted to inherit it at the expense of his brother.

"Continue," Alex insisted in a low voice. He needed to hear the rest.

"Douglas stopped his drinking and his gambling at least two years before he inherited Caldern. It seems the only thing he continued of his old life was his horses."

"That still does not prove murder," David Stanton interjected.

"I agree." Nathan uncrossed his arms and rubbed the back of his neck impatiently. "But you can no longer believe the story that he fell off his horse drunk."

"Maybe he was celebrating his engagement," Alex suggested. "You did say things had been finalized that night."

"That was what I thought, until I spoke with MacBain. The marriage settlement had been signed weeks earlier. For whatever reason he and Miss Tremayne had kept the engagement secret until the day of his death.

"He still might have had an accident."

"True." Nathan leaned his head back against the wooden bedpost and shut his eyes. "We will probably never know what happened, but we do know what has been occurring to you."

David Stanton cleared his throat. "That is what I have been trying to tell Alex. He needs to be careful."

Alex turned back to the window and gazed out at the sun-drenched flower gardens. A timid rabbit peeked from beneath the shrubbery and then dashed across the lawn to the safety of the woods. Alex silently cheered. Jenkins, his gamekeeper, would not have been so generous.

He turned back to the muted light of the bedroom. "What shall we do?"

"You refused to have us accompany you before," David reminded him. "I think you must now accept it."

Alex tried to ease his tension by flexing his shoulders. He winced at the pain that traveled down his arm. It was one more reminder of what was at stake. He could no longer deny the problem.

"What about the ice storage?" he asked with a lifted eyebrow. "That could not have been planned."

"That hatch had been deliberately sawn through," David stated quietly.

"What?" Alex's voice rose in surprise. "Why did you not tell me before?"

"You needed to recover from your injuries." David rubbed his nose, his voice mildly defensive. "You were in no condition to deal with it. After the doctor had finished fixing you up, I went back and checked out the area. There is no doubt that someone planned it."

Alex sat down, putting his head in his free hand. "That is why there were no candles," he murmured to himself.

"Candles?"

"There are always candles and a tinderbox with flints at the entranceway," Nathan interjected. "I expect whoever planned the accident took them away so that Alex would have no other choice but to open the hatch."

"Exactly," Alex agreed with a groan. "And I fell right into their plan."

"You could not have known," Nathan said with a shrug.

"Can you be certain it was deliberate?" Alex asked, his voice now strong with determination.

"The hatch was sitting on the frame by less than an inch of wood. All of the hinges had been removed and the surrounding area of grass had been lifted."

"For what purpose?"

"I suspect they had loosened the mortar that was holding the domed roof of the cavern in place," David suggested with a shrug of his shoulders.

"It would be quite simple to work their way back from the hatch, making it impossible for anyone to see the weakened condition until actually stepping on it," Nathan finished with a small whistle. "Brilliant."

"What they did not count on was the buildup of wet straw below the hatch."

"Or me being able to protect my body as I fell," Alex added dryly. "Very nearly a perfect accidental death."

"Except you survived," Nathan murmured.

"And more than once." David began to pace around the room. "That is what concerns me."

Alex raised an eyebrow. "I would have thought that was the least of our problems."

David waved aside Alex's words. "Your survival must be angering whoever is doing this. That means they will become less cautious."

"And less fearful of being caught," Nathan added. "We have to find out who is responsible before any more attempts are made."

"You have made certain that no one can come near me," Alex observed sarcastically. "That should end the attempts for the time being."

Nathan looked down at his feet, his lips pursed. He glanced over at David and then to the floor again. Alex noted the hesitancy in his brother's manner. There was something that they were keeping hidden from him.

"What?" he demanded harshly.

Nathan looked up at him. "It may be unimportant."

"But it is something that concerns you," Alex guessed. "I need to know."

"I found it strange that Douglas should die the very night he announced his engagement."

Alex stared at his brother for a few seconds, his brain refusing to understand the meaning of his words. What possible connection could Douglas's engagement have to him?

"Sarah," he whispered, fear clenching his heart.

Nathan nodded. "You have done more than become engaged. You are now married and that would be a threat."

David frowned. "I think Sarah is safe," he assured. "The whole household probably knows that Alex spent his wedding night alone."

Alex had thought that he was past the age of embarrassment until his brother looked at him with open amusement. He leaned back in the chair and forced himself to swallow. Nathan would never let him forget this.

"Not a very auspicious beginning, little brother." Nathan grinned broadly.

"There were reasons," Alex growled.

"I can only imagine," Nathan teased.

"The important thing is that Sarah should be safe," David reasoned.

"Because there is no chance that she could produce an heir," Nathan added.

Alex's heart sank again. Even though they had not consummated the marriage, there was still the chance that Sarah might be pregnant. The perpetrator might even deduce that, given the circumstances of their marriage.

"We must find the culprit." Alex stood up and went to his wardrobe. "Help me dress."

"You are not leaving." David blocked Alex's way. "Nathan and I will take care of it."

"I will not sit back and allow this person to destroy my family." Alex pushed David out of the way and went into the dressing room. He came back out with some breeches, a shirt and jacket.

"Everything is fine as long as you stay put," David insisted.

Alex shook his head. "This person will go after Sarah."

"Why?"

Alex sat on the bed and pulled on his trousers. "There are numerous reasons," he insisted. "The first is that it is the surest way to get me to leave my room. The second is that they may surmise that Sarah may be pregnant, despite the wedding night."

Nathan nodded his head. "You are right, of course."

"I do not understand." David helped Alex remove his arm sling and then held out his shirt for him.

"People will assume that there was a reason for the speed of the marriage," Nathan explained.

Alex winced as he slid the shirt over his arm. "I will not chance Sarah's life. Where is she?"

"She is safe," David reassured. "She has stayed away from the family and is spending most of her time in the sewing room."

"We need to find out who is trying to kill you." Nathan stooped and helped his brother pull on his Hessians. "God, these are tight."

"Hobson usually helps." Alex eased into a brown riding jacket. It was less snug than his other coats. "Let's find Bryan."

"Why him?" Nathan stood up.

"He was the one who insisted that I look at the ice storage."

"How long ago was that?"

"Day before the accident."

"You thought he was responsible for the saddle being cut also," Nathan mused.

"I thought it was a prank," Alex added as he tied a quick knot in his cravat. It was not perfect, but at least he would look presentable.

"Not when you consider everything else," David observed. "Bryan is the logical one. He is the only one who gains by your death."

"Yours and Douglas's death," Nathan added grimly.

Alex only nodded. The sooner he found out who was responsible for his accidents, the easier he would feel. He had fought many battles during the war and had never felt the deep fear that now gripped him. He could not bear the thought that someone might try to harm Sarah.

He did not believe that Bryan was responsible for the strange accidents, but Alex could not risk it. There was too much at stake now. Bryan must be confronted and, if guilty, stopped.

The three men left the room and headed for the library. It was empty.

"Where else could he be?" David asked.

"The stables," Nathan and Alex replied in unison.

Quickly they left the house, almost running in their eagerness. When they reached the stables, Alex sought out Jacobs.

"My lord," he exclaimed with a smile. "I thought you were in your bed. You're a sight better now than the last time I saw you."

"Thank you for helping with my rescue." Alex patted Jacobs on the back. "We are looking for Lord Bryan. Has he been here?"

Jacobs shook his head. "Strange that one. He hasn't been riding since you took your tumble, my lord."

Alex frowned, but only nodded. "He must be back at the house."

The three men left, waiting until they were out of earshot to speak. "Unusual for Bryan to forgo his daily ride," David commented.

"Very," Alex agreed. "Still he may have his reasons."

They walked into the house and stood in the main hallway. "I will have Johnson find him," Alex decided.

Before he could ring the bell, a voice called from the second floor. "Find who?"

Alex looked up and smiled grimly at his brother. "We were looking for you. I would like to speak to you in the library."

"So serious," Bryan sneered. He sauntered down the stairs and stopped in front of Alex. "I thought you were confined to your room."

"Obviously you were mistaken."

"What do you wish to speak to me about?"

"In the library," Alex instructed coldly. He was in no mood to banter words with his brother. If Bryan were in fact the person responsible for Alex's accidents then he wanted him stopped now.

Bryan tilted his head sideways, started to open his mouth to protest, but hesitated. He shrugged his shoulders and walked into the library.

"Well," he demanded once inside the room.

Alex waited until Nathan and David were in the room before shutting the door. He looked at his brother's bored expression and wondered how much of it was an act.

Alex went over to his desk and leaned against it. Nathan was standing by the library window and David had remained at the door, making it impossible for Bryan to escape.

"I have only one question for you," Alex stated calmly. "Have you been trying to kill me?"

Sarah held the bedsheet away from her. There were jagged rips scattered throughout it, but these paled in comparison to the foot-sized strip of linen missing from the center. No amount of darning could repair this. With a sigh she tossed it onto an already large pile of scrap cloth. At this rate she would be done in a couple of days.

The thought of leaving the sewing room sent a shiver up her back. It was her refuge from the family. She had even stopped taking meals with them. She could not forget that one of them might have tried to kill Alex.

Sarah stretched her arms over her head and stood up. Keeping busy was the only escape she had from worry. Her mind was numb, her stomach in a constant knot that refused to ease, even after the doctor had said Alex would recover fully. Sarah inhaled sharply at the thought of how close she had come to losing the man she loved.

Every night she kept watch over him, measuring his breaths, counting each one a blessing. Sometimes he would murmur her name in his sleep and tears would come to her eyes. How could she have ever doubted him?

A sharp knock at the door brought her back to the present. It must be Daisy with her lunch. She frowned. It seemed as if she had just eaten breakfast.

"Come in." Sarah moved away from the table.

The knock came again and Sarah went to the door and opened it. Her eyes widened in surprise and then she smiled.

"I was not expecting you." She walked back into the room and pulled out a chair. "Sit and visit."

Sarah turned. The sound of a dull thud followed by sharp pain echoed through her head. She gasped as shards of light splintered across her eyes. Sarah opened her mouth to protest, but another blow hit her. She shuddered, falling to her knees. Her last thought before slipping into unconsciousness was that she had to warn Alex.

Chapter 28

"What?" Bryan yelled, his mask of boredom leaving his face instantly. "Are you insane?"

"Hardly," Alex countered. "Someone has been arranging little accidents for me and you seem to be the most logical one."

"I will not listen to this outrageous accusation." Bryan had recovered his composure and started to walk to the door.

"Stop," Alex commanded. "You will stay until this matter is settled."

Lord Bryan turned around. "Who do you think you are?" he snarled. "You have no right to hold me here."

"I have every right," Alex insisted. "You are a guest in my house."

"How dare you?" Bryan sneered. "This is more my house than yours."

"How can you say that?" David's voice rose in outrage. "Alex is the Marquess."

"He ran away," Bryan spat out loudly. "Just like Douglas, both of them cowards."

"Some people would consider you the coward," Nathan defended. "A man unwilling to leave his father's protection."

"That is ridiculous," Bryan snorted. "It took more courage to remain than to leave."

"You stayed because it was easier," Nathan goaded. "Did you think you would be rewarded for your loyalty?"

"Yes," Bryan shouted, his eyes wild with anger. "I should have inherited Caldern. I put up with Father, while the rest of you left."

Alex crossed his arms over his chest. "The estate is entailed."

"Perhaps you thought to increase your chances of inheriting by murdering your brothers?" David Stanton suggested with a sneer.

"No," Bryan denied loudly.

"Then what did you mean by saying Caldern should have been yours?" Nathan asked with a raised eyebrow.

Bryan pulled out a handkerchief and mopped his forehead. "You are twisting my words," he cried.

"Explain," Alex demanded sternly. His brother was visibly upset by their questions, but Alex could not stop now. If Bryan was trying to kill him, he needed to know now.

A shudder seemed to pass through Bryan and he sagged down in one of the leather reading chairs. "I never tried to kill you. You had been gone so long that I just assumed you would not live through the war. When you did survive, it was easy to convince myself that India would be too harsh for you," he confessed with a sob.

Alex closed his eyes briefly. Wishing someone dead and actually doing something about it were two very different sins. "What about my saddle? Did you tamper with it?"

Bryan shook his head. "Why would I need to? No one can win against me."

Alex looked over his shoulder at Nathan who shrugged and shook his head. For whatever reason, Nathan believed Bryan. Alex believed him innocent, too. He did not think Bryan had the nerve to actually plan and execute murder. They would have to look elsewhere for the culprit.

"Did you see anyone near my horse that day?"

Bryan looked up, his lips twisted into a sneer. "Can you not accept that you fell?"

"Easily," Alex agreed with a smile. "If that were the case."

"Someone deliberately cut the strap," David Stanton explained in a mild tone, moving away from the library door. He stopped a couple of feet away from Lord Bryan. "It was not a fair race."

"And you suspect me of being a cheat?" Bryan shouted indignantly. He started up from the chair, but David pushed him down.

Alex almost grinned at his brother's reaction. He seemed more upset at being accused of cheating than of murder. Before he could say anything more, the door was flung open.

"What is going on here?" Lady Caldern's shrill voice demanded.

Alex turned and bowed slightly to his stepmother. "By all means, come in dear Fanny. We were just having a cozy family discussion."

Lady Caldern looked about the room, her eyes narrowing suspiciously. "Your voices were raised. The whole household can hear you."

"Then we will not have to repeat ourselves." Alex moved away from his desk, closing the door before taking Lady Caldern's arm and leading her to a chair. "Please make yourself comfortable."

Lady Caldern pulled the black silk skirt of her gown to one side before sitting. She looked over at Nathan standing at the window. "I will not stay in the same room as that man."

"You will," Alex insisted. His voice had hardened and he glared at his stepmother coldly.

"I am still mistress here."

"That has changed." Alex turned away from Fanny and walked back to his desk. "Have you forgotten my marriage?" he asked without turning around.

"Hardly a marriage," Lady Caldern harrumphed. "Where is your wife now?"

"Safe." Alex smiled as he faced Fanny. He had no intention of letting his stepmother distract him. "We were discussing the strange accidents that have befallen me."

"If you insist on running around the estate on your own then you must expect problems." Lady Caldern folded her hands in her lap.

"Like being shot at?" Nathan moved away from the window. His lips were pursed and he barely looked at Lady Caldern. "What about the roof falling down or a saddle being cut? Are these things Alex should expect?"

"Nonsense." Lady Caldern straightened her shoulders. "I meant that Alex should send workmen to inspect things."

"But Mother," Lord Bryan interrupted. "You asked me to tell Alex to check the ice storage."

Lady Caldern stiffened. "You were not being spoken to, Bryan. Kindly keep quiet."

"Ah, but his observations do interest me," Alex interjected quietly. "Please, continue."

Bryan cleared his throat, his eyes darting nervously from his mother to Alex. "I may have misunderstood what Mother said."

"Perhaps you heard correctly," Alex suggested smoothly. "What made you take a sudden interest in the repair of the estate?"

"I love Caldern."

"But you let it go to ruin while Father was alive." Alex's voice hardened and his jaw clenched tightly as he considered the extent of the neglect.

"I did the best I could," Lady Caldern stated smugly. "If you were so concerned about Caldern then you should have come home to help."

Alex clenched his hands tightly. "Is that why you have tried to make certain Bryan will succeed me?"

Lady Caldern's eyes widened, her mouth opened and shut, but no sound came out. Alex crossed his arms over his chest and watched her dispassionately.

"Are you suggesting I tried to kill you?" Lady Caldern asked finally. "That is preposterous."

"Not only have you tried to kill Alex, but you succeeded with Douglas," Nathan added.

Lady Caldern looked at Nathan and shook her head. "I do not understand what you are talking about. Douglas died of a riding accident. He was drunk."

"Douglas had given up drinking long before he inherited Caldern."

"How would I know?" Lady Caldern defended, her voice rising indignantly. "He locked himself into the library every night. Not so much as a polite good evening to his family. I assumed it was the habit of a drunkard hiding his disgrace."

"You did not have a very pleasant opinion of Douglas." Alex felt a shiver of disgust at his stepmother's callousness. It brought back all his memories of growing up in a cold, uncompromising household.

"Why should I?" she demanded querulously. "Both you and your brother were never good for anything. When you left, it was a blessing. The only regret I have is that both of you came back."

"So you decided to murder us?"

"Never," Lady Caldern defended. "I had no need."

"It would certainly be easier for you if Bryan succeeded to the estate and title."

"Perhaps," Lady Caldern agreed, her lips twisted in a tight smile. "That does not mean I would do anything about it. I am sure there are plenty of people who would like to see you dead."

"I had no idea I was so unpopular." Alex thumped his fingers against his desk, his forehead furrowed in a frown. "Perhaps you could enlighten me?"

"You do not have to look any further than this room," Lady Caldern advised with a shake of her head in Nathan's direction.

"Nathan?" Alex asked incredulously. "Why would he want to harm me?"

"Jealousy."

Alex snorted inelegantly. "Of what?"

"He is older than you," Lady Caldern said with a shrug. "Mayhap he wants to make sure you do not get what should be his."

Alex looked over his shoulder at Nathan who was shaking his head in disbelief. Alex knew deep within his soul that his brother would never harm him. Even though they had been separated for years there was an unbreakable bond between them.

"Nathan would never hurt me," Alex asserted.

"But you believe Bryan would?" Lady Caldern stiffened with displeasure.

"Actually, no," Alex explained with a sigh. "If Bryan had done anything, I was certain it was only meant as a prank."

"There are others in the household. Any one of them might be responsible, but I think it is unlikely." Lady Caldern stood up from her chair. "You have been the victim of a few accidents."

"I wish that were the case. Unfortunately there is evidence that someone has deliberately tampered with my saddle and the roof of the ice cavern."

"Impossible," Lady Caldern stated. "It must be your suspicious nature to think someone wants to see you dead. Or is it a guilty conscience?"

"Neither," Nathan interjected. "I think it would be wise for us to solve this problem now."

"Or what?" Lord Bryan finished with a sneer. It was obvious that he had recovered his composure.

"We will have to bring this matter to the attention of the magistrate and it will become a scandal," Nathan threatened. "I am certain no one wishes that."

Lady Caldern glared at Nathan, her hands clutching at the back of the chair she had just vacated. Nathan's own gaze did not waver from Fanny's face. Alex cleared his throat, forcing the two combatants to look at him.

"I think we can solve this without bringing in outside help."

"How?" David Stanton asked quietly. "It has already gone far enough. If neither of these two are responsible, then you have no other recourse."

Alex felt the knot in his stomach tighten even more. To expose the family to censure was not his wish. All he wanted to do was to stop the accidents and send the culprit away from Caldern. Scandal was not to be tolerated.

He rubbed his hand over his chin, flexing his jaw muscle. "No scandal," he stated firmly. "We will settle this within the family."

"Then send them all packing," David advised with a nod. "It is the only way you can be certain of safety."

"This is outrageous," Lady Caldern cried, shaking a finger at Alex. "It was a sad day when you came home."

"Calm down," Alex instructed coldly. "I have no intention of sending anyone away."

"I should hope not." Lady Caldern straightened her shoulders. "We are your family."

"Family or not," Alex observed dryly. "I will not countenance any more attacks. It has to end."

Lady Caldern opened her mouth to protest, but a commotion outside the library door made her stop. Alex turned to the noise and frowned. It sounded as if the doctor had arrived and was yelling at Johnson.

"Find out the problem, David."

David moved to the door, but before he reached it, it was flung open. A wild-eyed Dr. Caruthers stood there, panting for breath.

"There is smoke coming from the fourth floor."

"Smoke!" Nathan and Alex exclaimed at the same time.

"Where?" Alex asked, pushing away from the desk and moving toward the doctor. Alex's nose did not smell anything, but they were a good distance away.

"The north wing."

"Sarah," he whispered. His chest constricted in horror as he remembered that Sarah was in the sewing room. He pushed past the doctor and started to run up the stairs.

"Wait," Nathan shouted from behind him. "You will need help."

* * *

A throbbing pain seared through Sarah's skull. She groaned and struggled to lift herself. The pounding in her head was excruciating. Her chest felt as if it were on fire. She tried to ease it by inhaling, but acrid smoke filled her lungs. Her body was racked by a coughing spasm. When it was over she lay her head down.

Sarah felt the hardness of the floor under her, but could not remember how she had gotten there. She blinked, trying to focus her eyes, but they refused. Instead, the room spun and black billows of smoke hovered above her, in the distance a blur of flickering orange lights.

Sarah closed her eyes, willing away the image. When she opened them it was the same. Her stomach churned with nausea and she fought the urge to scream. Sarah's heart beat frantically as she tried to stand up. She did not have long before the fire reached her.

She pushed up with her arms, but they gave way and she collapsed back onto the floor. Her body felt as if it were wrapped in yards of rope. The heat of the fire burned her nostrils with each breath. Somehow she must escape. Slowly she pushed her body back a couple of inches. A single thought surfaced. Alex.

She must warn him. Brief images of his beloved face flitted through her mind. Her body shook with a longing to touch him once more. She had to tell him that he was right about their love being all that mattered. Sarah forced herself back another few inches before the blackness of unconsciousness descended.

* * *

Alex was past hearing anything but the frantic beating of his heart. Sarah was in danger, perhaps already hurt, or worse, dead. His mind shied away from that thought as he pushed his way past the servants. Somehow he must reach her before it was too late.

When he reached the fourth floor, he hesitated a second. Smoke had already filled the hallway and he brought his handkerchief out of his pocket to cover his nose and mouth. His eyes watered and his nose twitched with the acrid smell.

"Let me help," Nathan panted from beside him. "You will not be able to carry her out with that shoulder."

Alex nodded and the two raced down the hall to the sewing room, ignoring the sound of footsteps behind them. The room was ablaze by the time they reached it, flames of fire licking up the curtains and consuming the piles of linen that littered the tables and floors.

Alex's eyes watered and he squinted to see through the haze. His chest hurt with the effort of breathing. He coughed and pain shot through his arm and shoulder, but he pushed on. Frantically he moved chairs and tables out of the way. Nathan motioned for him to leave, but he shook his head. Sarah needed his help.

He stumbled further into the room, falling to his knees as he gasped for air. He crawled forward, feeling with his hands, searching desperately for his wife. Nathan grabbed him by the arm.

"She may have got out," he said before coughing racked his body.

"She is here," Alex insisted. "I can sense it."

He went forward a few more feet, now unable to see with his eyes. Every survival instinct within him screamed to leave, to find safety. He ignored it and swept the floor with his hand.

Nathan began to pull him away by his feet, but Alex kicked at him, struggling to inch forward. His hand stretched out, grasping for hope. He caught a piece of fabric and yanked. The fabric did not move.

"I have something," he yelled at Nathan.

Nathan let go of his legs and moved up beside Alex. "Where?"

Alex pulled on the fabric, his other hand patting along its length until he felt skin. His heart leapt in his chest. "It is Sarah," he screamed.

Nathan nodded and moved ahead of Alex, following Alex's arm. The two men pulled together, moving the body slowly toward the opening of the room. When they were within a few feet of the doorway, other hands began to help them in their struggle.

Once in the hallway, they were hustled by a line of servants who were passing buckets of water. They were doing their best to douse the fire before it engulfed the whole house. Alex barely noticed them as he moved past, coughing and gasping for air. Ahead of him, the doctor and David were carrying Sarah.

Her arm hung down limply, its skin black with smoke. Tears of fear and doubt threatened to overcome him. He would never forgive himself if something happened to Sarah because he had forced her to marry him. Alex struggled to stand up, grateful for Nathan's assistance.

"You take care of Sarah," Nathan instructed. "I will stay here and make sure the fire is out."

Alex nodded and followed the men carrying his wife down the stairs. When they reached the second floor they hesitated.

"Take her to my room," Alex shouted, moving ahead to open the door.

The doctor and Stanton hurried into the room, their breathing heavy with the effort of carrying Sarah's lifeless body. They placed her on the bed. David moved away, but the doctor bent over her and put his ear to her nose.

Alex picked up one of her hands and started rubbing it. "Sarah," he pleaded. When there was no response he looked up at the doctor, who shook his head slightly.

"No," Alex denied firmly. "I will not let her die."

Chapter 29

"Get my bag," the doctor directed David Stanton. "It is in the hallway downstairs."

"Why are you waiting?" Alex demanded, frantically rubbing Sarah's hand. "She needs air now."

"I have my tube for artificial respiration in my bag," the doctor explained. He moved Sarah's head back, leaving her neck taut.

Alex pushed the doctor away. "Let me try."

He had seen men revived from drowning before and instinctively he began to work on Sarah in the same way. Often there was no time to search for a tube to put in the nostril. Alex pushed on her stomach, as if expelling water and then closed her mouth and one nostril. He breathed air into the open nostril and then pushed on her stomach to force the air out again.

"What are you doing?" Dr. Caruthers asked forcefully.

"This is how we revived men in the navy."

"I have never seen it done without a tube."

"It is effective," Alex said between breaths. "Time is crucial if she is to recover."

"Breathe," Alex whispered, pushing in Sarah's stomach again when there was no response. Her chest seemed to expand and he pushed again. A sputtering cough was his reward.

"Move," the doctor ordered, pushing Alex out of the way. He put Sarah onto her side and began rubbing her back and pulling the blankets over her.

Alex sagged back against the bedpost; his hands limp at his side. He watched intently as the doctor worked on Sarah, gradually coaxing her to breathe. When her breathing had started to sound more regular Alex crawled up beside her, pushing her hair away from her face.

"Do not leave me," he whispered. Sarah's eyes fluttered and Alex held his breath.

"Someone has hit her on the head," the doctor stated professionally. "I doubt she will be awake for some time."

David Stanton rushed into the room at that moment. "Here it is," he panted, handing a small black bag to the doctor. "Is she alive?"

"Barely," the doctor said curtly, opening his bag with a snap. "I need space. You gentlemen will have to leave."

"I am staying," Alex insisted firmly.

The doctor looked at him, his eyes full of sympathy. "You can do nothing here."

Alex stared at him for a few seconds. Every nerve in his body wanted to stay beside his wife, but he also knew the doctor was right. She was breathing and there was nothing else he could do at this moment, but watch.

Alex nodded his head and stood up from the bed. "Keep her alive," he ordered quietly before leaning down and kissing Sarah on the forehead.

He followed David from the room, shutting the

door behind him firmly. He closed his eyes and leaned his head against the wall. He winced as pain shot through his shoulder.

David cleared his throat and Alex opened his eyes.

"Someone started that fire."

Alex frowned. "Yes," he agreed. "They also meant for Sarah to die."

"You have to find out who is doing this."

"Well I suppose we can take Bryan and Fanny off our list," Alex mumbled with a twisted smile.

"So we have no ideas then." David sighed and rubbed his eyes with his hand. "This makes no sense."

"It is the work of a lunatic," a voice stated from the stairway. Nathan Carter walked toward the two men.

"How is the fire?" Alex moved away from the wall, meeting his brother halfway.

"It is out now." Nathan was covered in black soot, his clothes soaked with water.

Alex gripped his brother's shoulder. "Thank you."

"Why is it the work of a lunatic?" David Stanton asked as he joined the men.

"No one else would try to set fire to the house in broad daylight. Whoever it is, is getting desperate."

"And must have thought Sarah was a risk," Alex mused, looking over his shoulder at his closed bedroom door.

"How is she?"

Alex turned back to Nathan, warmed by the sincere concern in his brother's voice. "She is breathing now. The doctor says she was hit on the head."

Nathan nodded. "She is strong."

"I hope so." Alex's voice broke and he turned away, swallowing back his fear.

The servants rushing down the stairs with their buckets broke the silence in the hall. Alex watched them as if from a distance. His body was numb to everything around him. All he could do was concentrate on Sarah fighting for her life.

He cursed himself for a fool. He should have taken these accidents more seriously. Instead, he had forced Sarah into a marriage that had placed her life in jeopardy. He would never forgive himself if she did not survive.

Johnson, the butler, brought Alex back to the present. He came up the stairs quickly. "My lord," he exclaimed loudly. "You must hurry."

"What is it?" Nathan asked.

"It is Lady Julianna. Curtis, the stable boy, saw her on the roof."

"The roof," Alex repeated.

"She is leaning over the edge."

Alex frowned and glanced at Nathan. Had Julianna been forced to the roof because of the fire? Before he could speak, Lady Caldern and Lord Bryan rushed up the stairs.

"Do something," Lady Caldern demanded.

Alex nodded and made his way up to the fourth floor and then to the roof. Nathan and the others followed. When he reached the outside, he scanned the roof hurriedly. Julianna was nowhere in sight.

"Over there." Nathan pointed toward the front of the house where the parapets had fallen almost a fortnight earlier.

Alex squinted, the sunlight almost blinding in its intensity, and made out the slight figure of his sister. She stood on the furthest end of the damaged section, holding tightly to a broken piece of stone crenellation.

"Julianna," he called.

Julianna turned her head and stared at them for

a second before raising her hand. "Do not come near."

Alex had begun walking toward her, but stopped at her words. "Let us help."

"No one can help now."

"Julianna, come down," Lady Caldern instructed in a stern tone. "Your behavior is unacceptable."

"I can never please you, Mother," Julianna cried.

"No lady of breeding would act in such a manner as you are doing. Come here immediately."

Julianna only shook her head, clinging to the narrow upright parapet. A slight breeze blew her pale yellow skirt outwards, giving her the appearance of a specter. Her hair had fallen to her shoulder, a mass of knotted curls and ribbon.

Alex put his hands on his hips. He had to convince Julianna to come down, but he had no idea what drove her there in the first place. It was obvious that she was angry with Fanny.

"Did you and Julianna have an argument?" he asked, turning to look at Fanny.

"No." Lady Caldern straightened her shoulders and glared at him. "I would never argue with anyone."

Alex clamped his jaw tightly. Frustration and annoyance threatened to overcome his usual calm. Every nerve in his body wanted to be with Sarah and instead he was on the roof.

"This is nonsense," he shouted at his sister. "Get down."

"I understand your anger," Julianna sobbed. "I never wanted to hurt Sarah. She was the only one who ever treated me kindly. I had no choice."

Alex inhaled sharply, staggering backward with the force of Julianna's words. Nathan gripped his good shoulder, steadying him from his shock. Alex had always thought his sister the gentlest of creatures. How could she have possibly started the fire?

"What have you done?" he asked in disbelief.

"It was what Mother wanted," Julianna wailed. "Nothing I do is ever enough, though. She is always asking for more."

Alex's lips whitened with fury. He turned cold accusing eyes on his stepmother. "Explain."

"She is lying," Fanny refuted.

"No, Mother." Julianna's voice raised hysterically, her whole body shaking precariously from its perch. "You said this morning that you wished Sarah were dead. She had ruined everything."

Fanny stared at her daughter in horror, shaking her head in denial. "You cannot have thought I wanted you to kill her."

"Of course," Julianna said in a childlike voice. "I always do what you want."

Alex closed his eyes briefly and threw his head back. His sister's confession pierced his soul. Her efforts to get her mother's approval had led her to attempt murder. Was she responsible for his accidents? Alex walked slowly toward her, stopping about ten feet away.

"Did you also try to hurt me?" Alex asked quietly. Out of the corner of his eye he saw Nathan and Bryan move closer.

"I did not want to," Julianna confessed. "Mother was so upset when you returned to England."

"And Douglas?"

Julianna nodded her head. "He was not nice like you. It was easier."

Alex's stomach turned, nausea threatened briefly, but he forced it back. Later he would be able to digest the full horror of his sister's actions, now he needed to know the truth.

"It must have been difficult to arrange Douglas's death," he suggested in a conversational tone.

"He was easy," Julianna said with pride. Her eyes gleamed with an inner light. "He always took a ride in the evening. I think he went to see Lila," she giggled. "What a surprise she must have had."

Alex cringed inwardly. Lila Tremayne was still trying to recover from her loss. His sister had no concept of the pain she had inflicted. "How did you do it?"

"I waited by the stone fence in the north field. He always went cross-country. It was dusk, so he did not see the board I had put across the fence. It was too high for his horse to jump."

Alex frowned. If his sister had already arranged the fence, why did she wait for Douglas? He inhaled quickly as realization hit him. She wanted to make certain he was dead. "What next?" he demanded softly.

"I had to hit him with a rock a couple of times." Julianna looked down at her clenched hands and shrugged. "He seemed glad to see me at first, but I could not let that sway me. Mother had been most specific. Douglas should not be alive. He did not deserve Caldern."

"And me?"

"Mother hates you," Julianna stated simply. "Even more than Douglas."

"I see."

"She says you have no respect for what is proper." Julianna frowned thoughtfully. "I think you are nice, but I have to do what Mother wants. You understand, Alex."

"Yes." Alex sighed.

As much as Alex abhorred his sister's actions, he knew that she had thought she had no choice. Years of doing as she was told and struggling to please a woman who could only find fault had twisted her mind.

"I suppose I am lucky that you did not lay in wait for me, too."

"But I did." Julianna looked up at him, her brown eyes wide with sincerity. "Sarah was always there, though."

Looking back, Alex realized that Julianna was right. Sarah had always come to his rescue. She was his savior, he realized with a tightening of his heart.

"What about the saddle?" Lord Bryan had moved up beside Alex.

Julianna looked at Bryan, her eyes full of confusion. "Douglas's?" she asked.

"You cut his saddle too," Alex surmised.

Alex could now see the whole event clearly. Alone on a dusky night, Douglas's thoughts focused on meeting the woman he loved, he had not checked his mount. When the horse had gone down, he had been thrown, his saddle cut to make certain he would fall. That is when Julianna had hit him.

"No." Bryan kicked his foot against the roof. Alex put his hand out and touched his arm. Any sudden movement might make Julianna fall.

"Bryan means my saddle," Alex explained in a soothing tone. "The day of the picnic."

"I just wanted Bryan to win." Julianna looked over at her mother. "Remember you said that Alex needed to be taught a lesson?"

Lady Caldern nodded her head slowly. Her eyes had sunken into her head and her whole body seemed to have aged in the short time they had been standing on the roof. Alex felt a twinge of sympathy for Fanny. Julianna's confession was devastating.

"I think we understand now." Alex held his hand out to his sister. "It is time to come down."

Julianna shook her head. "No."

"We are not angry," Alex soothed. "Please take my hand."

"It is Mother," Julianna whispered.

Alex strained to hear his sister's words, moving a couple of feet closer to her. "Your mother is not angry."

Julianna giggled again. "She is happy," she confided. "But I cannot do as she wishes anymore."

"You will not have to."

"I will," Julianna insisted firmly. "There is always something bothering Mother."

"Perhaps we can arrange for you to live away from her?"

"That would be nice." Julianna smiled and seemed to move toward Alex, but hesitated, her face losing all of its animation. "You want to send me away."

"Just away from your mother. You will like living on your own," Alex coaxed. He moved another foot closer, sensing Nathan and Bryan move to either side of him.

"Can I go to London?"

Alex nodded. "Anywhere you want to. Now please come down from there," he pleaded.

Julianna tilted her head. "If you promise."

Alex nodded, holding his breath as he watched Julianna make a small step toward him. She released her tight grip on the stone and started to bend her knees when suddenly she froze. She looked over his shoulder, her eyes pierced with pain.

The shrill voice of Lady Caldern rang through the air. "You are not taking my daughter away from me."

Alex turned quickly. "Stay where you are," he commanded.

Lady Caldern ignored his warning and moved

forward. "I know what is best for her. I will make certain that she is taken care of."

"No," Julianna shrieked. "I cannot listen to you any longer, Mother."

Alex turned back to his sister, her fragile frame outlined against the morning sun. His heart ached for her torment even though he could not condone her actions. Julianna looked over her shoulder and Alex knew that he could waste no more time.

"Grab her," he shouted to Nathan and Bryan.

Alex ran toward Julianna at the same time Nathan and Bryan did, but they were too late. Without any final farewell, she pushed herself away from the parapet. Alex reached the edge just as Julianna slipped from life. Her body lay lifeless on the drive below them.

Alex groaned and put his head down on the cold stone parapet. "Why?" he mumbled under his breath.

Bryan leaned over the side and then looked back at Lady Caldern. "Do not look," he instructed sternly. He pushed away from the edge and walked to his mother. "I will take you to your room."

Alex listened to their retreating footsteps and when they were gone he straightened up. Nathan leaned against the parapet that Julianna had clung to, his head in his hands. David stood a few feet away.

"There was nothing we could do." Alex rubbed the back of his neck, weariness seeping throughout his body.

"No," David agreed. "Now you know who was responsible for your accidents."

"Do we?" Alex walked slowly to the roof door.

"She confessed," David exclaimed.

Alex looked back at his friend and shook his head. "She carried out the actions, but she was not the only one responsible. Fanny must carry a portion of the blame."

Alex left the roof, walking down the dark stairway, past the charred ruins of the sewing room. He would arrange for Julianna's body to be carried inside and prepared for burial. Then he would go to Sarah.

After witnessing the tragic consequences of a suffocating love, he knew what he had to do. If Sarah lived, he would give her freedom. He loved her too much to force her into a marriage she did not want. He had always thought that only good could come of love, but now he knew differently.

Chapter 30

Sarah opened her eyes, squinting at the bright light shining through the window. She moaned, bringing her hand up to her throbbing head.

"Does it hurt?"

Sarah turned and looked into Alex's dark eyes. They were soft with concern. He was pale and she put her hand out to him. He brought it up to his lips.

"I was so afraid you would not wake up."

"How long have I been sleeping?" Sarah's throat felt scratchy and she could barely speak.

"Since yesterday." Alex sat down on the bed beside her. "We were worried that you had inhaled too much of the smoke."

Sarah closed her eyes, images of the previous day flooding back. "Julianna," she rasped.

"Do not worry about her." Alex brushed her hair from her face, forcing her to look up at him. "She will never hurt you again."

"She came into the sewing room." Sarah tried to sit up, but Alex eased her back into the bed.

"She confessed everything," Alex explained gently.

Sarah frowned. "Julianna was upset. I asked her to sit with me. After that, everything is a blank."

Alex rubbed his hand over his eyes and sighed. "She did not tell you what she had done?"

Sarah inhaled quickly, her chest constricting in pain. Alex looked away from her, as if trying to avoid her question. Sarah knew instinctively that something horrible had happened.

"What happened in the sewing room?"

Alex looked out the window and sighed. "There was a fire. You were unconscious when we reached the room, and we had to revive you."

"I had no candles lit." Sarah struggled to remember what had happened after Julianna had come to visit. Sarah had turned away to get a chair and then pain—sharp, piercing pain on her head. "Julianna hit me," she exclaimed.

Alex nodded his head. "She struck you unconscious and then started the fire."

"Why would she want to hurt me?" Sarah puzzled. "She was a friend."

"She liked you, too." Alex clasped Sarah's hand tightly. "She was unbalanced."

Sarah stared at Alex for several seconds, trying to understand what he was telling her, but her mind refused to cooperate. If she had been found in the burning room, that meant Julianna had left her there. Why would she do that?

"Was Julianna trying to kill me?" she asked in a faltering voice.

"Yes."

"Then she tried to hurt you, too?"

"And Douglas," Alex said with a nod of his head. "I found it almost impossible to believe, but Julianna told us everything before . . ." Alex's voice cracked and he looked down at their clasped hands.

"Before what?" Sarah nudged.

Alex took a deep breath. "She jumped off the roof."

Sarah closed her eyes tightly, trying to block Alex's words, but it did not help. Julianna had taken her own life. A knot of regret formed in the pit of Sarah's stomach. "What drove her to such a horrible end?"

"She thought she was pleasing her mother." Alex cleared his throat. "It seems whenever Fanny wished harm to a person, or even death, Julianna complied."

"How horrible," Sarah cried.

Alex nodded his head. "I found it hard to believe, but there was no disputing her words. In the end Julianna could not face her mother making any more demands."

Sarah looked away from Alex, letting the tears gently fall down her cheeks. Julianna had been such a sweet, fragile person. It was hard to believe Lady Caldern did not know what she had been doing to her daughter.

Alex moved closer to Sarah, gathering her into his arms as he lay beside her on the bed. "Hush, my love," he cooed.

Sarah turned around and buried her face in his chest. The tears that had started so gently now became sobs. Alex rubbed her back and held her close, rocking her until her despair had passed.

"What will you do?" Sarah hiccupped.

Alex shrugged his shoulder slightly. "Bryan has decided to take his mother to his estate in Somerset. Hopefully he will be able to salvage his life there."

"It will be hard," Sarah murmured. She could

not even begin to imagine the devastation he must feel at knowing his sister had killed for him.

"Yes." Alex rubbed his chin against Sarah's head. "He seemed so subdued, almost a broken man after Julianna's confession."

"You must be feeling the same." Sarah looked up into Alex's eyes, noticing the weariness for the first time. "She was your sister, too."

"She was only a babe when I left," Alex reminded Sarah with a sigh. "It was my fault for staying away so long. She never knew me as a brother."

"You did what was necessary." Sarah could not bear for Alex to blame himself for Julianna's actions. "You could not know that Lady Caldern would twist her mind."

"True, but I should have tried. I have been so caught up with my concerns and needs since I arrived at Caldern that I never made an effort to know either Julianna or Bryan."

Sarah could not deny Alex's words. When there had been an occasion for the family to be together, Alex had tried his best to antagonize them. He had his reasons, but that would not bring him comfort now. Time was the only cure.

Sarah squeezed Alex closer. "I love you," she whispered. "Let me help."

Alex brushed her hair from her face. "I have failed you most of all," he confessed.

"No," Sarah denied firmly. "You only tried to love me. It was I who would not allow you to get close."

"I forced you into marriage," Alex said hoarsely. "I arrogantly thought that would solve all of your problems. Now I see that I was wrong. You cannot bully another person into loving you. Julianna taught me that."

Sarah blinked back her tears. "I should have trusted you. Trust has to be a part of loving someone."

"I was a fool."

Sarah shook her head. "I was."

Alex looked at her, his eyes widening with surprise. "What are you saying?"

Sarah took a deep breath, her eyes never wavering from Alex's. "I want to stay married to you."

Alex smiled slowly, his face lighting up with joy and disbelief. "I never thought I would hear you say those words. Tell me you are serious."

A bubble of happiness rose up in Sarah's chest. She nodded her head. "I knew when you fell down the cavern that I could not live without you. I fear losing you more than I fear marriage."

Alex pulled her close and kissed her. His lips were full of triumph and victory. Sarah could not resist his demands and surrendered eagerly. His tongue slid across hers, caressing and teasing until Sarah pulsed with excitement.

When the kiss ended Sarah was panting, her lungs screaming for air. She watched Alex through half-closed lids, his chest rising rapidly. She melted at the look of love in his eyes. He hid nothing from her. She swept his hair back from his forehead with her hand.

He trembled at her touch. A surge of desire raced through her veins. She leaned forward, kissed his eyes shut and then brushed her lips across his forehead, nose, and cheeks. Her tongue grazed his chin, relishing the texture of his slight stubble. Sarah captured his lips, nibbling, teasing, and soothing until Alex was groaning.

"Do you know what you are doing to me?" Alex's voice was hoarse.

Sarah smiled. "Loving you."

Alex exhaled; his eyes did not waver from her. "Never stop."

Sarah leaned forward, her lips trailing kisses across his face until she reached his neck. The stiff corners of his cravat tickled her nose. She leaned back and untied it, casting the crumpled linen to the floor. She pulled at his jacket, but it would not budge.

"You have too many clothes on." Sarah could not contain her frustration.

"So do you, my love." Alex sat up and yanked off the offending garment. He began to undo his shirt, but Sarah stopped him.

"Let me."

Sarah's fingers shook as she plucked at the first button. Her hand skimmed across Alex's chest, sending a shiver of awareness through her. Instinctively she kissed his exposed skin. Alex inhaled sharply and an answering surge of desire filled Sarah. She needed to see all of him. With trembling hands she tugged the shirt away from his pantaloons and pulled it over his head.

She blinked back the tears as she gazed upon Alex's exposed chest. With tender fingers she stroked the bandages that still remained around his ribs. Her heart ached when she saw the bruising and redness, but most of the cuts and scrapes were almost healed. Sarah coaxed Alex back onto the pillows before she began to caress each bruise and cut with her lips. As her mouth moved lower, her fingers toyed with the fastening of his pantaloons. With a twist of her hand she had them undone.

Alex jumped, but Sarah eased him back, letting her lips roam over his chest freely as she made her way to his mouth. She kissed him hungrily, savoring the taste and feel of Alex beneath her. He pulled her close, his arms encircling her, his fingers massaging, until her body hummed with desire.

Fire burned in Sarah's body, its flames all-consuming. Restlessly she moved against Alex. She craved more than kisses. She needed to be a part of him, to feel him deep within her. Only then would her fiery yearning be quenched. She ended the kiss, her heart raced frantically and her body trembled with passion. Sitting back from Alex she began to pull at the waistband of his pants.

"Let me." Alex's voice was barely audible. He grimaced with effort as he pulled off his boots and then his pantaloons. When he was finished he reached for Sarah, but she evaded his hands.

"Lay back." Her voice was hoarse. She watched with bated breath as Alex slowly positioned himself on the pillows and surrendered to her wishes. A jolt of desire twisted in her womb.

Alex motioned to her nightgown. "I must see all of you."

Sarah nodded and with a seductive smile lifted the edge of the gown. Alex's eyes widened and his breathing became more ragged. An answering thrill of anticipation raced through Sarah. For the first time in her life she understood the power a woman could have over a man. Her love for Alex made it sweeter.

The lacy edge of her silken nightdress scraped across her thighs. Sarah licked her lips, watching as Alex's eyes darkened with desire. Exciting Alex was arousing her to a fevered pitch. With slow and deliberate movements she eased the gown higher up her body until all of her legs were exposed.

Then with a swift flick of her hands she pulled it over her head.

Alex groaned. His eyes ravished her body hungrily. Sarah sat back on her feet, relishing her body's answering response. Moist heat filled her inner core and every nerve ached with need. She let her fingers skim up the side of Alex's leg, brushing seductively near his hardened manhood. He reached for her, but she moved away. Her fingers danced across his other leg before she followed with her lips.

With slow, lingering kisses she devoured every inch of his legs until his body quivered beneath her. Every lick, every touch of her lips, sent a tremor of heat throughout her until she was ablaze with passion. She hesitated only a second before she let her tongue glide up the full length of Alex's erect penis.

"Oh God," Alex said through gritted teeth. "You must not."

"Do you want me to stop?"

Alex shook his head against the pillow. "No. Quite the opposite."

Sarah took another tentative lick of Alex, enjoying the slightly salty taste of him. His hips moved restlessly beneath her, but she continued to stroke him with her tongue and mouth until they both throbbed with need. Only then did she sit up and straddle him.

"Are you certain?" Alex's words came between gasps for air.

"I love you."

Sarah leaned forward and nibbled at Alex's lower lip before soothing it with a kiss. Then she moved her body back until the engorged flesh of her moist inner thighs was touching Alex's swollen shaft. Her breath caught in her throat as she gazed into Alex's eyes. They were full of love and understanding.

"I trust you." Sarah slowly eased herself back onto Alex, luxuriating in the sensation of him filling her completely.

"I chose you for my husband."

Sarah rocked against Alex until she found a rhythm that sent spirals of delight throughout her. Alex guided her with his hands, thrusting his hips upward to meet her. Waves of bliss cascaded through her body. She quivered on the edge of rapture until suddenly the world exploded into a million points of ecstasy.

Sarah collapsed onto Alex's chest. His arms embraced her and with one, smooth motion he swung her beneath him. His lips caressed hers, soothing and coaxing, until a tremor of renewed passion was ignited deep within her. Her inner muscles tightened around Alex's hard penis, exalting at his slow and lazy strokes. Her body vibrated with sensation.

Only then did Alex's mouth leave hers and begin to nuzzle her neck. His hands caressed her breasts, his fingers brushing over her already sensitive nipples. She arched her back as a jolt of heat flooded her. Sarah did not think she could stand anymore. She was taut with need, panting for release.

Alex quickened his pace, thrusting deeper with each stroke until he carried them to the heights of ecstasy. He claimed her mouth in a searing kiss just as their bodies shattered together in release. Sarah shook as waves of rapture burst within her. Tears filled her eyes at the sheer splendor of their love-making.

* * *

Much later, when the sun had already started its descent into dusk, they lay under the covers completely satiated. Sarah smoothed her hand across Alex's chest, absently curling the short black hairs in her fingers.

Alex put his hand over hers. "You will pull them out at this rate," he teased. "Leave some for our old age."

Sarah chuckled and gave him a quick kiss of apology. "I was just thinking how lucky we are."

"You will never regret our marriage," he reassured. "I promise to make you happy."

"I will be happy." Sarah's whole body felt bathed in contentment. Alex's love had given her the confidence to live again and she intended to enjoy every moment of it.

"I will let you do whatever you want," Alex continued. "You can continue with your herbs and I will not interfere. I will be a model husband."

Sarah looked up at Alex and smiled indulgently. "You will protest the first time I leave your bed to tend a sick tenant after dark."

"Never," Alex denied.

Sarah looked at him steadily, watching as his face slowly reddened. He grinned sheepishly. "I will try not to interfere," he corrected.

"I know you will try." Sarah snuggled closer to her husband. "It will be hard for us to work through our differences, but it will be worth it."

"You are starting to sound like me," Alex joked.

"I understand you better now," Sarah explained. "Your love for me makes you protective."

"Very," Alex agreed.

"We will make a life together," Sarah promised. "And every day I will be thankful for your love."

Alex lowered his head, nipping her lips gently

with his teeth before lathing them with his tongue. Passion stirred deep within and Sarah sighed contentedly. Alex had shown her the beauty of love. She would cling to that and let it guide her the rest of the way.

Epilogue

Alex sat in the bedroom, a single candle flickering in the darkness. It was late. The clock had chimed midnight almost twenty minutes ago. He stretched his legs when he heard the soft opening of the door.

"Was it successful?" he asked, pushing himself out of his chair.

Sarah stood in the doorway, her hair falling about her tired face. She closed the door and smiled. "A beautiful, healthy boy."

"Wonderful," Alex enthused, gathering his wife into his arms. "I hope you did not tire yourself."

Sarah shook her head. "I am fine."

"You can never be too careful," Alex scolded gently.

Sarah moved away and took off her dark cloak, flinging it onto the chair Alex had just vacated. Alex's breath caught in his throat. She was beautiful. Even after ten years of marriage, he could not take his eyes off her.

Sarah's dark auburn hair still retained its youthful appearance, not a strand of gray to mar its perfection. Her eyes sparkled with contentment and Alex prided himself on that. It was the one promise he had made her that he had kept. Happiness.

"I am concerned about you doing too much." Alex stretched out his hand and rubbed her rounded tummy.

"There is nothing to worry about," Sarah reassured. "This is our third child and everything is going wonderful. I feel better than I ever did with the boys."

Alex began to rub Sarah's shoulders. "Do you want me to order a bath?"

Sarah shook her head. "It is late. Tomorrow morning will be fine."

Alex went over to the washbasin and dipped a cloth into the lukewarm water before handing it to her. She wiped her face with the cloth and sighed.

"This is wonderful. That cottage was too warm."

"Perhaps you should get out of those clothes," Alex suggested with a wink. "I could help give you a sponge bath."

Sarah grinned at her husband. A bubble of joy gurgled inside of her. Ten years of marriage had brought many things, but it never failed to delight her. Alex was a strong and, at times, difficult man to love, but he always made it worthwhile.

They had their arguments, mainly about decisions Sarah made and Alex disagreed with. They patched things up quickly, though. Alex was always willing to give her the freedom she needed. Once the boys had been born, their world had seemed perfect.

Sarah rubbed her tummy protectively. This pregnancy had been unexpected, but welcomed. Sarah was beginning to feel as if her children no longer needed her. Douglas, who was nine, spent most of the year at school. James, at seven, would soon follow his brother. Now she would have another baby to dote on.

"Unfasten me." Sarah turned her back to Alex.

"No extra persuasions needed?" Alex asked in mock surprise.

"Your offer is too good." Sarah looked over her shoulder at Alex and winked. "At my age it would be foolish to refuse a man's offer."

Alex began loosening her gown. His lips nuzzled her neck as his expert fingers made their way down the back of her dress. Within seconds, she was standing in her chemise.

Sarah turned to face her husband, kissing him gently on the lips and guiding his fingers to her. When Alex had dealt with the last bit of material that stood between them, he lifted her into his arms and carried her to the bed.

"Alone at last," he sighed. "I have waited all evening for this moment."

"So have I," Sarah confessed.

"No more late night deliveries," Alex begged.

"I will try," Sarah whispered, giving Alex's ear a slight nibble. "You will have to talk to the babies, though."

Alex chuckled. He captured his Sarah's lips in a searing kiss. She returned his passion with fervor; luxuriating in the depth of the ecstasy he always carried her to. Their lovemaking, fantastic even in the beginning, had only gotten better over the years.

Alex's hands roamed over her body, touching all the places that made her wild with desire. Sarah surrendered. Alex had promised her a life of happiness and he had given her so much more. She had never regretted the risk she had taken in trusting Alex and their love. Love had healed her. Love had made her whole.